What the critics are saying…

ONE WILD WEEKEND

4 ½ Stars! "...a quirky plot filled with humor and sizzle. The characters in this delightful tale are fresh and appealing." ~ *Susan Mitchell, RT BOOKclub Magazine*

"Delightfully sexy and guaranteed to make you smirk from time to time. ...one wild ride that you should not miss!" ~ *Dee Harge, In The Library Reviews*

"Get ready for one hysterical story. Man or woman, you are sure to find delight in this book. A must read summer story." ~ *Bea, Fallen Angels Reviews*

"A wild ride....a magnificent story with sensuality that will blow the reader away, while the comedy will make you laugh until tears roll down your face." ~ *M. Jeffers, The Road to Romance*

"From almost the first page, this amusing and entertaining story will have you laughing out loud. The characters are genuine and the story line is definitely one of a kind." ~ *Amelia Richard, eCataRomance Reviews*

WILD BY NIGHT

"A powerful, sexy story about a woman who needs to realize that she has found the man for her life and succumb to her feral needs. Full of sexual tension...this book will enthrall the reader to the very end." ~ *Valerie, Love Romances*

"A great novel that will reach out and grab hold of you and won't let go until the book is through. I found myself up at 2AM because I could not put this book down until I finished it. ...this one is definitely going on my keeper shelf." ~ *Angel Brewer, Romance Junkies*

"A fun and romantic story that will definitely tug at your heartstrings as you read about Candy and Duane's struggle to become one." ~ *Sarah, Fallen Angels Reviews*

"Well done! A very entertaining story with some truly tender moments that just make you feel warm and fuzzy all over. Here is hoping Ms. Copeland will continue the magic with Carrie's love story." ~ *Keely Skillman, Coffee Time Romance*

JODI LYNN COPELAND

INNER Urges

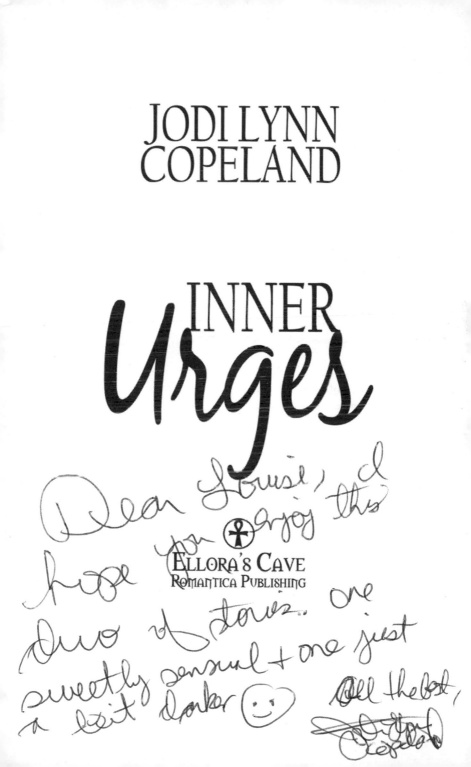

ELLORA'S CAVE
ROMANTICA PUBLISHING

Dear Louise,
I hope you enjoy this
duo of stories... one
sweetly sensual + one just
a bit darker :)

All the best,
Jodi Lynn
Copeland

An Ellora's Cave Romantica Publication

www.ellorascave.com

Inner Urges

ISBN # 1419953281
ALL RIGHTS RESERVED.
One Wild Weekend Copyright© 2004 Jodi Lynn Copeland
Wild By Night Copyright© 2004 Jodi Lynn Copeland
Edited by: Briana St. James
Cover art by: Dawn Seewer

Trade paperback Publication: December, 2005

Excerpt from *Naughty Mistress Nita*
Copyright © Jodi Lynn Copland, 2003
Excerpt from *Son of Solaris: Taurus*
Copyright © Jodi Lynn Copeland, 2004

Warning:

The following material contains graphic sexual content meant for mature readers. *Inner Urges* has been rated *E-rotic* by a minimum of three independent reviewers.

Ellora's Cave Publishing offers three levels of Romantica™ reading entertainment: S (S-ensuous), E (E-rotic), and X (X-treme).

S-*ensuous* love scenes are explicit and leave nothing to the imagination.

E-*rotic* love scenes are explicit, leave nothing to the imagination, and are high in volume per the overall word count. In addition, some E-rated titles might contain fantasy material that some readers find objectionable, such as bondage, submission, same sex encounters, forced seductions, etc. E-rated titles are the most graphic titles we carry; it is common, for instance, for an author to use words such as "fucking", "cock", "pussy", etc., within their work of literature.

X-*treme* titles differ from E-rated titles only in plot premise and storyline execution. Unlike E-rated titles, stories designated with the letter X tend to contain controversial subject matter not for the faint of heart.

Also by Jodi Lynn Copland:

Contents

Wild by Night

Prologue

"She actually said that?" Duane Livery stilled with the pizza slice midway to his mouth and gaped across the restaurant table in disbelief. "That you gotta get in touch with your feminine side? Oh, man, how cheesy is that?"

"Tell me about it," Nathan Anderson agreed with his long-time friend. Considering the number of women the press had linked him with in the six months since his outdoor superstore chain, *The Sports Wharf*, had surpassed the fifty million profit mark, the claim wasn't just cheesy, but absurd. While Nate hadn't been with all those women, he'd been with plenty; more than enough to know he had the female psyche down to a science.

They all wanted the same thing, at least the ones not related to him. His money, followed closely by the tanned, blond good looks shared by all five of the Anderson siblings, two of which happened to be women. He knew women. Knew what they wanted, knew what made them tick.

"As much as I hate to play devil's advocate, did you ever think that she might have a point?" Nate's older brother Joe asked. "I mean, yeah, you know women, know a hell of a lot of them more intimately than I even want to think about, but do you really *know* them?"

Nate snorted. Joe did *not* hate to play devil's advocate. Call it the older brother in him, but he lived for tossing potential hurdles his siblings' way. It wasn't that he wanted to see them fail, Nate knew, rather he wanted to help them succeed by pointing out problems that might arise before they could. Only this time there wasn't a problem, and Joe couldn't be any farther off base. "I *know* women."

"You know women," Joe repeated, his look speaking volumes to the fact he disagreed. "In that case, how does Jill feel about her family? Is she close with her parents? Are they even still alive? What about sisters or brothers?"

How did his ex-lover feel about her family? Nate didn't know and he honestly couldn't say that he cared. "Why?"

"You were together for almost a week, which might not be much for some but is an all-time record for you. She had to have mentioned her family at least once during that time."

Jill had mentioned a lot of things. Things like where she liked to be touched, how much she loved the feel of his mustache chafing against her sensitized skin, her endless delight over his staying power. Nate had a sneaking suspicion not one of those things would impress his older brother. He shrugged. "We didn't do much talking."

"Exactly my point."

"And my kind of relationship," Duane put in with a smirk.

Joe glanced at him. "*You* are the last person to be getting involved in this conversation."

Duane went on the defensive. "What the hell's that supposed to mean?"

"That the most meaningful relationship you've ever had was with your own hand."

Duane didn't even try to argue, and Nate knew it was because his brother spoke the truth. He also knew the reason why Duane steered away from anything more significant than a one-night stand. Because the poor sap only wanted one woman, Nate and Joe's sister Candace. And, Candace, God love her, had barely spared more than a glance Duane's way since the man had moved back to Clarion Heights almost two months ago.

"The point is you do *not* know women," Joe said firmly, pulling Nate's attention back to the topic of his wisdom where women were concerned. "You know what they want sexually, maybe even what they want for dinner or their taste in drinks, but you don't have a clue about what's going on in their heads or their hearts."

Nate grunted at the last words. He should have known this was heading toward feelings. Up until a year ago Joe didn't have a single damned idea what the word even meant, then he'd met Gracie and fell head over ass in love. And that was clearly why Nate was getting the grill session now. Big brother Joe had deemed it time for him to settle down. Too bad for big brother Joe, Nate had no such intention. "I don't have time for a relationship. Even if I did, there isn't a woman in this city who could keep me entertained for more than a week or two."

The pretentious city of Clarion Heights bred beauties by the droves. Beauties whose idea of a good time was sunbathing by their daddy's pool, or heading out to one of the local clubs for a hard night of partying. As entertaining as that might have been once upon a time, the appeal for Nate had long run thin. He'd had more than his fair share of debutantes, and he didn't want another one. At least, not right now. What he wanted now was a woman who found adventure in the world around her, who wasn't afraid to break a nail while dangling thirty stories up off the face of the mountain. A woman who could share his love for both the outdoors and the bedroom without falling in love with him herself.

"Then expand your scope," Joe said. "It's not like you have to stick to Clarion Heights. You're jetting off to parts unknown every other damned day."

"For business."

"In the form of sporting events," Joe amended. "Ones I find it awfully hard to believe there isn't a single woman at who can keep you entertained, both mentally and physically."

There were women at the events all right, and they came in two forms. Those who were there for the express purpose of meeting a muscle-bound man and those who were there to prove they could kick a muscle-bound man's ass. Neither of them particularly appealed to Nate. A lot like this conversation.

He tossed his napkin onto his emptied plate and glared at his brother. "What part of 'I don't want a relationship' don't you understand?"

"The part where you won't even give one a try. I don't get you, bro. When we were kids all you ever talked about was having a family of your own someday. About wanting a wife and a dozen kids. What the hell happened?"

He'd grown up and realized everything wasn't white picket fences and lazy Sunday afternoons spent playing baseball with the family. Up until roughly a year ago, Nate had invested all his time and effort into seeing the *Wharf* became a success, and now that he'd accomplished his goal he wanted time to reap the benefits that came with being a single, sought-after millionaire. Benefit number one was the ability to take off to wherever it might be he wanted to go without so much as a moment's notice. Benefit number two was not having a wife nagging him to come home and stop acting like a kid. "I'm thirty-two, not eighty. I have every intention of settling down one day, presuming I find a woman who can stand up to her claim she loves both the outdoors and me and isn't just saying that to get at my bank account. That day isn't today or anytime in the foreseeable future."

Joe stared across the table at him in stony silence. Finally, he said, "I don't think you know how."

"What do you mean?"

"You've been playing the jet-setting bachelor for so damned long I don't think you know the first thing about forming a real relationship. I bet you can't even have a normal conversation with a woman you find attractive for more than five minutes."

The words were as inaccurate as any Nate had ever heard and still they managed to prick at him, just the way he knew Joe had intended. "I know how, just like I know women. I can sure as hell talk to them."

"About something other than sex?"

"Yes," Nate said calmly, fighting back the irritation that came with his brother's doubtful expression and tone, "about something other than sex."

The skepticism in Joe's eyes faded and he smiled. "All right, prove it."

"I will, in a few years."

"Now."

"Why?" Duane asked, pulling both men from their staring match to focus on him.

"Because I don't think he can." Joe looked back at Nate and his smile grew to a knowing grin. "Prove it to me, little brother. Find a woman who you're attracted to and who shares your tastes and get to know her. The *real* her. *Out* of bed. And just in case the concept has failed to enter your realm of comprehension, what I'm suggesting is called a friendship with a member of the opposite sex."

It was true that Nate didn't have any female friends outside of those related to him, but that wasn't because he didn't know how to handle a nonsexual relationship with a woman. He'd just never had the desire to have one. He could have one easily. No, he *would* have one. If for no other reason then to get Joe off his back. That and because he hadn't backed down from a challenge any other time in his life and he wasn't about to start now. "Say I agree and take you up on the challenge, where do you propose I meet this woman? And don't say abroad. I'm not about to start a long distance relationship to prove some ludicrous point."

"At the *Wharf*," Duane suggested.

Nate shook his head. "I don't use the store to meet women."

"Then you'd best start thinking of places," Joe said.

Nate could only laugh. Thinking of places to meet women for the express purpose of friendly, relationship-building conversation. He would put that on the top of his "things to do" list. Yeah, right. "As much as I would love to continue discussing this, I have to run. I promised Jan I'd come in today so she could take off early."

"What about her?" Joe asked. "She's not a customer."

"She's got a nice ass," Duane added.

That she did, along with a decent rack and miles of thick red hair. She also happened to be Nate's most dependable manager. On the extremely off chance he really couldn't keep a relationship with a woman he found attractive nonsexual, he wasn't about to risk tossing Jan into the equation. "She has something going on with Rex and, even if this is just about friendship, I don't want him seeing the two of us together and getting the wrong idea."

Nate grabbed the check and headed for the restaurant's front counter. As he drew closer a bright yellow flyer taped beside the register caught his attention. "Ninth Annual Wild Woman Weekend" was written in bold black letters and pictures of women camped out around a fire and several others hiking and white water rafting made up the lower half of the sheet. He vaguely recalled donating supplies to the event in the past.

Duane's hand slapped over his shoulder and he nodded toward the flyer. "Check it out, man. I do believe we have found your place."

"My place?"

"To meet your woman."

"She's *not* my woman," Nate clarified, his gut tightening at the far from pleasant thought of a woman moving into his life and taking over. Yeah, he wasn't ready for that. Not even close. "As it seems you've failed to notice, you might check out the print on the bottom. It's for women only."

"Yeah, as in a hundred or more nature-loving females all alone in the big outdoors. I'm sure I don't gotta tell you what they do at those things."

If the pictures were anything to go by, they sat around fires and went hiking and rafting. If Duane's lecherous grin were anything to go by, they sat around fucking each other. "Let me guess, it's one big female orgy?"

"Couldn't have said it better myself."

"I have serious doubts on the whole orgy thing," Joe said, coming up behind them, "but he might not be so far off about it being the place for you to test out this supposed friendship skill of yours. The women who attend that thing have to be into the outdoors. Enough so that even you ought to be able to find something to talk to them about."

Nate shook his head, noting his brother still thought he was incompetent where inter-gender friendships were concerned. "Thanks for the vote of confidence, but I'll wait for something better to come along."

"Scared?"

Nate was handing the check and two twenties to a middle-aged, matronly-looking woman when the taunting word reached him. He glanced back at Joe. "Of what?"

"That if I'm right and all those women are into the outdoors, you'll never be able to last an entire weekend on conversation alone, that you'll find one you just can't resist and end up nailing her. Or worse, that you'll get to know one of them for more than their ability to put their legs behind their head, and actually start caring about her."

Nate collected his change and started toward the door. "I'm not scared of shit. I'm also not a woman, and I would say that ends this conversation."

Reaching the door, Duane turned and cast him an assessing gaze. He shrugged. "I dunno, man. I'd say you could be a woman pretty damned easy."

"He can?" Joe asked the same time as Nate said, "I can?"

Duane frowned. "What, neither of you ever dressed in drag?"

"No," Nate said resolutely. "And I've also never had to lie my way into a woman's feelings any more than I've had to lie my way into one's pants, and that's exactly what you're suggesting I do."

Joe smirked. "The reason you've never had to lie your way into a woman's pants is because they all know you have money. Not to mention, if the tabloids are to be believed, a dick the size of your arm. As far as feelings go, you've yet to convince me you have ever experienced such a thing or given any in return. If Jill's parting comment is a sign, I would say you haven't even come close."

Nate pushed through the restaurant's front door and struggled to force back the growing frustration his brother could stir in him like no other. "It really doesn't matter, since it isn't going to happen."

"Because you're scared of opening yourself up and getting close to someone," Joe pressed from where he walked beside him.

Nate came to a halt and met his brother's overconfident smile with barely tethered exasperation. "I am *not* scared."

"All I'm asking is for you to prove it, little brother. Go to that weekend full of outdoor-loving women and show me you can make friends."

Nate's frustration cracked with the absurdity of the challenge. He felt like laughing or maybe rearranging Joe's face. He nodded instead. "Fine, I'll go and I'll make these friendships you seem to think I'm incapable of handling, and when I do, I don't want to hear another word from you on feelings or relationships and sure as hell not on getting in touch with my damned feminine side. Got it?"

"Got it."

"Good." He turned to Duane and spoke words he wished to God had never found their way into his mouth. "Show me my feminine side, Duane. Make me a woman."

Joe laughed, obviously enjoying the hell right out of this. "You seriously think you can make him look like a woman?"

"Oh yeah, man," Duane said, all confidence. "Just wait and see. This time on Friday 'Natalie' here will be so hot he's gonna want to jump his own bones."

Chapter One

Seated behind the wheel of her Jeep, Kelsey Stuart scanned the area twenty yards in the distance. Trees, bushes, and patches of marshland surrounded the foothills of the Eagleton Mountains. In the middle of it all was an open stretch of ground where women of all ages, shapes and sizes scurried about, setting up tents, breaking out coolers and grills, and arranging their temporary homes.

Laughter filtered through her open window and Kelsey breathed out an edgy sigh. She should have stayed home.

The only reason she'd agreed to come to the Wild Woman Weekend was because of her best friend Jan. Jan, who had canceled at the last possible minute. Jan, who Kelsey had a sneaking suspicion hadn't come down with the flu at all, but merely had better plans in the form of her new boyfriend Rex. Jan, who if she hadn't been best friends with since kindergarten, she would sever her relationship with permanently.

They had been friends that long. On top of the length of time they'd known each other, Jan was one of the few women Kelsey felt she could be herself around. Which was exactly the reason she ought to turn around and head back home.

The thought of exiting her vehicle and throwing herself into that bramble of chattering females twisted her gut into knots. Still, she had to do it. She'd not only already paid for the weekend, but had driven for over an hour and a half to get here. And, honestly, she'd been looking forward to it. On top of the fact the dense and variegated foliage and rolling landscape of the mountains would provide some prime footage for the latest in a series of nature books she was writing, time away from Grayson City could only do her well. More notably, time away from thoughts of Todd, her latest error in judgment, and even better, the whole male population.

She could do this. Relax and enjoy herself amongst strangers without Jan by her side to ease the way. With any luck she might even make a few lasting friends. Or she wouldn't make a single one and end up being paired with women as unexciting as she was for all the partner events.

"You are *not* unexciting," Kelsey scolded herself.

She wasn't. In fact, Jan had told her more than once that she was one of the wildest women she'd ever met. She just appeared unexciting, not to mention peculiar, to those who didn't know any better. She would simply have to make sure these women knew her. And if getting to know her, the *real* her, meant opening up and revealing things about herself she rarely shared, then so be it.

She would have fun this weekend. As much fun as Jan and Rex were having. Thoughts of sweaty, tangled limbs and undoubtedly naked events they were most likely taking part in even now flashed through her mind and she laughed shortly. That much, or rather type, of fun wasn't bound to happen this weekend. Still, she would have a great time and not allow her anxiety around strangers to unveil itself as clumsiness the way it too often had a tendency to do.

Clinging tight to the confident thoughts that belied the restlessness of her belly, Kelsey pushed open the driver's door. Intent on coming across as self-assured from step one, she bounded out of the Jeep with both feet forward. The soles of her hiking boots touched down on earth made slippery by a week of on-again/off-again rain, and she was airborne before she could do a thing about it. She landed with a painful thwack on her backside, chunks of mud plastering her bare arms and legs. The shriek of surprise that tore from her mouth ensured those who hadn't seen the mishap were looking at her now, many of them smiling. All of them, she guessed, fighting laughter.

Heat rushed into her cheeks and she hid her face in her hands and groaned. "Why couldn't I have just stayed home?"

* * * * *

Nate breathed a sigh of relief that the attention of the cluster of women below was focused on something other than him as he exited his truck. The cute though obviously balance-challenged brunette floundering in the mud and talking to herself was as good a distraction as any. Duane had said he would turn him into a woman so hot Nate would want to jump his own bones. While he'd never considered his looks to be even remotely feminine, Nate had to admit Duane had done a decent job. He wasn't so hot he would chase after himself, but between the honey blonde wig, carefully applied makeup and generously padded bra, he might take himself home after a few too many drinks.

That is, until he stood up and realized how damned big he was.

Hell, who was he kidding? The odds he would be able to pull this off were less than slim. There might be women here as tall as he was, many with gym-honed bodies, but it was doubtful they would be as obviously built. He should leave right now before someone spotted him. Only the image of Joe's cocky smile wouldn't let him.

His brother had come over to see Duane's handiwork this afternoon. If Nate had thought there was a chance Joe would let up on his belief he couldn't handle a friendship with an attractive woman, then he'd been wrong. Between his brother's smile and parting words of "See you tomorrow" when he knew damned well the event lasted all weekend, it was clear he expected Nate to fail. He wouldn't fail. He never failed. And if he allowed this time to be a first, he would never hear the end of it.

The brunette stood and, grabbing a towel from the back door of a red Jeep, started wiping the mud from her body. She draped the towel around her back, then holding an end in each hand, rubbed it along her ass like she was waxing a car. It was the strangest damned thing Nate had ever seen. The strangest and oddly one of the most unexpectedly arousing. His cock stirred to life, expanding within the confines of the cup and spandex shorts that covered it. He gritted his teeth, and gazed down at the black nylon unisex pants. As much as the layers of confining clothes and plastic might hurt at times, they hid the bulge that would otherwise be an obvious giveaway to his gender.

Too bad they didn't mask the effect his suddenly stampeding testosterone had on the rest of him. His heart rate picked up and his fingers itched to reach out and have a nice, long feel of the cute little brunette's nicely round rear end.

And that is exactly what he wouldn't be doing this weekend.

Drawing in a cooling breath, Nate mentally calmed his erection. When the distressingly snug feeling of the cup was alleviated, he took a look in his truck's driver's side mirror. Even if it weren't for the makeup, he looked incredibly different than he had a few short hours ago. Different than he had in the seven years since he'd first started wearing a mustache. The remainder of his facial hair grew slowly and came in sparse. For years he'd hated the fact he couldn't grow a beard, then he'd simply accepted it and grown a mustache instead. Now that too was gone, and he felt oddly different. Not quite like himself. Not like a monster of a woman named Natalie either, but just not like himself.

He would be himself soon enough. Until then he had a weekend ahead of him, surrounded by women. Women he would be bonding with mentally instead of sexually. It was merely a change of pace. One that sounded almost as exciting as the Tuesday nights he spent at the bingo hall with his grandmother. At least there he had entertainment, watching Earl spit endless streams of tobacco into a plastic cup or old lady Jennings tooting out a symphony so gassy it had the whole place ready to explode with the first match lit.

Boring or not, he wasn't turning back. With one last glance in the mirror to ensure everything still looked as it should, Nate started toward the growing throng of women. He'd taken a few steps when an engine gunned to life. He glanced over in time to see the brunette backing her Jeep out of the muddy lot. She turned it around and headed toward him on the narrow trail.

The vehicle came to a stop several feet away, and the woman looked at him through the windshield, obviously waiting for him to move out of her way so she could leave. He started to move to the side then stopped. Why was she leaving when she'd only just gotten here? Not to mention when he'd already pegged her ability to make a scene as the best means to keep the attention away from him?

She poked her head out the window and peered at him through clear gray eyes. Her face was free of makeup and between her smooth complexion and shiny, straight hair, she looked exceedingly young.

"Um, could you please move?" she asked.

"Going somewhere?" Nate paused at the feminine sound of his voice. He had a deep voice, one that had a tendency to sound brash whether he wanted it to or not. During his visit today, Joe, who was head of engineering at a technology development plant, had given him a voice alteration device to wear over his vocal cords. The downside was to keep it camouflaged he had to wear a turtleneck or at least a high collar shirt regardless of the early summer humidity. The upside was that it worked. Amazingly well.

"Home." The brunette's eyes narrowed slightly and fine lines marred her forehead, the effect stepping her age up from somewhere in her late teens to her early to mid-twenties. Though her voice remained warm, he could tell she didn't appreciate him blocking her exit.

Too bad for her he had no intention of moving. He planted his feet a little wider, hoping the action didn't look as masculine as it felt. So far she seemed oblivious to the idea he was anyone but the woman he'd done his best to look like. It would be asinine to blow his cover over one wrong move. "You're not staying for the weekend?"

She looked away and muttered, "I never should have come."

He didn't miss the slight catch in her voice or the subtle streak of color fanning along her neck. Obviously that fall she'd taken had embarrassed her. He didn't have a mind or generally the time for cute women who turned red at the slightest incident. Today, he didn't have a choice but to make time. "You aren't into the outdoors?"

She looked back at him and frowned. "Yeah, but..." She shook her head. "Nothing. Have a great time."

Her window started to rise and Nate's heart beat faster. He wasn't one to be fazed easily, but at the moment he was counting on the distraction her clumsy nature would supply more than his next breath. He hustled to the side of the Jeep and blurted the first thing that came to him. "It would be better if I knew someone."

The window stopped its slow ascent then returned to its wide-open state. The brunette bit down on her bottom lip and eyed him curiously, as if she couldn't quite decide to trust him or not. Finally, she asked, "You're here alone?"

He fought back a triumphant grin. There was acceptance in the question, acceptance in her eyes as well. Acceptance that said he had her. She was about to give in and stay. Clearly, she was one of those women into helping others, the kind who picked up strays and took them home.

Though he'd had more than a few women offer to take him home, had allowed many of them to do just that, he'd never been called a stray before, far from it. Right now he wasn't about to mince words. What he was about to do was lay on the "poor me" act as thick as he could get it.

"Yeah. I just moved to the area and don't know anyone." He glanced to the group of women in the near distance, noted most wore shorts and T-shirts that showed off legions of succulent female flesh and feigned a shiver. "There are just so many of them. It's..." Like a dream come true. *All those women, all outdoor lovers, and just one me.* How the hell could've he ever been upset with Joe for pushing him into this? He glanced back to the brunette and shrugged. "It's pretty intimidating."

"Yes, it is." Her gaze roamed the length of him, from the long, blonde wig to the plain, black running outfit with its top zipped to his chin. Nate forgot all about the legion of womanly curves in the near distance and fought the uncomfortable sensation to justify his appearance. He was used to being thought of as good-looking, perhaps even arrogantly so at times. He wasn't used to feeling disconcerted for a second. He sure as hell wasn't used to feeling intimidated. Though he had claimed to feel so for the sake of drawing her in, he honest to God felt that way under her intense scrutiny.

None too soon, she returned her attention to his eyes. "You don't really seem like the type who would be intimidated easily."

He wasn't. Not until you stuck him in the middle of the woods with a case of makeup, a padded bra and a duffel bag of women's clothing as his only means of defense. He shook off the thought. No matter how his gut suddenly felt knotted with tension, he wasn't intimidated. A little out of his element perhaps, but never intimidated. Least of all by a shy, little slip of a woman. "Because I'm big?"

Color streamed into her cheeks and she bit down on her lip once more. "Uh, yeah, though I didn't mean it to sound quite so rude."

He smiled at her discomfort, able to well imagine just how much more so she would be if she knew who she was really talking with. She wouldn't find out. At least, not if he could help it. If somehow it did leak to the press he'd spent the weekend parading as a woman he would simply play it off as a marketing tactic. Learning what it was the female outdoor enthusiast wanted by submerging himself right into the thick of things. "It wasn't rude, just a fact. My whole family is big." Remembering he was supposed to be playing to her sympathetic nature, he continued, "I don't mind really, just sometimes it can turn people away. They seem to think that because I'm big I'm an ogress or something. That I don't have feelings. I *do* have feelings."

The sniff he'd added for effect obviously spoke right to her tender, little heart as her eyes turned a soft shade of ash and she sent him a soulful look. "I don't get that impression about you at all. You seem like a wonderful person."

A twinge of guilt hit Nate in the gut. When he'd agreed to come here and make friends he hadn't put much thought into what would happen after the weekend was over. More importantly, how his new friends would deal with his sudden disappearance. Seeing the genuine concern in the brunette's eyes now, he was thinking about it in a big way.

He might not currently have any female friends, but having grown up with two sisters who were routinely upset with something the other or one of their girlfriends had said or done, he knew just how much women allowed their feelings to get wrapped up in things. Unless he selected the right women to befriend this weekend, his leaving without so much as a goodbye could cause some serious hurt. He wouldn't harm anyone over a stupid challenge, and that meant he'd simply have to find someone to make nice with who was far stronger than his current companion.

Settled by the thought, he said, "You aren't the type."

A flare of something that looked surprisingly like temper entered her eyes. "Just what type do you think I am?"

Cute. Innocent. Gullible as hell. The type of woman he veered away from at every turn even if she did happen to have a nice ass. "Warm. Outgoing. The type who isn't afraid of coming alone to an event like this because she knows her personality will have her being the center of attention within the first hour she arrives." That last part was true anyway. She'd had most of the camp staring at her within two seconds of exiting her vehicle.

The temper left her expression and a smile tugged at her lips. One that continued to grow until it blossomed fully and turned her undeniably plump lips a most appealing shade of pink. Her eyes lit until they sparkled and a dimple emerged in her cheek.

Nate swallowed hard at the sudden desire to lean forward and run his tongue over that sexy as hell indention. The transformation that had just taken place before his eyes was almost too unreal to believe. Gone was the bashful girl without any friends, and in her place was a siren just waiting to be uncovered. She might not be wearing the most alluring of clothes, sure as hell not the tight, slinky dress and strappy heels the women he generally spent time with favored, but she was a looker all the same. One that, between that exquisite divot in her cheek and the salacious lips she seemed intent on keeping moist, had his mind voyaging into an area it knew better than to go.

The thought of stripping her T-shirt away and tugging her shorts and panties down her long legs until her sweetly rounded curves were exposed to him was too tempting to pass up. All the blood in his body cruised through his veins on a due south journey as he envisioned unhooking her bra to find her nipples standing on end, impatiently waiting to be pulled into his mouth and sucked on. He worked his tongue against his inner cheek almost able to feel their texture, taste their sweet and salty mix. He'd bite down tenderly, sink his teeth into her aroused flesh just far enough to make her nerves stand on end and those full, pouty lips of hers to part and release throaty mewls of sensual pleasure. Cries that would grow all the louder when he trailed his tongue over the gentle swell of her breasts and down her belly to feast from the wet, swollen lips of her pussy.

"I guess if it would make you more comfortable, I could stay."

Nate's ball-tightening thoughts came to a staggering halt as her softly spoken words caught up with him. He smothered a laugh at their irony. Five seconds ago he'd have said that was exactly what her presence would bring him. Comfort among the masses. Now, as his throbbing cock pinched painfully against the sides of the cup and he moved closer to the Jeep to hide his hand as he made a seriously necessary adjustment, he knew just how wrong he'd been. She and her unexpectedly enticing smile and the carnal pull that came along with it weren't going to bring him comfort in the least. What they were going to do was make this weekend harder than he'd ever imagined.

Harder, and yet he had no choice. He'd already backed himself into a corner by making it clear he wanted her to stay. Resigned to continue as he'd begun, he forced his eyes wide. "Oh, no. You can't stay just for my sake. I'm sure you have much better plans for this weekend than spending it at some silly outdoor event."

She shook her head, her face coming more alive, her eyes more expressive with each passing second. "It's not just for you. I love the outdoors. Actually, I'm in them more often than not for the sake of my job, but my friend bailed at the last minute and I was considering doing the same." She nodded toward the parking spot she had vacated moments before. "Just give me a second to park and I'll walk down with you." She started backing the Jeep up and then stopped and leaned back out the window. The dimple reappeared in her cheek as she smiled. "I just realized I didn't get your name."

And he just realized how bad a judge of character he was. Not only was she not friendless or soft and shy the way he'd assumed, but that damned dimple might just be the death of him. Or at the very least the death of his assurance he could handle a nonsexual relationship with a woman he found attractive. "Nate, er, Natalie." Er, hell, why had he ever let Joe talk him into this?

"Kelsey. Be right back."

"Take your time. I'll be here." *Wishing to hell I wasn't.*

Nate breathed out a sigh and glanced back at the swarm of women who milled about in the fading daylight. All those women, all that succulent female flesh, and just one him. Oh, yeah, this was going to be one hell of a long, hard weekend.

Chapter Two

Why did she feel so comfortable with Natalie?

It was the question Kelsey had been asking herself since the moment the giant of a woman had lumbered into her path. It was the question she was still asking herself as they sat with a couple dozen other women around an immense bonfire over an hour later. Natalie had claimed many women were put off by her size, that they made it a point to steer clear of her. Kelsey had to admit that her first inclination was to do just that. Then they'd started talking and she'd soon realized how bad her snap judgment had been. Both rude and completely inaccurate.

She didn't feel dwarfed or intimidated by Natalie's size the way she thought she would. She felt comfortable, and not in the way she felt around Jan either, but the way she typically only experienced around men.

It was that comfort level Kelsey managed to achieve around men that always ended up leading her toward a painful goodbye where relationships were concerned. Whether it had to do with being primarily raised by an older brother who lived, ate and breathed the outdoors or something else altogether, she could simply relate to men better than most women, and for that reason she also found herself trusting them way too easily.

It was amazing—or maybe stupid was the better choice of words—but no matter how many times she trusted a man only to learn he was a lying jerk weeks to months later, she just had to go back for more.

No longer. She was tired of being a doormat. Tired of having men like Todd and every other idiot who passed through her life lead her on a journey that seemed filled with promise only to be filled with lies and heartache. She wasn't taking it any more, just like she wasn't going to think of men any more this weekend.

"You're up."

At the sound of Natalie's voice, Kelsey turned to find the woman looking at her through night-rimmed eyes. She had noticed her eyes the moment she'd stepped up to the side of the Jeep back in the parking lot. They were a striking shade of amber, almost gold, and fringed with long, thick lashes. Right now the firelight danced in them and cast shadows over the harsh angles of her face. To put it nicely, her new friend was put together very oddly. She wasn't really ugly, or even homely for that matter. She was just…different. In a big sort of way.

"My turn for what?" she asked, realizing she'd lost track of the conversation.

Natalie smiled. "Tina just went through a rough break-up. We were sharing bad experiences with dating or men in general to help her see she isn't alone."

Natalie's smile grew wider with her words and flames from the fire flickered light through her eyes, making them appear mischievous. It was a strange reaction to have when someone was clearly upset, but even stranger was the warmth that stirred to life in Kelsey's belly.

She pressed a hand to her stomach and turned to face the group. The warmth in her belly had nothing to do with the light in Natalie's eyes. It was more likely she was suffering indigestion from a supper of bratwurst and beer.

From all sides of the fire, women looked her way, expectancy in their eyes, as if they were hanging on her every breath and cared about what she had to say. The idea they could care was enough to prompt Kelsey into making herself a liar. She had just told herself she wouldn't think of men any more this weekend and yet she was about to do so aloud, because for whatever reason she felt comfortable and like herself around this group of near strangers.

She took a quick drink of beer, then set the can back in the holder built into the armrest of her canvas chair and once more looked out at the women. "My experience with men... To sum it up quickly, it's been pretty bad. I have this uncanny ability to attract jerks. The kind that like to romance you with candles and wine, and then you find out a few dates or maybe weeks later that they've only been after one thing all along and that thing isn't romance or love."

"Sex," a chorus of voices rang out.

Kelsey couldn't stop her smile. Maybe it was Natalie and the odd bond they seemed to share that made her feel confident or maybe these women just honestly understood her. Either way, she found she wanted to keep talking. To get all those things that had been eating at her for weeks off her chest. "Right, sex. And to make things worse I can never see it coming. I'm too trusting I guess, taking men at their word when I should be taking them at the action going on beneath their belts."

"You got it, honey. They couldn't talk to us with their little heads, they wouldn't talk to us at all," a woman called out.

At the sound of Natalie's very unladylike snort, Kelsey turned to see her mouth was tipped in a wide grin and her eyes filled with what could only be laughter. Obviously she found something about this conversation funny. It wasn't funny. At least not to anyone who had ever been on the receiving end of the pain. She couldn't keep the emotion out of her voice, so she didn't even bother to try. "What about you, Natalie? Do you find this conversation amusing?"

Natalie's lips fell flat and she glanced at Kelsey, sympathy replacing the amusement in her gaze as their eyes locked. Her lids narrowed slightly and she shook her head. "Hell no, I don't find it amusing. I would never do something like that. I make damned sure we both know it's just about sex going in."

Laughter cascaded around them, and where she'd been upset moments before, Kelsey found she had to fight to contain her own laugh. "I actually meant what were your experiences like, but I guess that pretty well tells us."

"Oh. Yeah. I guess so."

It was hard to be certain in the light of the fire, but it looked as though Natalie was blushing. She was embarrassed because Kelsey had accidentally put her on the spot. Recalling how Natalie had said she found the group of women intimidating, Kelsey waited until the conversation started back up around them and then leaned over in her seat.

Bracing her hand on the arm of Natalie's chair, she whispered near her ear. "I'm sorry about putting you on the spot. I didn't mean to embarrass you."

A barely audible hiss escaped Natalie's mouth and she jerked in her seat. Her arm shot from her lap lightning quick and clasped Kelsey's wrist in a painfully strong grip as she spun to stare at her. A squeak came from somewhere in Kelsey's throat. A squeak that faded to stunned silence as Natalie's gaze meshed with hers. The intensity of the look had her stomach doing flips. The heat that chased from Natalie's hand up the length of Kelsey's arm had her mind turning circles. Then Natalie's thumb moved, trailing ever so gently along her pulse point and Kelsey's stomach stopped doing flips to curl with sizzling warmth she couldn't pass off as indigestion even if she wanted to. And she did want to. Desperately.

Her heart galloping in her chest, she tugged at her hand until Natalie's grip lessened enough to pull her wrist free. She placed it in her lap and continued to stare at the large woman beside her, shaken, stunned, and mostly mortified at the carnal sensations rioting through her body. Her blood sizzled with awareness and her sex tingled with a desire evident in the dampness of her panties.

Just that look, that simple touch, and her pussy throbbed so badly she felt as if it had been stroked deep inside.

Kelsey swallowed back a gasp with that last realization and swore under her breath. Oh, God, she was aroused from another woman's touch. Judging by the suddenly anxious look in that other woman's gaze, she knew it too.

Wasn't that just the way her life worked? She'd managed to make a friend in less than an hour, a friend she felt comfortable around, and the woman thought she was a lesbian. What the hell was she supposed to say now?

"Sorry about that," Natalie said. "I was listening to Pat talk and the sound of your voice so near startled me."

If only it was just the woman's quick reflexes that had her cheeks aflame and the rest of her trembling with a desire she refused to think any farther on. For now she would be thankful that Natalie was oblivious to her discomfort. "Right. Uh...right."

Natalie's blonde eyebrows winged together and she frowned. "Is something the matter?"

Kelsey bit back the nervous laughter that bubbled up in her throat. Wonderful, she wasn't out of the woods yet, and it was her own fault because she couldn't stop staring and wondering how she could possibly feel this stimulated. It had to be the beer affecting her or...something. It couldn't be actual attraction for the simple fact she did not get turned on by other women. Not that she had a problem with homosexuals. She had friends who were, but *she* wasn't one.

"No. I..." *Am clearly losing my mind.*

Frantic to move past the awkwardness of the moment and clueless as how to do it, she could have cried when a raindrop pinged her in the nose. She tipped her face upward to the starless sky and was greeted with several more drops. "I thought I felt a raindrop."

"You did," Carla, one of the event coordinators said from beside her. "They were predicting we might get another shower tonight. I was hoping it would hold off a few more hours, but it looks like that won't be happening."

The rain picked up, coming down in fat, cold drops. The women vacated the quickly dying fire in a mass, some scurrying for cover while others hurried to put up a tent they hadn't gotten around to assembling before dinner.

Unfortunately Kelsey belonged to the latter group. By the time she and Natalie had arrived the women had already been starting to prepare dinner. Not about to lose her chance for some early bonding, she'd set her gear aside to assist with the food. Natalie had followed suit and now their equipment and bags were being drenched.

"We should have waited to help out with breakfast I guess," she yelled as they ran to where they'd left their gear, and started pulling out their tents.

"Hindsight," she heard Natalie mumble, then ignored her completely as she went fast to work on getting her tent assembled.

Thankfully, she had camped in it many times and within a couple minutes she was hooking the rain cover in place and tossing her duffel bag and sleeping gear into the tent. She crawled inside and shivered at the sudden chill that had overtaken the night. Rain plastered the canvas over her head, and her T-shirt and shorts clung to her body. Feeling soggy, miserable and, thanks to Jan's desertion, alone, she reached for her duffel bag in search of dry clothes. Loud swearing stopped her mid-search. It was Natalie's voice. And she didn't sound happy.

Unzipping a side window, Kelsey looked across to where Natalie had left her gear. A large, dark figure dashed around, and blistering curses singed the air.

"Damn." She obviously couldn't figure out how to put up the tent. The darkness and biting rain couldn't be helping things.

She should leave her out there to fend for herself. After all, the woman had come to an outdoor event where sleeping in a tent or under the stars was mandatory. It therefore followed the attendees knew how to assemble their gear. It might follow, but at the moment logic wasn't going to solve a thing.

Neither was putting off the inevitable.

Even if to do so would ease her mystified state of mind and more so body, Kelsey was too nice to leave Natalie out there on her own, shivering in the rain. Nice and sensible. Natalie was a woman she had befriended and already felt a connection with, she assured herself. A connection that was about friendship, not sex.

Opening the front flap of the tent, she poked her head out and shouted toward the small flash of light she presumed to be coming from a flashlight. "What are you doing?"

"I can't seem to figure this out," Natalie yelled back, her irritation clear.

"Well, by the time you do, you're going to be soaked." Kelsey unzipped the canvas door the rest of the way and flung it back. "Get in here. You can share mine for the night. It's a two-person."

Natalie halted her erratic movements and stared at her. "Share yours?"

She couldn't make out her face, but her tone sounded stunned, as if the idea were the worst thing she'd ever heard. It confirmed what Kelsey had guessed back at the fire. Natalie thought she wanted her. Nerves reawakened in her belly with the notion, and she was determined to bring her into the tent and prove otherwise by not groping her while she slept. "Yes. Unless you'd rather stand around and get wet."

Natalie remained still for another few seconds then shook her head. "No. I don't want to do that."

"Then get in here."

"Okay. Just let me grab my stuff."

Kelsey watched long enough to see the other woman grab her bags and start toward her, then moved back into the warmth and dryness of the tent and prayed she hadn't just made a terrible mistake.

* * * * *

He had never felt more incompetent in his life. If Duane was here right now he'd be laughing his ass off. Nate had put up hundreds of tents through the years, possibly thousands. He'd never put a single damned one up when he was wearing a bra with enough padding to sink a ship. And more notably, more than enough to prohibit him from maneuvering the tent poles into position.

It was Duane's fault he had such a damned big chest. Duane just kept stuffing the bra, saying how big-boned woman were typically big-breasted too. Duane, who he had to thank for the long night ahead, in the last place he wanted to be. In Kelsey's tent. With Kelsey's warm, tempting body mere feet away from him. Kelsey's vivid eyes closed and her ripe, lush mouth susceptible to his kiss while she slept.

Hell, he shouldn't be going into that tent. Not after the jolt of pure sexual arousal he'd gotten from the heat of her breath in his ear. Her whispered words had done far more than awaken his cock from the flaccid state he'd managed to keep it in throughout dinner. They had momentarily turned him stupid, enough so to make him reach out and caress her pulse, feel it pounding beneath his touch. The heat that sparked in her eyes ensured she hadn't missed the magnetism between them. It also ensured she'd been scared as hell by the idea of finding another woman physically appealing.

No, he shouldn't be going into that tent. Not by a long damned shot. But into that tent was exactly where he was going.

It was either that or sleep in the truck. So long as he had breasts the size of melons he couldn't put up his own tent to save his life. While he'd planned to use the excuse his presence here was a marketing tactic should he be caught, he realized now using this weekend to gain professional insight was actually a good idea. He understood women just fine, that didn't mean he knew what they wanted from a sports outfitter. He would spend the next two days making a mental list, starting with a chest-friendly tent.

Reaching Kelsey's tent, Nate tossed his belongings inside the front flap. He shook the excess rainwater from his wig, then climbed in backwards and tugged off his muddy boots, leaving them beside hers by the entrance. He zipped up the door and blackness surrounded him. Darkness broken only by the slight rustle of what sounded to be clothing, and barely audible breathing coming from just behind him.

Both sounds were way too intimate. They made him think of rumpled sheets and sweaty skin. Of breathy sighs and frantic moans. Of the hungry look in Kelsey's eyes when he'd touched her at the campfire, of the cries of ecstasy he'd evoked when he tongued her in his vision hours ago. He groaned inwardly at the way his penis responded to his thoughts, growing hard in an instant, then turned when a light flickered to life. He blinked, adjusting to the sudden intensity, and followed the beam to its source. An oil lantern was settled off to one side of the tent, and two short feet from it was Kelsey. Naked.

Oh, Christ.

"What the fuck are you doing?" The question was automatic, and the second it was out of his mouth, Nate regretted it. Even more so when she turned to frown at him. She wasn't naked, which if he'd been looking anywhere but at all that smooth, supple skin exposed for his viewing pleasure he would have known. She'd just taken off her shirt to reveal the sheerest looking black lace bra he'd ever seen, and he had seen plenty.

His aching cock grew harder yet within its snug confines, and he cursed the fact she wasn't wearing camping underwear. He could have handled camping underwear. Damn it, why the hell wasn't she wearing camping underwear!

"Getting out of these wet clothes. I'm soaked and don't care to get sick."

Hearing the slight edge to her voice, he dropped his gaze from the small, firm breasts that were even more appealing than they'd been in his vision and focused on her belly. He sucked in a breath at the silver and purple ring adorning her navel, and his penis stiffened to an entire new level of painful hardness. "Oh, hell, that is so hot."

"What?"

Nate's gaze flew to Kelsey's face. Her forehead was creased with fine lines and her eyes held something between horror and shock. Not that he would look any different if the situation were reversed and it were a man ogling his half-naked body with such open appreciation. Actually, he would look different. By now he'd have that man by the throat and be leveling a few choice words his way if not a fist or two.

He struggled to form conversation that didn't involve sexual connotations. "Ah, your belly button ring is...hot. I've...ah...been thinking of getting one for myself. Now that I've seen how sexy they make a girl look, I know I want one for sure."

"Oh." Her forehead evened out and she shrugged. "It was either that or a nipple ring. I figured with my tendency for bad luck a nipple ring would catch on my clothing and get ripped off. And frankly, I'm not into that kind of pain."

He sucked in another breath as the candor in her words took their toll on his body, cramping his balls so tightly in the cup there was a good chance they would never be the same again. He was here to make friends, Nate reminded himself sternly. He was here to prove to Joe that he could handle getting to know a woman he found attractive on a personal level without wanting her on a sexual one as well. He was not here to indulge his overzealous libido. Yet, as much as he knew all that, he still couldn't stop his attention from roaming back to Kelsey's breasts.

It was her own damned fault. The way she was all but asking him to look at her nipples, he just couldn't say no. He *could* be objective. After all, it wasn't like he hadn't seen plenty of nipples in his life.

Just not any quite as dusky pink and visibly standing on end the way hers were right now, Nate realized on a hasty gulp. Damn, the thin lace of her bra held so little back she might as well not have bothered with one at all. Her erect nipples pointed straight toward him, looking exactly as they had in his vision earlier tonight. Only in his vision he wasn't nearly so far away.

In his vision he was right in front of her, pulling those tight, hot buds into his mouth and aching to fondle her pussy with his fingers. In his vision he'd proceeded to do just that, only with his tongue.

His hand came up on instinct, ready to reach for her. The barely audible squeak that escaped Kelsey's mouth had him dropping it back to his side. He lifted his gaze slowly to find pale red streaked over her upper chest, then looked higher and found the shade had taken over her neck and face too. He connected with her eyes then and the blend of panic and hunger that burned there couldn't have been any more clear.

He was a bad, bad man to make her have such awful thoughts as the ones that must be going through her head right now. He ought to come clean with her, only to do so would ruin the entire point of this weekend. If she knew the truth, the odds she would stand by and help him were slim. And then there was the fact that if she knew the truth, she wouldn't let him into her tent any more. As much as that would probably be a good thing, at the moment he couldn't convince himself of that fact.

Several more seconds of silent staring passed before Kelsey finally turned her back on him. "Anyway... I, uh, need to find some pajamas."

She crawled to her duffel bag and bent over in search of what he guessed to be the aforementioned pajamas. Nate had no idea if she ever found them, because all he could see was her shapely ass waving in front of his face. Mocking him. Telling him just what an idiot he was. An idiot, he realized as his pulse ascended to a potentially dangerous level, who his brother might have been right about. He just might be incapable of developing a friendship with a woman he found attractive.

Or maybe it was just this woman.

That had to be it. Kelsey had taken him by surprise. His first impression of her was that she was cute, innocent and naïve. The truth was she wasn't a single damned one of those things. And now that he knew that beyond a doubt, he could work around it and get back to his whole point of being here.

Not to fantasize about wrapping his tongue around a sexy as hell belly button ring or slicing it down the sticky, sweetness of her center, but to develop friendships.

He could do that. He would do that. Starting with Kelsey first thing in the morning. After his cock had a chance to relax and the image of her tight rear end and nipple-hardened breasts was flushed from his mind.

Chapter Three

Some part of her mind told her to not scream with the mind-bending feel of the tongue suckling at her pussy, but Kelsey wasn't up to listening.

Closing her eyes to the blackness of night, she relaxed against the covers and let the impassioned cries come out while her hands moved to the back of the man between her widespread thighs. His powerful tongue sliced over the swollen lips of her cunt and liquid warmth gushed from deep within. Tension pulled at her from every angle. His teeth bit down, grating against her clit, tugging at the nubbin with teasing nips, and it was all she could do not to dig her nails deep into his muscled flesh.

The nips subsided and hot breath caressed her slit, sending a delightful shiver coursing through her body. A shudder that was forgotten when his mouth fitted over her sex an instant later. His tongue returned to her sheath, flicking deep into the arousal-slackened valley of her pussy and threatening to push her over the edge.

She was so close, so very close…

Kelsey bowed up and pressed her cunt harder against his gifted mouth, demanding more pressure, longer, firmer strokes. His large hands palmed her naked ass and tipped her hips higher, granting his tongue deeper access. He took it immediately, increasing the strength of his flicks, pushing into her vagina faster, fucking her with his mouth and tongue until she couldn't stop from mindlessly writhing beneath him any more than releasing a second round of restless screams.

"Todd! Oh, yes, baby, right there! God, I love it when you lick me there."

His tongue stilled and he asked in a raspy whisper, "Where is there, sweetheart? Where am I licking you?"

The barely audible question halted Kelsey's desperate writhing, her racing heart. Todd had never asked her to talk dirty before, but it seemed that's exactly what he wanted. Why shouldn't she indulge him? It would benefit them both. "My pussy. You're licking my pussy and it feels so good. I love it when you fuck my cunt with your tongue. I love it even more when you're filling me up with your big, hard cock."

A rolling laugh drifted to her. A laugh that didn't sound like Todd's. It sounded far softer, feminine almost. But that was ridiculous, a trick her mind was playing on her. It had to be Todd in her bed. It might be dark and the middle of the night, but she still knew where she was, in her home, with the man she loved.

"So you want to feel my big, hard cock inside you, do you? Buried between those sweet, plump lips of yours or maybe deep in your pretty, little pussy, or is it the other end you're after? Do you want it from behind, sweetheart?"

Every suggestion reached Kelsey as a rough whisper of heated words that turned her stimulation from steamy to sizzling. She wanted to answer him, wanted to tell him exactly where she wanted to feel him, how she wanted to be loved. Before she could do or say anything, the hands at her thighs moved to her sides and rolled her onto her stomach. She bit back a whimper as her belly brushed against something cool and hard. Something that didn't feel like her warm, soft mattress. It didn't feel nice. In fact, it hurt a little, as did Todd's hands. He'd never been this aggressive before.

As if he knew her thoughts, his hands moved from her sides to palm the cheeks of her buttocks. One large finger teased the center of her ass and she drew in a ragged breath as that same finger reared forward and entered her from behind. Fear chased through her mind, followed quickly by urgent longing as he began to move within her.

43

Her pussy pulsed, heavy with the juices of arousal, and Kelsey bit back a jagged cry that he give her more, take her fully, fuck her from behind.

God, how she wanted that. She'd never done it before, never trusted a man enough to try it, but she wanted to try it now with Todd. "Yes. More. Please."

"You want my cock in your ass, do you, sweetheart?"

The voice was teasing, grating, and once again held a feminine ring that sounded nothing like Todd. The part of her mind that had told her not to scream now told her not to give in to his playful taunting. She shouldn't, but she had to. Her blood burned, her pussy ached to be filled and her nipples were so hard and hot it felt as though his hands were on them even now. They weren't on her breasts though. They were on her buttocks, palming her, fingering her. Bringing tears of awe to her eyes over the immense sense of ecstasy his touch rendered.

Kelsey wriggled back against his probing finger and bit her lower lip as sensation after blinding sensation coiled in her cunt and filled her limb to limb. She couldn't silence her shouts. "Yes! I want that! I want to feel you in my ass!"

She expected further conversation, more teasing words before he gave into her wishes. No words came. Only the feel of his hand moving beneath her to palm her belly, then the unmistakable feel of a swollen and precome-lubricated cockhead rubbing against the seam of her buttocks. The hand at her belly slipped lower and long fingers threaded through the soaked curls at her mound. Two moved further, dipping to her feminine lips, then going further still to bury deep into her inflamed sex.

She cried out with the contact, and his big fingers moved against her pussy, fingering her throbbing clit, tangling in her pubic hair, coaxing her to come undone.

"Come for me, sweetheart." His low voice mimicked the silent plea in his actions. "I know you want to. I even know what will make you do it."

She didn't have time to wonder over what that might be, as he reared back, then thrust forward and pumped his swollen cock into her ass. The breath caught hard in her throat with the force of entry. His hands moved to her breasts and he held her tightly to him. Warm flesh pressed against her back and long, silky hair caressed her neck and shoulders. Hair that wasn't hers.

Kelsey's breathing came even harder with the thought. Todd had short, neatly trimmed hair. Hair that wouldn't touch her neck or her shoulders. That being the case, who the hell was it that held her so intimately now?

Panic clawed at her belly, panic she strove to hang onto as the stranger in her bed turned up the pace. His fingers toyed with her aroused nipples. His cock stroked the sensitive inner muscles of her buttocks. The air around them ignited with the heady sweet scent of sex.

The part of her mind that had forewarned her not to give in, attempted to be heard one last time. But it was too late. She couldn't hold back another second, couldn't escape this stranger's arms and the pleasure he wrought. She could only give in to sweet mercy in the form of gratifying shudders of ecstasy that claimed her head to toe.

"Oh, God, I'm coming! I'm coming. I'm coming."

The chant continued, followed her into a hazy state of euphoria, then suddenly rescinded as a rush of pale light spilled against her closed eyelids and the pleasure that racked through her died an instant death.

Kelsey squeezed her lids tighter and groaned.

It had only been a dream. It wasn't even dark out. The only reality here was the man in her bed, cupping her breasts. The man who was clearly Todd doing his best to get some early morning loving. She should make do with the dream orgasm and get up and ready for work. Only the way he was stroking her through her sweatshirt, the way his hard, lean body felt pressed against her back, the strength and security his embrace provided… It all made it too hard to open her eyes and face the day just yet.

The stroke of his fingers grew faster, more insistent, and he caught an erect nipple and twisted and plucked at it. Heat coiled low in her belly and the liquid warmth in her pussy that resulted from her dream turned to a pool of burning desire. Her cunt throbbed, aching for release, to feel his fingers buried inside its warm, wet interior, thrusting deep and hard the way she thought they'd been doing moments ago.

The hand at her breast lifted, then touched down beneath her shirt. His fingers felt rougher than they had in the dream. Callused. She didn't recall Todd ever having callused hands any more than he'd ever had long hair. She liked the abrasiveness though. Liked the way the hard pads of his thumbs chafed across her nipples and shot raw need from the swollen tips direct to her core. She could imagine easily how amazing they would feel rubbing against her clit.

The dream orgasm had been good, but it wasn't the real thing. She wanted the real thing, needed those strong, capable hands on all of her, needed her own on him as well.

She'd used words to coax him into making his next move in the dream. But he hadn't been the same Todd in that dream. In real life, she wasn't certain he would respond to dirty talk. Actions however had always been a thing he understood.

Moaning in the back of her throat, Kelsey slipped her hand beneath her shirt and caught his. Wordlessly, she pulled his hand lower, indicating the place she burned for his touch. With the aid of her guidance, he moved to the edge of her sweatpants and then beneath the waistband. She sucked in a sharp breath at the first contact of his hand on her mound, his fingers coaxing the dewy curls, and then groaned her impatience when they didn't continue to go farther.

Thanks to that amazingly lifelike dream, she was unbearably wet, hot and eager to explode. All it would take was one stroke of his thumb over her clit and she would be climaxing. They'd been together long enough that Todd had to know how close she was to coming. Even if he couldn't read her body's desperate moves, he had to hear her jagged breathing, the hasty beat of her heart, the dampness that permeated the lips of her cunt to moisten her pubic hair. So why was he holding back?

Maybe he really did want dirty talk. Or maybe it was just more action on her part he was after. Both were worth trying.

"I want you, now, baby. I want to feel you fucking me. I want to feel your fingers deep inside my pussy. I know you want that too."

A low grunt followed her words and the hand at her mound clamped down. Taking that for his response and that he was in complete acceptance, she ground her ass against his groin and reached behind her. She latched her fingers onto his buttocks through a thin pair of shorts, squeezed hard, virile flesh…and froze.

Seconds ago, Kelsey's heart had felt close to beating out of control. Now it stilled and the breath cruised from her lungs on a painful huff. Todd had a decent rear end, but as was the case with the long hair from her dream and the calluses she'd first detected on this person's hands moments ago, he didn't possess the one she currently grasped. Worse, far worse, was the fact this was no erotic fantasy she was about to wake up from. This was cold hard reality. A stranger held her, a stranger who had his hands down her pants because she'd put them there.

Her eyes snapped open as panic once more reared. Struggling to forget the hand that still cupped her sex, she looked to the one that lay on her hip. Morning was just dawning and inside the canvas walls of the tent the lighting wasn't the best. Still, she could make out the hand, the long fingers tipped with red polished nails.

Red… Polished… Nails…

Kelsey's heart slammed into her ribs and she wheezed back a gasp as clarity dawned. It hadn't been Todd who infiltrated her dreams and left her wet and horny. It wasn't Todd who held her now. It was Natalie. Natalie with the long, silky hair. Natalie with the strong, callused fingers. Natalie with the feminine voice and magical tongue.

Oh...my...God!

Inhaling long, calming breaths, while her sanity threatened to run far and fast away, Kelsey slid her hand beneath the waistband of her sweatpants and guided the hand she'd moments ago led into her pants back out. Cautiously, she moved from the ground then resettled Natalie's hands on the sleeping bag. Natalie didn't make so much as a sound. In fact, aside from that one grunt, Natalie hadn't made a sound the entire time she'd been touching her. Kelsey could only pray that meant she was asleep, that she'd been asleep the whole time and if anything presumed the whole thing to be the same kind of wet dream Kelsey had had. Or maybe nightmare was the better choice of words here.

Kelsey didn't turn back to verify things one way or the other, but grabbed her boots and darted out of the tent and into the early stillness of morning.

She hustled to put distance between herself and the tent, venting to herself as she went, "What is wrong with you?!"

How the hell could've she been so stimulated by another woman's touch? It would have been bad enough had things ended with the dream, but they hadn't. She'd been awake and wanting Natalie so badly she'd actually begged her to sink her fingers into her pussy. She'd been on the cusp of rolling over and wrapping her legs around Natalie's waist, to taking Natalie's non-existent erection into her hand, for God's sake!

The fact the woman didn't have a penis should have been clear when Kelsey had rubbed so urgently against her groin and encountered nothing more than a solid surface that had clearly been the hard ridge of her mound or pelvis. Only it hadn't been enough, not by a long shot. She'd felt that gently rounded surface and had gone right on rubbing, right on writhing. Right on silently pleading for more.

Damn it, she did *not* do these kinds of things with other women! One of the points of inviting Natalie into her tent had been to prove that very fact, that she could get through a night without groping her.

She hadn't made it.

But that didn't have anything to do with her wanting Natalie. She'd been confused in both the dream and real life. She'd thought she was still with Todd and it was he who'd stroked her nipples. He who'd worked his fingers into her pubic hair. He who'd had her pussy throbbing with the need to make her dream one big, Technicolor reality.

"Oh, God!" She was not going to think about that.

She was going to…to…visit.

The sun was only just beginning to rise, but there was already a small fire made and a handful of women milling about. Women she felt she could be herself around. Her outdoor-loving, heterosexual self.

* * * * *

Dumbass. What the fuck had he been thinking?

First off, Nate had been thinking that Kelsey was asleep. He never imagined in a million years she would come into his arms and proceed to rub against him until he was too aroused to stop himself from reaching out to her otherwise. He sure as hell never thought she would ask him to fuck her, then proceed to take his hand in her own and stick it down her pants.

Christ, she'd been so wet, so aroused…

He hadn't even touched her pussy and he could feel the heat coming off from her, feel her wetness soaking her pubic hair, smell the essence of her sex on the air. Between the dirty talk and her erotic scent, he'd been a lost cause. He'd been on the verge of saying to hell with it and fucking her right then and there consequences be damned, when she'd finally came alert and stopped him.

Not that her stopping him made things any easier in the long run.

Nate had thought last night's leering and subtle touch had been bad of him, but this morning's moves were downright evil by comparison. Kelsey's head had to be spinning with thoughts she didn't care to entertain. His own was thick with the wonder of how the hell he was supposed to treat her like a friend after touching her in a way that was anything but friendly. Somehow he had to forget the way her breast filled his palm, the soft, husky sounds she made deep in her throat when she was aroused, the intoxicating as hell scent that filled his nostrils whenever she was within two feet of him. That somehow wasn't going to be easy considering his cock was pulsing and his balls ready to explode out of the damnable cup at the mere thought of her.

Difficult or not, he would do it. He would show her that he was just another one of the girls with a feminine side a mile wide and not the slightest in the way of same-sex tendencies. And after he'd convinced her and they'd had a chance to do some of the bonding Joe believed he was incapable of, he would move on to befriending more women.

He could form nonsexual, inter-gender friendships as much as the next person. Right after he did any necessary touch-up shaving and saw to his morning makeup routine, he would prove it too.

* * * * *

Partner hike. Two words that to Kelsey sounded a lot like isolating yourself in the woods with the woman you spent the morning avoiding.

She couldn't ignore Natalie forever. She'd already walked away from her question without so much as a word of response. It was rude and very unlike her. At that moment saving face was not on the top of her list of things to worry over. Natalie had joined the morning campfire less than a half hour after Kelsey woke. It was enough time to hope she hadn't been awake during the touchy-feely session, but it wasn't nearly enough time to set Kelsey's mind at ease.

Regardless of her fears, she couldn't be edgy or rude any longer. Women were quickly pairing off for the hike and if she didn't act fast someone else would claim Natalie as their partner. Allowing someone else to claim her would probably be the best thing Kelsey could do. At the risk of being stuck with someone who made her even more uneasy than Natalie, if such a thing were even possible, or worse, being stuck alone, she wasn't about to let that happen.

She hurried over to where Natalie stood talking with a small group of women and tapped her on the shoulder. Heat surged through her fingertips and she took an automatic step back and sighed. It was not awareness the subtle touch had evoked, it was simply a shock. The kind a person could receive from something as inanimate as a door or a pair of freshly washed jeans. Just a shock.

Natalie turned and smiled. Unlike most of the women who didn't bother much with their appearance during this weekend away from the bulk of civilization, she wore makeup. Not enough to look garish, but enough to nearly conceal the slight hint of a mustache and bring out the golden hue of her eyes. "Hi. I thought you had already picked a partner and took off."

Kelsey returned her attention to the slight trace of a mustache just visible beneath the brilliant rays of the morning sun and bit back a nervous laugh. It wasn't enough she was having strange feelings for a woman, but she had to pick a woman who clearly battled to keep herself from looking masculine. "No. I thought you planned to partner with me today."

Natalie's eyes warmed. "I do. I've been looking forward to partnering with you since last night."

Kelsey swallowed hard at the implication that seemed to be hidden in the response, and for the first time a thought occurred to her. What if Natalie didn't just think she was a lesbian, what if Natalie was one herself and was using this weekend to meet a new girlfriend? Oh, God, what if Natalie had been awake this morning and not only enjoying every minute of it, but was aware just how into it Kelsey had been?

Anxiety lurched in her belly even as a rush of wet warmth gathered in her panties. She blinked back the shock that came with the unexpected stimulation the idea caused and drew a long breath of cool morning air. When words finally made their way out of her mouth, they weren't even close to the ones she wanted to say. Those words were, *"Sorry, I changed my mind about this weekend. I have to go home now and pretend we never felt each other up."* "Uh, okay. Well, if you're ready..."

"Just let me grab my pack."

Kelsey used the time it took for Natalie to round up her gear and rejoin her to take several more long, deep breaths and regain her senses. She was behaving like an idiot, letting her imagination run wild and turn something that was merely a blossoming friendship into something that she didn't even want to digest. At least her mind didn't want to digest the way Natalie aroused her. Her body seemed to have its own plans. Her sex was still heavy from the memory of this morning's encounter and as the thoughts assailed her now, her nipples stiffened as well.

Cursing her reaction, she crossed her arms firmly over her chest. She was building this up in her head, is all. She honestly didn't feel anything sexual toward the other woman. She couldn't, and if she didn't stop thinking she did and get back to her normal self, the one that Natalie had first met last night, the other woman was going to get paranoid and stop talking to her altogether. She refused to let that happen. She liked Natalie, felt they had already started to bond, and she wouldn't lose her friendship over foolish fears.

Kelsey took one last calming breath as Natalie returned and they started on their journey up the winding mountain trails. The first fifteen minutes of the hike they were accompanied by other women, then the group slowly dwindled until it was the two of them on their own narrow path. Kelsey managed to keep her edginess to a minimum and even that died away when the path opened up to reveal a valley of wild flowers and dried mountain grass. A Monarch butterfly with blazing orange and black wings soared past and she practically salivated as the photographer in her took over.

Using a knee-high tree stump as a table, she dropped her pack onto its lichen-coated surface and took out her camera. She attached the telephoto lens and repositioned the settings to best suit the area and lighting. Then unable to hold back a moment longer, she breathed in the untamed beauty of her surroundings meshed with the scent of the overnight rain and began snapping.

Nate was certain he had never witnessed anything more equally appealing and terrifying as the woman Kelsey had become the moment they stepped into the clearing. Her eyes were the color of smoke and a smile claimed her unpainted lips so widely that the dimple in her cheek looked ready to burst with pleasure. She was the embodiment of natural beauty, alive in her surroundings, so much so that warmth and excitement radiated from every inch of her. And he was harder than he'd ever been in his life.

The blood pumped in his veins and his cock was pressed so snugly against its tight confines he had to bite back a grunt of pain. A smart man would turn away until she was done playing photographer and that arousing as hell dimple left her cheek. Apparently he wasn't smart, because he couldn't make himself turn away for anything.

Moving her hiking pack aside, he took a seat on the stump and made a quick adjustment that took some of the pressure off his shaft and balls. He watched as she moved through the lush valley, taking pictures like a woman possessed. She circled around and returned to him some fifteen minutes later. She snapped a picture of him, then moved the camera from her vision and smiled.

The pressure Nate had managed to remove from his cock and balls returned stronger than ever and he found himself grinning right back, thinking the last things in the world a man out to establish a platonic relationship should be thinking. Things like how soft, sweet and sensual her lips looked right now. How the gleam of excitement in her expressive eyes and her wind tousled hair made it seem as if she'd just emerged from a lover's arms and not a field of wild flowers. And by far the worst thought of all, how badly he ached to make his brother right about him and finish what she'd started this morning.

The setting was perfect. He would lay her back on the mossy ground and slowly strip away her clothes until only his hands and his body covered her ripe, rounded curves. He'd palm her breasts, suck on her distended nipples and then slide into her damp pussy with his fingers. He'd fuck her as she'd asked him to do this morning, not stopping until she was on the verge of exploding. Then he'd take her with his mouth, lick and bite at her swollen cunt until she couldn't hold back a moment longer and she cried out her ecstasy while releasing her heady essence onto his tongue.

"That really gets you off, huh?"

Kelsey's mesmerizing smile vanished. The camera fell to dangle from the strap at her neck and she pinned him with a distraught look. "What do you mean, gets me off?"

Nate blinked at the shock in both her question and expression. The words he'd spoken in the midst of his reverie registered and he bit back a groan. He'd thought his blurted comment over her belly button ring last night had been obtuse, but this one beat it hands down.

And once more it was her own damned fault.

She did things to set herself up for his ogling and out of place remarks. Things like taking pictures of ordinary butterflies and smiling so hard over the feat you'd have thought she'd captured Big Foot on film. Didn't she see how that type of behavior could affect a man, make him lose his judgment and fantasize over things he knew damned well better than to imagine?

No, she most likely didn't see it, because he was probably the only man on the planet who felt ready to come from such an innocent action.

Checking his thoughts, he stood. "I don't think that came out quite right. I meant you enjoy taking pictures."

Her gaze softened and she nodded. "Oh, yeah. It's part of my job."

Jobs. Now there was safe territory. There was nothing even remotely sexual in talking about jobs, and better yet, it would give him a chance to get to know Kelsey on a more personal level—his whole point of being here. He hefted her pack over his arm and started slowly down the trail. "So, what do you do?"

When she didn't respond, he turned back to find her standing where he'd left her, looking after him. An odd expression was back on her face. Not exactly distraught as it had been before, but not exactly relaxed either. "What's the matter?"

She sent a pointed glance at his shoulder. "You don't need to carry my bag."

"Oh." He swung the pack from his shoulder and handed it to her. "Habit, I guess. My brother and his wife and I take turns escorting my grandmother around. She's had a lot of problems with breaks this past year. If I can help it, I try to stop her from carrying anything too heavy."

The look Kelsey shot him said she wasn't sure if she believed him. The irony was it was probably the first time he'd told her the truth all morning. Her lips fell flat after a few seconds and she moved past him along the path. When she finally spoke her voice was low and uneven. "That's nice. I used to be close with my grandparents too."

The ache in her tone was subtle, but Nate heard it nonetheless. It started a slow pressure building in his upper chest. A pressure that told him he'd been right about women and their feelings. How they dragged them into a relationship and let them all hang out. It also reminded him of the reason he'd hadn't established a friendship with a woman in the past.

She made him feel sympathetic, made him want to ask even more questions in an attempt to soothe her. "They're passed on?"

"Yeah."

The one word answer was direct, enough so to make it clear she didn't want to share more. And since he had no real longing to uncover any further emotions, he moved past the subject. "What about your parents? Do they live around you?"

Kelsey paused an instant, before saying in a tight voice, "Gone too."

He bit back a grunt. He could dismiss her grandparents' deaths, but not her parents' quite so easily. Not when she clearly still grieved over their loss, and certainly not when he thought about how close he was with his own. "I'm sorry. I can't imagine."

"Don't be, it was a long time ago. I just don't generally talk about it." She glanced back at him and smiled. "Anyway, you were asking about my job. I work for the Green County Conservation Department. While they've never given me an official title, I guess you could say I'm a naturalist. Mainly my work entails documenting nature in print."

Nate didn't miss the way she sped past the topic of her parents and while he was tempted to ask more, her latest revelation had him temporarily forgetting his questions. That and the fact she'd turned back to continue along the trail in front of him.

He followed the hypnotic sway of her firm ass, lust hammering through his bloodstream and any chance of his cock softening in the next twenty-four hours dying away completely. His mind filled with fresh ideas on how he might make her forget any lingering sadness she felt over her parents' and grandparents' death, and it was all he could do to stop himself from reaching out and dragging her to him. Not that sex would erase her sorrow permanently, but it couldn't hurt things either.

Nothing but his peace of his mind, that is.

Kelsey might be a naturalist, and therefore about as outdoorsy as a person could get, and she might have a dynamite body and a smile that made him feel as randy as a teenager, but she wasn't on his list of women to make his lover. Not that he actually had a list, but even if he did her name would have no place on it. He was here to make friends, and friendship is what he would have with Kelsey.

While it might be easier to move onto making friends with someone less tempting, it wouldn't verify what he'd come here to prove. That he could handle having a nonsexual relationship with a woman he found attractive. And he had to prove it, because the closer he got to Kelsey and the more he learned about her on a personal level, the more he found himself doubting his claim.

Needing to eliminate any tension that might still be between them, he concentrated his efforts on making friendly conversation. "If you're into documentation, does that mean I can expect to see that shot you took of me in some future paper?"

"Actually, it would be in a book if anywhere, but I doubt I'll use that one."

"I take it I'm not pretty enough for you?" The words were out of Nate's mouth before he could stop them. It was a habit, casual flirting. One he wished to hell he'd have left at home this weekend along with his libido.

She stopped short and glanced back at him, shaking her head. Red fanned up her neck and streaked her cheeks. "Of course not! You're a very attractive woman."

While he wanted to eliminate the tension between them, the response was so unexpected he couldn't quite contain his grin. "You think so, huh?"

The red in Kelsey's face turned to deep scarlet and she looked away and started walking again. He could just hear her mumbling under her breath. It reminded him of the moment he'd first set eyes on her, floundering in the mud the evening before. He'd thought her clumsy at the time, the perfect distraction to take attention away from him, but since that moment she hadn't done anything remotely awkward. Well, outside of sliding what she believed to be another woman's hand down her pants and proceeding to grope that same woman's ass. As far as being distracting, she did have that part down. Only the person she was distracting, namely him, wasn't the person or rather persons he had intended to be.

"Should I take your silence as a yes or a no?" Nate asked when a few seconds had passed and she had yet to respond.

She glanced back again, the red was gone from her face, but her eyes still shifted from side to side, pointedly ignoring his. "I think you're attractive, plenty enough to be in one of my books. It's just that I don't normally include people in them. It tends to be purely wildlife."

He nodded his understanding. It was a reputable response. One that didn't say much about the fact she'd admitted to finding another woman appealing and yet also didn't put down his looks. He'd been right about that much in his initial assessment of her at least. She was a sympathetic woman where others were concerned.

"So, uh, what do you do?" she asked.

"I own an outdoor…" He droned off and shook his head. He did not own an outdoor superstore chain. Not this weekend anyway.

"A what?"

Good question, what the hell was it that he did? For some reason in planning this weekend Nate had put a lot of thought into how he would convince the women around him that he was one of them. He hadn't put a single thought into what it was he did for a living. He'd just borrow Duane's shop for the weekend. No way the man would mind. Or ever know for that matter. "I co-own a Sporties store."

Kelsey responded without turning back. "They rent kayaks and things like that, right?"

"Yeah."

"Which one?"

"What?"

She shrugged, but kept walking. "There are a few of them around here. One of them is only a couple blocks from my house."

How convenient. Could he be so lucky as to have her turn up at it Monday morning asking where Natalie was? "Where do you live?"

"In Grayson City."

"Nice area." Not only was it over an hour away and not the city where Duane's store was located, but it was both the perfect change in topic and the opportunity for him to develop their relationship a bit more. "One of my sisters used to live there. She moved out of state a couple years ago. Do you have any siblings?"

"Just an older brother."

As it had when she'd spoken of her parents and grandparents, emotion entered her voice. This time it was edged with a happiness that suggested a smile lit her face. It also brought unexpected warmth into his heart. The reaction was about relief and nothing more, Nate assured himself. Relief to think she wasn't alone in the world. That it mattered to him if she were or not was something he'd worry about later. "You're close with your brother?"

"Yeah. Though we don't see each other nearly enough. Andy travels a lot. I used to go with him, but..." Her voice droned off and she hesitated a few seconds before continuing, as if trying to decide how much she wanted to share. "I didn't have any real place to call home for so long I guess you could say I felt the need to establish roots. I still go with him whenever I can, but now I have a home and a job to come back to."

Compassion erupted inside him with the answer. If she didn't have any real place to call home then what did it say of her childhood? How long ago had her parents died and where was she raised? He shouldn't want to know the answers. He'd never wanted to know such intimate details about a person before. It had to be his feminine side showing through, the side effects of getting close with a woman. "Your brother sounds pretty great."

"He is," Kelsey agreed, happiness once more apparent in her tone. "Actually, you've probably heard of him. Andrew Stuart. He's on the sports channels quite a bit. ESPN2 aired a week-long special on him last month."

Nate's rambling thoughts came to a standstill, as did his feet. He stared after her in shock. "Andrew Stuart is your brother? The man who will take any challenge put before him no matter how death-defying it might be? The one who's broken more bones in his body than most people even are aware they have and yet he keeps going back for more? The one who's climbed Everest not once, but three times? *That* Andrew Stuart?"

Several yards in the distance Kelsey swiveled around. The gleam of sisterly esteem in her eyes was practically tangible and that sexy as hell dimple flashed in her cheek. "The one and only, and I'll take it by the goofy grin you already know more about him than I could probably ever tell you."

He might, and he might not. What Nate did know was the more he learned about Kelsey the harder he was finding it to resist her and the attraction that was practically screaming to life between them. Not that he wanted her more because of who her brother was—a man he'd respected to the fullest, but hadn't yet had the pleasure to meet. It was the fact she was proud of her brother and not only fully supported his risky stunts, but did her best to tag along with him on his travels that had his heart beating harder and his testosterone shooting through his body at a potentially lethal rate.

It was as if the embodiment of everything he'd ever hoped to find in a wife stood before him now. And Kelsey thought his reaction was all about her brother. He couldn't have asked for a better interpretation on her part. As much as she might be everything he'd ever wanted in a wife, she wasn't what he wanted in a lover. Looks-wise, she was perfect. Sexually, oh yeah, she had that one down to a science. It was the feelings part where things became messy.

She'd admitted the night before how easily her emotions became involved in relationships, and that she wasn't the type to have sex on the run. He wasn't the type to have it any other way. At least, not for the time being. It was good they were on such opposite ends of the playing field. Knowing she was off limits would make keeping things between them to a friendly level much easier.

"Hey, don't feel strange about wanting my brother," Kelsey said. "Andy has that effect on women of all ages. You mention his name, and their brains and various other parts of their bodies turn to mush."

He smiled at the truth in her words. Andrew Stuart had that effect on many men too, Nate knew. Not the mush factor, but the awe factor. It was the latter the man had on him, but he would leave it up to Kelsey to interpret things how she might. "I'm glad you feel that way, because I think I'm in love with your brother."

She laughed. The sound was high and melodious and rich with relief. "If you want, the next time he's around the area I'll be happy to introduce you."

His smile fell flat and his gut churned. He'd wanted to meet Andrew for years and now he had the opportunity to meet him face to face and with only the man's sister in tow. His sister, who, if Nate turned down her gracious offer any woman in their right mind would sell their body to obtain, would assume he was after her. His sister, who if he didn't turn down, would eventually come to think of him as an untrusting asshole who made plans with no intention of following through on them.

He could handle looking like an asshole. Or rather Natalie could. He could even handle never getting to meet Andrew Stuart the legend. He would do it, because he owed it to Kelsey to set her mind at ease. More importantly because agreeing to meet Andrew meant seeing Kelsey again after this weekend was over. And that meant telling her the truth about him and dealing with the consequences. More, it meant hurting her. She might be strong and she might be capable, but knowing the way she considered most men to be lying jerks out for a fuck and little else, he knew she could never forgive him. He couldn't hurt her like that, by admitting he'd deceived her. Knowing who her brother was and therefore how their parents had been killed in a boating accident years ago, one that had clearly left her with considerable emotional scars, he wouldn't even consider it.

Nate forced a smile into place. "I would *love* to meet your brother."

"Then consider it done. After all, what are friends for if not for introducing each other to their good-looking single brothers? Speaking of which, you said you had a sister, what about a brother? Anyone you care to introduce me to? Let me rephrase that, any man you care to introduce me to who I can trust for more than a few hours?"

He shook his head at the actuality in her words, and how big of a factor trust was for her. He didn't know a single man like the one she spoke of. Including himself.

Chapter Four

Kelsey was impressed and relieved. Impressed because she never thought Natalie would be able to keep up with her once they reached the steeper and more rugged mountain terrain and relieved because the other woman clearly wasn't harboring same-sex tendencies the way she'd momentarily considered. And that made two of them.

Smiling over both her relief and Natalie's admission she had a thing for Andy, Kelsey braced her feet for better balance and turned to regard the other woman.

Natalie sent her an expectant look. "Tired?"

"Nope. Just hot." The cooler air that had been left behind from the rain had gone and the sun was now high in the sky and beating down upon them. The higher they ascended, the more humid the air became. Sweat beaded in thin drops on Kelsey's forehead and her sweatshirt clung to her body.

She should have gotten rid of the shirt long ago, but they had such a great pace going she had hated to stop for so much as a drink of water. Now that they were stopped she wasn't going to let the opportunity pass. She shook off her pack and positioned it between her feet to keep it from rolling down the steep path. Dragging in a breath of fresh air, she stripped out of the bulky shirt. The slightest of breezes rolled over her flesh and the heat of the sun caressed her bared skin with a sensuality she was certain only another nature lover would truly understand.

Tiny goose bumps of bliss raised on her flesh as she stuffed her shirt into the top of her pack. She pulled out her water bottle and, taking a thirst-quenching drink, glanced back at Natalie. She frowned, trying to guess the woman's thoughts. Her attention was fixed somewhere around waist level and there was an emotion in her amber eyes that was unidentifiable.

The gleam of perspiration that lined her wide forehead wasn't unidentifiable however. She had to be roasting with all those layers on. Yesterday Natalie had worn a black running suit that was zipped to her chin and hid ninety-five percent of her body. Today she wore a white nylon suit zipped just as high. "Aren't you hot?"

Natalie looked up from whatever it was she'd been looking at and shook her head. "Not really. I hike a lot. So far I haven't even broken a sweat."

Typically there was only one person who could prick at Kelsey's temper, and that was Andy. Yet, Natalie had managed to do it last night at the campfire with her out of place smile and again now with the accusation that seemed to be hidden just beyond her words. She sounded as if she thought Kelsey were incapable of going any farther without taking a break. The truth couldn't be further off.

"I hike a lot too," she said, not bothering to hide the bite in her words, "and am by no means winded; however, I am starting to get sweaty. It has to be close to eighty-five and muggy as hell out."

What looked to be amusement flickered through Natalie's gaze. She dropped her pack from her shoulder and unhooked her water bottle from where it was mounted to the bag's side. She downed a long swig and pressed the cap back down. "You're right, it is hot out. Maybe I'll change when we get back to camp. I don't have a T-shirt along."

Whereas Kelsey's temper rarely unleashed itself around anyone but Andy, neither did the urge to gloat. That urge coursed through her now and she couldn't stop her victory smile. Natalie grinned back, clearly not missing the reason beyond her expression, and the affinity she felt toward the woman grew to an all new level. A few hours ago the closeness might have bothered her. Since learning she had nothing to fear with Natalie and nothing to fear of herself but an overzealous imagination and the way she allowed it to get to her, she embraced it. "You have a bra on, right?"

"Yeah."

"Then just wear that. It's not like we're going to run into any men up here."

Natalie's mouth fell flat and she reattached the bottle to her pack. She hoisted the pack to her shoulder and nodded toward the trail. "I'm really not that hot. Now if we're going to be back on time for the afternoon events, we had better get moving."

Kelsey nodded and settled her bag on her back. She didn't miss the tremor of uncertainty in Natalie's words. She was clearly lying about not being hot. She was also clearly embarrassed. She should just start walking and let things slide. She didn't do it because she hated the idea she was at the source of the woman's discomfort. "I'm sorry. That was pushy of me. I know not everyone's comfortable with their body. To be honest, I am usually the last one to be comfortable around someone I've only known for a short while, but I am with you."

She frowned at the reality that came with voicing those words. She was more at ease with herself at this moment than she'd ever felt with another person aside from her brother. While she never spoke of her parents' death to anyone with the exception of Jan, she found she wanted to tell Natalie everything, from the threatening phone calls they'd received in the weeks leading up to the boating explosion to the final, "You were warned," call that had come in the day after. If Natalie asked about her parents again, she would do just that. "It's strange, but I feel more relaxed around you than I feel around friends who I've known for years. I feel like I can be myself around you, that I can trust you. Do you know what I mean?"

Natalie stared at her, her gaze intent and her mouth pinched together in an unyielding line. Finally, the firm set of her lips relented, and she gave a slight nod. "I think so."

She thought so? It wasn't that strange of an answer really. It was the look in Natalie's eyes that seemed so strange, the expression on her face. It was almost as if she hadn't wanted to voice the words aloud, Kelsey thought as she continued to trek up the mountainside. Did it have something to do with this morning, had she been awake the whole time and as a result afraid of what Kelsey wanted from her? Or was it merely the fear of beginning a friendship only to never again talk after this weekend? Either way, Natalie had nothing to worry about.

This morning had been a fluke, one that would never be repeated. As far as their friendship went, she still didn't know where Natalie lived, but wherever it was she would keep in touch with her, as well as make good on her words to introduce her to her brother. Not that Andy would go for Natalie. Or for that matter that Kelsey wanted Andy to go for Natalie. She loved her older brother, he'd been all that she'd had for years, but he wasn't known for his relationship skills or for dating women that weren't both superficial and flawless.

Nate stared at Kelsey's back as they neared one of several mountain crests. She hadn't spoken a word to him since they'd stopped over fifteen minutes before. He could tell by her slightly irregular breathing she was starting to get tired, but he had it on good faith that wasn't the reason for the silence.

She thought she had embarrassed him and was maintaining her silence in an effort to not do so again. She hadn't embarrassed him. The instant she yanked off her sweatshirt to reveal a thin, white sports bra, she had blindsided him with a bolt of sexual desire so strong it had been all he could do to jerk his attention from her breasts to her waist before she caught his wolfish ogle.

He had wished she'd had on camping underwear last night, had believed if she was in camping underwear instead of a slip of black lace someone had obviously told her was a bra he wouldn't be so damned turned on by her. He had been wrong, painfully so. The sports bra was every bit as arousing as the black lace had been. The sight of her tanned, lightly-sculpted back and arms glistening with a fine sheen of perspiration had been one of the most erotic sights he'd ever seen. It had taken almost more control than he possessed to keep his hands at his sides and not run them all over her sumptuous body the way he'd ached to do nearly from the first minute they'd met.

It was peculiar as hell. He had seen plenty of women perspiring in sports bras at the gym and various outdoor events. He had seen more than that wearing nothing at all and perspiring for a much more pleasurable cause than fitness. Yet, for some reason not one of them had turned him on so completely as Kelsey in a plain white cotton sports bra, hiking along a mountain trail.

It had to be sexual deprivation. It had been almost two weeks since he'd last had sex and obviously it was catching up with him. It couldn't be that he was honestly this attracted to her. That she blindsided him so completely with each and every new thing she revealed about herself. It had to be sexual deprivation that made his guts knot at the thought of keeping things between them on a friendly level. Almost as badly as they had knotted when she'd admitted to trusting him.

Worse than trusting him, she'd expected him to understand. To feel the same damned way!

It was ludicrous. More ludicrous than spending the weekend parading as a woman while sweating to death beneath two layers of too damned snug spandex and nylon. No, he wasn't this attracted to her or so caught up in her intrigue that he couldn't keep his cock from pulsing with the need to fuck her and his mind free of thoughts of doing the same. He was simply so hot he was becoming delirious.

"Wait until you see this, Natalie! It's incredible!"

Delirious, Nate reminded himself sternly, as his balls tightened at the sound of Kelsey's excited voice coming from the other side of the rise several yards ahead. Not captivated. Not aroused. Not hard as hell and wanting to screw her pretty little brains out until thoughts of her unhappy past and how he might make her present a whole lot more enjoyable left his mind permanently. Just delirious.

He crested the rise a moment later and the breath lodged in his throat. The mountain peak had leveled off to reveal an open glen of flowering trees and shrubs and several acres of mossy grass. A river ran through it all, and in the center of that river was Kelsey. The water came to just below her breasts and she'd obviously been under completely at one point because her nipples strained against the soaked bra and her hair hung in long, dark strands to just below her neck.

Nate's heart took off, slamming against his ribs as he met her eyes. Their ashen depths sparkled with life, with energy, with vitality. With an exuberance reflected in her brilliant smile and the sinful dimple in her cheek he knew he had to run his tongue over if it were the last thing he did.

"I know you said you aren't that hot, but c'mon, Natalie, this is just too tempting to ignore. I'm telling you, it feels like pure heaven. Give it a try."

He groaned at the whisper of excitement in her words. Groaned even more as his cock hardened further still and his blood heated to fever pitch.

Oh, hell, he *was* delirious. Going out of his goddamned mind with it. Judgment was gone. Reasoning was gone. Everything was gone, but his ability to move forward and do just as she suggested and give her a try.

Halting long enough to toss his pack aside, he strode to the riverbank and down its side. Cool, crisp water worked its way past the many layers of his clothing and offered divine relief to his sweltering body. Divine and yet not the relief he craved. That relief he found when he reached Kelsey's side several seconds later.

Mirth rallied through her expressive eyes for another instant then vanished as a hunger she couldn't have concealed if she had wanted replaced it. He slid his gaze from her smoldering eyes to her full pink lips and the primal groan that escaped his mouth said more than any words could have. Her lips parted and a breathy gasp stole out. He returned to her gaze, expecting her to make a hasty retreat. She didn't move.

Just remained still, her lips parted and raw need burning in her eyes.

Christ, he wanted her. Wanted her in a way he'd never before experienced. Wanted her in a way that was not logical. Wanted her in a way that refused to be denied, so Nate didn't even bother to try.

He reached for her and she seemed to fall into his arms, to lock onto his mouth, to need his kiss every bit as badly as he needed hers. He'd thought of her as many things since he had first laid eyes on her, as her hands gripped his arms with a wild strength and her lips pressed demandingly against his own, he realized he'd left out passionate. Her mouth waged a mad siege, pressing ruthlessly against his lips, insisting he open to her, and when he didn't do so immediately her teeth took over, nipping into the soft pad of his lips, teasing with playful bites and pushing him ever farther over the edge.

Unwilling to remain immobile a moment longer, he moved his hands over her, feeling every inch of sleek contours. She was muscled enough to prove she spent time seeing to her body's fitness and curvy enough to ensure she was all woman. He filled his palms with the firm globes of her ass and delved his tongue past her lips. Her grip on his forearms turned stronger and she suckled at his tongue, licking and kneading with the force of her own.

He skimmed his hands from her buttocks along her naked sides, pulling her body flush to his as he went, needing to feel the wet heat of her cunt pressed against his cock regardless of the consequences. First, he had to get rid of the damnable cup. And he would. Soon. For now he reveled in the feel of her sex riding his thigh, the press of her pussy lips grinding against his hard muscles. He moved his hands higher, dipping beneath the edge of her drenched bra to palm her bare breasts, and connected with her plump, aroused nipples. He drew one rigid crown between his fingers and squeezed. A moan exploded from her mouth and into his, and she arched into his touch and ground her cunt harder against his thigh. The feel of her pussy parted beneath the thin layers of her clothing to rub repeatedly against his thigh the way he ached to feel it rubbing over his throbbing cock was too gratifying, too stimulating, too damned intense to ignore.

A groan of ecstasy bubbled up in his throat and he drew back from her mouth to plant hot, wet kisses along her jaw, down the supple line of her neck on a journey to the breasts he had to taste, to the nipples he had to have in his mouth, to the rest of her tantalizing body he wanted to sample one slow, lazy lick at a time.

He ran his tongue along the hollow of her neck and the intoxicating scent of her that had filled his nostrils all morning exploded in rich sweetness. The taste was too natural to be perfume, but it was something. Something that made his head spin and his blood boil ever hotter. Something noteworthy. "You are so damned sweet. You make me want to come and we've barely even touched yet."

The feminine voice registered to Nate's ears the instant the words left his mouth and he knew that it had registered with Kelsey as well because she went from writhing and purring with rapture to irrevocably still.

She shuddered within his arms and he lifted from her throat to meet her eyes. They had been closed, but now they parted to reveal bewilderment. Slowly, her lips parted as well, and words trembled from her lips, "Oh...my...God..."

Nate didn't want to blow his cover. He didn't want to admit that Joe had been one hundred percent right about him and that he really was incapable of having a friendly relationship with a woman he found attractive. But he couldn't handle the punch of guilt that came with the disbelief in Kelsey's expression, couldn't stand the thought that even if they never touched again this moment would bother her for the rest of her life. It would make her question her sexuality and everything she was. Knowing what he did about her, the last thing she needed was one more thing to put a damper on her life.

Grudgingly, he freed his hands from her breasts and rubbed his thumb over her swollen lower lip. His stomach turned with her lost look. He wanted to erase it, wanted to see the sexy smile that lit up her entire face and warmed him in turn. Admitting the truth would accomplish one, but not the other. He wouldn't be seeing her smile again and he would just have to deal with that. "It's okay, Kelsey. I'm a—"

"Well, I'm not!" she shrieked, hastily dislodging herself from his embrace.

She scrambled to the river's edge and tripped her way up its side. Righting herself, she looked back at him, like she wanted to say something more, but didn't know where to begin. Nate opened his mouth intent on explaining he wasn't bisexual or a lesbian or whatever it was she'd thought he'd been about to say. The words never made it out of his mouth. She'd already turned away and was crashing through the trees like the ogress he'd claimed people associated Natalie with was on her heels.

* * * * *

Oh God! Oh God! Oh God!

Kelsey shook her head, struggling to ignore the chanting. It continued incessantly as she hurried down the mountainside. How could it not continue? She was going to hear the words forever, followed by, "What the hell were you thinking?"

"Oh my God, I kissed a woman!" *And it had felt so good.*

No. It did *not* feel good. Natalie's big hands on her, cupping her ass, running over her breasts, plucking at her nipples did not feel good. But then why was her entire body quivering with longing and her panties wet in a way that had nothing to do with jumping into a river?

"Kelsey, stop!"

She wrenched her head toward the voice and drew in a sharp breath. Natalie was so close. If she stopped for even a second she would be upon her. And what would happen then? Would she attack her? Toss her to the ground and drive her mindless with searing hot kisses, fondle her breasts and nipples some more? Or would she not stop there this time? Would she strip away her clothes and touch her, bury her big, thick fingers deep into her pussy and coax her until she couldn't stop from climaxing the way that had happened in her dream, the way she'd longed to experience for real this morning? The way her pussy ached to feel even now.

No! She did not ache to come from Natalie's touch. She was just confused again. Natalie had managed to convince her she wasn't into women and so when she made it clear she actually was, it had scrambled Kelsey's mind. Enough to have her sinking into the other woman's kiss, to have her believing as they stood groping each other in the water that it was a man who held her, a man's hard body that rocked up against her own. God, she really was losing it.

But she was done with that now. No more confusion, no more jumble.

It was time to think clearly, to remember she didn't want the other woman in any way, shape or form outside of friendship. She would tell her that too, just not when they were alone in the woods with only her own fleeting logic to watch over them.

Later, after she'd had more time to relax and think this thing through, she would confront her. Until then, she could only pray Natalie would keep silent about the kiss. If she brought it up around the other campers...

She wouldn't. She couldn't.

But, if she did, Kelsey would simply have to deny the claim. She didn't dream about other women and she sure as hell did *not* kiss them. Not to mention get wet and needy feeling the moment she stared at one's strong, sensuous and mustache-lined mouth.

* * * * *

If she didn't stop moving away the moment he finally managed to get within five feet of her, Nate was going to have to take drastic measures. He didn't blame Kelsey for wanting her distance thinking the way she did, but her flighty movements from one group of chattering women to the next was starting to really piss him off. He wanted to make amends, to come clean and explain that it was all one big misunderstanding, that her sexual preference for men was still intact. He knew his explanation was going to be met with hostility as well as hurt, but both emotions would only be worse if he allowed her to go on thinking the way she did. He had to tell her the truth and get the hell out of here. Run back home to Joe and confess to being the sex-driven maniac he was.

But maybe he wasn't. Maybe it really was just Kelsey. And if it was, then what did it say about him? About them?

"Are you in for rafting?"

Nate turned from glaring at the back of Kelsey's head to force a smile for the woman who stood beside him. She was attractive, tall, built, and a redhead. Everything he'd always looked for in a bed partner. Given her presence here this weekend, she was also into the outdoors. She presented the perfect test. If he could spend the four hour rafting trip getting to know her and not feel the need to fuck her, then it would prove he wasn't a sex-driven maniac incapable of having an inter-gender friendship. At least, not with all women.

"Rafting?" he asked, realizing she waited for an answer.

Her smile blossomed to reveal straight, white teeth. "It's the next event. The groups are starting to assemble and I thought you might be looking for one to join. If so, we can use another person."

The redhead glanced over to a cluster of women Nate guessed to be the group in question. They were all in their late twenties to early thirties and decked out in tight tops and small shorts. Acres of sun-burnished flesh and creamy calves and thighs peeked out from frayed hems and rolled cuffs. If he could spend an entire four hours with seven gorgeous, athletically-inclined women and not want a one of them it would more than prove Joe's theory wrong. Not to mention make him worthy of sainthood.

It was a great plan, the only problem with it was that it left Kelsey alone with her anxiety for the better part of the afternoon. Unless she already had plans to go rafting with another group, in which case his staying behind would be senseless. He nodded toward the redhead. "Let me check. I think I might already be expected to go with another group."

"All right, just let us know in the next few minutes."

She walked back and joined the group. Nate watched her go, taking in the formfitting shorts that hugged her tight ass and the seemingly endless tanned legs that led to a pair of modest water shoes. It was obvious most of the women here dressed however they wanted because they thought no man was within range to worry over. It was also obvious his concerns over Kelsey's confusion were wearing on him more than he'd even realized. Not only wasn't he turned on by the sight of all that prime female flesh glistening in the distance, but the thought of spending four hours alone in a raft with the women suddenly sounded more like work than pleasure.

Frowning at the odd as hell thought, Nate turned back to where he'd last spotted Kelsey. She was gone, as were the women she had been talking with. His guess must have been right on and she'd already left to go rafting. Good for her, she'd made new friends. And if in making them she had ditched him, so what. He deserved to be ditched.

Deserving or not, it didn't remove the slight sting of rejection that crimped its way into Nate's gut. Refusing to marvel over why her rebuff bothered him so much, he turned back to join the redhead's group. It wouldn't be work sharing a boat with the beauties, he ensured himself. And as it turned out he was right. It wouldn't be work because he wouldn't be doing it. They too were already gone. At least they were making fast tracks in the opposite direction. And now their party of seven had an eighth. A quick glance revealed the same was true of all the groups still around. They were filled. And he was alone. Rejected by everyone.

The feeling was both unfamiliar and troubling. He was used to women and men alike fawning over him. He was used to being treated like the sought-after millionaire he was. He wasn't used to being rejected. Sure as hell not twice in one day.

Oh, how the mighty have fallen.

The thought was pure Joe, and Nate couldn't stop from laughing. He headed back to the center of camp, aware there would be a few stragglers about that he could spend the time forming friendships with. Or better yet he could catch a nap. He hadn't slept more than a few hours with Kelsey's warm, tempting body next to his last night. Unless he figured out how to set his own tent up or told Kelsey the truth and got the hell out of here before dark, he wouldn't tonight either.

Sleep it was. Not only was there a chance he might not be able to corner Kelsey until morning, but crawling into a tent alone meant he could free his aching cock and balls from their snug confines, and that in and of itself was a true nirvana.

* * * * *

She was out of her mind. Kelsey peered through the tent's small side window one last time. There were several women in the distance, sitting around the campfire, but other than that no one was within sight. As long as she was quiet, no one would be able to hear her either. What she was about to do was crazy. Insane. Something she normally only did in the privacy of her bedroom and then when all the lights were out, but she was desperate.

She needed to speak with Natalie, to explain there could never be anything between them more than friendship and then go on to prove it. In order to do that, she had to first vanquish her horniness. She'd reached the conclusion in the last couple hours that a too long unsatiated sexual appetite was the real reason for her confusion where Natalie was concerned. She'd always had a vigorous libido, and thanks to a hectic past few weeks, she hadn't had time to do anything about it. She would take care of it now the old-fashioned way. A touch here, a stroke there. No one would ever know what was going on inside the tent.

Drawing a calming breath, she quickly removed her shorts and panties, then slid into her sleeping bag. Her legs would be a bit cramped in the bag's confines, but there was a certain measure of security in knowing she wasn't totally exposed to any unaccounted-for prying eyes. Eased by the thought, Kelsey rested her head against her pillow, drew up her knees and moved her hand down to the warm flesh of her belly.

She jumped at the first touch of her hand on her skin. It was odd, probably even demented, but the idea she could be caught had her extra-sensitive. Her pussy was already heavy with arousal, and when she moved her hand even lower and rimmed her mound with the tips of her fingers she also felt how wet she already was.

This was going to be so easy. She would be climaxing in seconds and then she wouldn't be horny any longer. Of course, she'd still have to deal with Natalie, and why exactly it was the woman had claimed to want Kelsey's brother one minute and then had attacked her with her mouth the next, but she would worry about that later. Now she would relax, enjoy, and take care of business.

She sank her first finger into the slick folds of her cunt and sighed at the heat surging through her body. More fingers joined the first, working an erotic beat against her clit and creating slick friction along her pussy lips. Her eyes closed with the force of need spiraling from all angles to pool deep within her center, and a face floated into her mind. A face with no real definition, but stunning amber gold eyes and the sexiest of bad boy grins. Even as she sensed he could be bad, she also sensed he could be trusted. He was a man she could get lost in. Murmuring her pleasure with each deep thrust, she tipped her hips higher, sank her fingers deeper, and endeavored to do just that.

Chapter Five

The strangled sounds reached Nate the moment he bent down to unzip the front flap of Kelsey's tent. The noise was low, keening. A cross between something dying and something being born. It was coming from inside the tent.

An animal had to have sneaked inside and was now trying to tunnel its way out. He wasn't about to let that animal ruin the tent. Not when the bed he'd spent the last few minutes dreaming about crawling into for some much needed sleep was in there. Hunching down quietly so the animal wouldn't hear him and panic, Nate eased the zipper open far enough to look inside and see what kind of critter he was up against. The tent flap gaped a couple inches and he leaned forward, peered inside, and damned near fell over.

It wasn't an animal making the sound and it also wasn't one of panic. It was Kelsey and the sound was one of sheer ecstasy. She lay on her sleeping bag with her eyes closed and her head tipped back, sweat glistening on her brow as she quietly cried out her bliss. While he could guess the sleeping bag had covered her body at one point in time, it was now draped loosely around her ankles, and her bared thighs were splayed wide. The dark hair that covered her pussy was soaked with her essence and the deep pink lips of her cunt were parted to take in her thrusting fingers. Her other hand had pushed her shirt up to her neck and was filled with a breast, her fingers tweaking and tugging an engorged nipple.

The erratic thrusting of her hand grew faster, the slick sounds of the juices being milked from her pussy cruised to his ears and the blood pounded through his head so loudly it was a wonder she didn't hear it and open her eyes. His cock pulsed just as strong, his balls pinching painfully against the cup. His fingers itched to reach out and take over, to fill themselves up with her small, firm breasts, to fuck her to climax time and again.

Aware just how much he couldn't do that, any more than he could sit here and watch a moment longer, Nate reached with shaking fingers and rezipped the tent's flap. It was more than immoral to spy on her personal actions; it was threatening to his sense of self. From just the few seconds he had watched and listened, her image was already thick in his head. If he continued to watch and listen that image would be more than thick, it would be permanently ingrained in his mind. He didn't want any woman in his mind that thoroughly. Not now. And certainly not Kelsey, a woman he was already battling joint forces of sympathy and lust for.

His blood humming with erotic images of her fingering the swollen flesh of her pussy, bringing herself to blistering climax, he surged to his feet and moved slowly toward the density of the woods. When he was far enough away that she couldn't hear him, he turned his pace up several notches. His steps were harried by the painful bulge of his erection and when he had gone far enough to believe there would be no chance of being spotted, he lowered his nylon pants and spandex shorts to his knees and freed his aching cock to the air.

He was not a man who had a need for masturbation. He'd always had plenty of women at his beck and call, just waiting for his say so to jump into his bed. At this moment, he didn't have those women and he needed release more than he needed his next breath. He knew Kelsey felt the same way. It was the reason she had stayed behind while most of the others had gone rafting. She was every bit as stimulated as he was and clearly believed if she took care of things herself the carnal tension between them would die.

He wished her beliefs were accurate. Hoped they could be. But he was quickly developing more and more serious doubts. Still, he was willing to try anything to ease the constant ache she stirred in him and if that meant running into the woods and using his hand to get himself off, then so be it.

* * * * *

She had heard someone or something. The thought had crashed through Kelsey's mind the moment the orgasm had drained away and she lay still on the tent's floor, drawing in hasty breaths of air. She had allowed only a handful more breaths before she'd tugged on her clothes and darted out of the tent. There had been no one in hearing range and she had been in the midst of calming herself enough to join the women who ringed the distant fire when the blur of white snagged her gaze. The color had disappeared nearly as quickly as it had come into her sight, but she knew she had seen it, and she also knew who it had been.

Natalie.

Damn it, she'd thought the woman had gone rafting. Clearly, she hadn't. Instead she had stayed behind to spy on her.

It was a ridiculous thought. Kelsey had sneaked away to her tent while Natalie had been preoccupied. She couldn't have stayed behind to spy on her. She had merely stayed behind by coincidence and for whatever reason had decided to return to the tent.

Oh, God, how much had she heard? Had she known what was going on? She had to have. It was the only plausible reason for her hasty retreat. What about seen? Had she somehow managed to see what was happening?

The idea Natalie had been witness to her masturbation had Kelsey's nerves standing on edge even as her sex grew moist. She closed her eyes and sighed at the tingling deep in her pussy. She had given herself an orgasm to relieve the arousal Natalie's presence somehow stirred in her. She had believed it all had to do with being horny. But if that were the case, if she was just horny, then why was she stimulated again, so soon, by the thought of the other woman? Was it just the closeness she felt with Natalie, that she could be herself and reveal the secrets of her past to her that had her body and mind so messed up, or did she really and truly want the woman?

It was a question she didn't want to address. It was also one she had to have answers to. The time had come to face Natalie. With the majority of the women currently gone from camp, they could find a place to speak in silence and without their absence being noted. More importantly, when the conversation was over Kelsey could make a fast getaway and no one would be any the wiser.

Her heart pounding furiously and her legs trembling, she ventured into the woods where she had seen Natalie disappear moments ago. She'd gone a couple hundred yards when a vivid stroke of white appeared. Knowing she had to get this over with before she chickened out and retreated to the safety of her Jeep and then her home, she hurried toward the color. The closer she drew, the better she could make out the details of Natalie's large body. Her back was to her and she stood still. She had no idea why she would be standing there, not making any obvious movements until she took a few more steps and a low groan reached her. A groan that sounded highly sexual.

Kelsey froze, listening as more harsh grunts joined the first. She concentrated harder, able to just make out the divide between tanned flesh and white nylon now. She could also make out the movement of the woman's arms. It was obvious what she was doing, the same thing Kelsey had been doing moments before, but how was she doing it standing up and why?

Her hammering heart demanded she turn back and leave the woman to her peace or rather satisfaction as the case might be. Her spinning brain agreed wholeheartedly. Her feet didn't appear to be listening. She moved silently as possible, skirting the trees and foliage, never drawing any closer to Natalie, but merely gaining a better view. A side view. It was perverted, highly demented, but she had to see what she was doing. Had to know how she could pleasure herself while standing up and not have her legs give out on her. She just had to know.

And in the next second she found out.

A gasp escaped before Kelsey could stop it, and she clasped a hand to her mouth to silence any further sounds and stared in utter disbelief. Natalie's hand moved in quick, sure strokes, gliding up and down the length of a long, thick...penis.

Oh...my...God... Natalie was a hermaphrodite!

But no. She wasn't. The large hands, the firm lips, the slight trace of a mustache that had tickled her flesh back in the river, the taut ass she'd cupped this morning and that was exposed to her now. The hard male body she thought she'd felt rocking up against her... They were not female characteristics. And that meant Natalie wasn't a hermaphrodite. Not a lesbian either. No, she was something plain awful.

Natalie was a man!

Anger and relief assailed Kelsey as burning joint forces. She fisted her hands at her hips, boiling to lash out at him, to scream at him for making her trust him so completely, for allowing her to get close, to believe he could trust her as well and want to be her friend.

He didn't want her friendship. What he did want was pretty damned obvious. He wanted to spend a weekend amidst a bunch of women getting his cheap thrills out of watching them undress. Obviously that desire had turned to an even greater goal when Kelsey had revealed how easily she trusted men, fell victim to their wiles. With her admission, his goal had turned to not only watching women undress, but to reveling in her personal horror when he'd successfully led her to believe she was developing feelings for another woman. And not of the friendly kind.

Why, the perverted bastard!

He was exactly the same as every other lying, untrustworthy man she had ever met. The difference with this man and those other ones was she would not sit idly by and wait for the bitter sting of rejection and hurt. She would deal with him. Not by running over there and lashing out at him as she'd first been inclined to do. That reaction would let him off way too easy. What she had planned for him was far more deserving.

* * * * *

It took almost more patience than Kelsey had to bide her time throughout dinner and then sit long enough at the campfire to make her excuse she was tired and going to bed early plausible. Not that she had wasted the time. She'd put it to good use. She had broken out the Polaroid camera she'd bought on a lark for those times when she couldn't wait even an hour to see the results of her latest shoot. Tonight was one of those times. She had taken numerous shots of the camp and in particular of the man who called himself Natalie. The pictures were secured away for later use, and the time had finally come for action.

Kelsey stood, folded up her chair and said to the group in general, "I'm going to turn in. I guess the hike today took more out of me than I thought."

She started walking away, then turned back and glanced at the impostor she foolishly believed was her friend. Damn it, she'd thought Natalie had cared about her! Enough so that she'd been ready to share her past with the woman. Enough so that she'd secretly wished she were a lesbian because the bond that had developed between Natalie and she was stronger than anything she'd ever experienced.

Only, she wasn't a lesbian. And Natalie didn't even exist.

Kelsey's eyes wanted to slit and the venom was all but impossible to keep out of her voice. She forced a calm smile. "You're welcome to bunk with me again tonight, Nat. The tent's plenty big and it will save you from having to set up yours."

He nodded, his eyes lighting with what she guessed to be gratefulness because he thought she would be undressing for him again tonight. Or maybe in his messed up mind he believed tonight would yield even more than that.

He stood and folded his chair, quickly falling into step beside her. "Thanks. I'll take you up on the offer and join you right now. I'm pretty tired too."

She glanced away and snorted. She would be willing to bet her favorite camera he wasn't tired five minutes from now.

Kelsey nodded her response, and they continued on to the tent in silence. She fired up the lantern and waited for him to remove his shoes and close up the tent flap. She pulled the light sweatshirt she'd put on following dinner over her head, then yanked off her T-shirt as well. She had put on a red lace bra for tonight's events, and now her nipples beaded from both the cool night air and expectancy. He had yet to turn around, and she was counting on her words to accomplish that feat. "I'm glad you decided to turn in early too."

She put a slight husk into her voice and it had the desired effect, as he stopped digging through his duffel bag and turned toward her. His eyes went wide and, while he'd obviously been about to say something, no words made it past his open mouth.

He swallowed audibly and jerked his gaze from her breasts to her face. "Uh, you are?"

The tremor in his voice was priceless. She wanted to make him more than tremble; she wanted to make him sweat. Make him scream. Make him want her so badly that he begged. And then leave him high and dry.

Catching her lower lip between her teeth, she crawled to his side and nodded. "Uh-huh. We need to talk, Nat."

His breathing grew rapid and she took great pleasure in the confusion that riddled his features. "We do? I mean, uh yeah, we do."

She crawled closer still, and laid her hand upon his thigh, stroking the hard muscles she felt through the thin nylon as she fixed her attention on his mouth. The breathiness of her next words wasn't nearly as contrived as she would have liked. The memory of his kiss, the feel of his strong lips rubbing over hers, along her neck, fueled both her anticipation for the events ahead and the moment when she walked away. "You see the thing is, I like you. I *really* like you."

"And I like you, but—"

"When we kissed back at the river," she continued hastily, raising her hand from his thigh to his torso, "it made me uncomfortable at first, but now I've accepted it."

The heat that had begun to dilute his gaze was replaced by shock and he blurted in a thick voice, "You have?"

She couldn't release the laughter that came with his stupefied look, but she allowed a triumphant smile to blossom, knowing he would take it as a victory of another kind. "Yes. That kiss was really great. And I want to try it again."

Her hand reached his well-padded breast and his gaze shot toward it. He drew another loud breath. "Y-you do?"

Kelsey leaned closer still, cupping his fake breast in her hand as she rubbed her own highly sensitized ones against him. She tipped her head back to focus on his mouth inches away and licked her lips. She couldn't deny the honesty in her response. "Oh, yeah, I do. And that isn't all I want to try."

"What, uh, what else do you want to try?"

"Everything," she purred, rising up to nip at his jaw. "I want you to show me things, Natalie. I want you to show me how it is between two women."

"I...I..."

She leaned back and gasped. "You look stricken. Are you telling me you honestly don't want to do that? Am I not attractive enough for you?"

He nodded, his long blonde wig bouncing wildly around his head. "Of course, you are. You're hot as hell."

She smiled at his speedy response. Regret came into his eyes in an instant and she knew he'd spoken before he'd had a chance to think. What a pity for him, she thought sardonically, having to tell her the truth for once. "I thought you'd say that."

Releasing her grip on his breast, she reared back on her knees and fingered the smooth flesh and the cool edges of the small ring that adorned her navel. "You said you thought this was sexy. You said you wanted one for yourself, but I think the truth is you wanted your hands on mine. You want me, don't you, Natalie?"

His gaze fell to where she fondled the ring, stroking it sensually, purposefully goading him. The amber gold of his eyes darkened and while he had yet to voice a word, the answer was more than obvious. The reality of how badly he did want her had her blood humming and her pussy dampening with forbidden desire.

"It's okay to say yes, Nat," she continued, her voice raspy with an arousal she couldn't disguise. "I already told you that I want you too. I trust you. I really, *really* trust you. You're so honest, so pure. I've never met someone as virtuous as you before. At the campfire when all the other women were talking about feelings and you said for you it was just about sex, that was so brave."

"It was the truth."

"Because you always tell the truth, right?"

His gaze returned to her face and what looked like remorse flashed through his eyes. "I used to."

A tinge of sorrow tugged at Kelsey. She forced it away and recalled all the lies he'd told her, the way he'd allowed her to get close, to make her want him. To develop feelings for him. Having sex with him hadn't been her plan for this night. The plan had been to leave him wanting and exposed. She would still do all that, after she showed him just how good it could've been between them if he hadn't taken advantage of her trust. After she extinguished the need for him from her system once and for all. After she showed him how it felt to be used for a hasty fuck and then tossed aside. "Why did you stop, Natalie?"

"A challenge."

It was the truth. Somehow she knew it, and it ticked her off all the more. "A challenge? Like a bet or something?"

"Not exactly."

As much as she knew his previous answer to be a fact, something told her that this one was a lie. Or at least close enough to being one. Any sorrow she might have felt vanished. "I guess exactly what it was about isn't important any more. As far as I'm concerned there's only one thing that is important."

"There is?"

The slight tremor was back in his voice and she took full advantage of it, placing her hands firm on his chest and pushing hard. He didn't budge, but merely continued to stare at her. "Yeah, there is."

"Wh-what is it?"

"Your name."

He blinked, astonishment lighting his face. "What do you mean?"

She smiled harder, letting the animosity that ate at her for the way he'd treated her show in her smile. "Call me old fashioned, *Natalie*, but I like to know the name of the men I fuck."

"The men?" he gasped. "You know?"

"Your name," she demanded, pushing harder against his chest. "Tell me your damned name." She shoved one more time and he allowed her to push him to his back. She hastily covered him, the mixed sensations of power and lust rioting through her veins and quickening her pulse.

"Nate," he finally supplied. "My name is Nate."

Kelsey nodded, glad he hadn't supplied a last name or any other information. She could pretend indifference, but she wasn't indifferent toward him. Not even close. And the more she learned, the more she would feel pain when this was all said and done.

She leaned forward and tugged on the thick strands of his wig. "Well, Nate, this hair has to go. And so do these clothes."

He shook his head. "This is a bad idea."

"Are you afraid you won't be able to get it back up again so soon?"

Once more shock reigned in his gaze. "What do you mean, again?"

The moistness in her pussy grew, the liquid heat of arousal filling her cunt as the image of him masturbating in the woods filled her mind. She would know heartache come morning, she already regretted ever meeting him, but right now she also burned to feel the length of his thick cock buried deeply within her.

She laughed, high and throaty. "What? Did you really think I'd let you enjoy a free show without getting my own in return?"

"You followed me?"

"You watched me."

"By accident."

She nodded, already having guessed he had come upon her by accident. It didn't change the facts. "You liked it."

She could tell he wanted to deny her words, but the truth— the mad beat of his heart beneath her hands and the arousal thick in his eyes—was too obvious to be denied. He nodded. "Yes. I liked it."

"Then what's the problem? Afraid this might be about more than just sex? It isn't, Nate. It's just sex. That's all I want from you. Just a quick fuck."

"That's not your style."

Not even close. She never had casual sex. Feelings were always involved. Her feelings at least. That being the case, this couldn't be called casual sex either, because while she denied it aloud, her feelings were very much involved.

Not about to let those feelings show, she lowered her breasts to his chest and rubbed against him. She couldn't feel his erection through his pants, but she knew he had to have one, hidden by some means. She ground her pussy against his pelvis and juices dripped from her sex to soak her panties as she mewled her want.

"Yes, it is my style. It's what I do. What I've always done. The things I said at the fire were lies. This is the truth. This is the real me. I don't want promises. I don't want pretty words. I don't want a damned thing, but sex. And you're going to give it to me. You owe it to me for taunting me so long, for making me want you until I couldn't stop from touching myself, from making myself come.

"Now say the words, Nate. Say yes."

His golden gaze glistened with raw appetite and still he shook his head in denial even as he rasped out the one word she ached to hear. "Yes."

Her smile grew and her sex gushed with heady wetness and warmth. She rolled off him and sat back, waiting for the show to begin. The show where he removed all his feminine layers and showed her the man he was. The man, who thought to fool her, to make her feel like an idiot. The man, who after she'd had her fun with, would feel like the biggest idiot of all. "I'm glad we've reached a decision. Now strip. I've already waited too long and have no mind for foreplay."

Chapter Six

Things had moved seriously beyond Nate's control. He shouldn't be here in this tent with Kelsey, taking his clothes off. He shouldn't be hard as hell and burning with the need to kiss her soft, sweet lips, to finally bury his fingers, his tongue, and his cock deep into the warm, waiting walls of her pussy. To prove Joe right with his assumption he couldn't have a friendship with a woman he found attractive any more than he could last the weekend amidst a camp of women and not have sex with a single one of them. He shouldn't be doing any of this.

But he was.

He jerked the pins that secured the long blonde wig in place free and tossed the thick mane of hair aside. His gaze locked on the heat of expectancy in Kelsey's flushed face as he hastily went to work on removing his clothes. His hands shook and his fingers fumbled with the buttons of the jacket he had tossed on earlier this evening. He'd felt nervous since the moment he entered this tent, incredibly so, and that was strange as hell.

Nathan Anderson did not get nervous about sex. He loved sex. Considered it as much a part of his life as eating and breathing. Though the past couple weeks had been an exception, in general it was an active part of his weekly routine. So why the hell were his hands shaking?

He finally managed to work the last button free and shook off the jacket. He tugged the lightweight shirt over his head, then dispelled of the dramatically padded bra. Kelsey's tongue came out of her mouth, rolling slowly over her luscious lower lip as she gazed upon the defined muscles of his naked chest and abdomen. She'd looked eager before, now she looked voracious.

The nerves he hadn't been able to shake any better than he could explain evaporated under her appreciative gaze. He knew he had a good body. He worked out at the gym three days a week, ran laps around the neighborhood daily, and attended various sporting events to keep himself in shape. More than a few women had complimented him on his physique. Yet, not one of those compliments or his self-conceit could compare to Kelsey's famished smile.

He kneeled and reached for the snap of his pants, pausing when she continued to sit in silence, enjoying the show. As much as he loved her watching him, knowing how aroused it was making her, he wanted a little something of his own to look at. A little something more than the sinfully thin red lace bra that just barely concealed the dusky pink shade of her nipples.

"I want you naked, too."

She raised an eyebrow. "You're demanding in real life, huh?"

Yes, in a lot of ways he was. Demanding of those he knew he had a right to be. Kelsey wasn't one he had a right to be, however. He grinned. "Not at all. I just expect to get as good as I give."

Her lips twitched for an instant, then curved into a wide smile that revealed her sumptuous dimple. "Oh, you will, Nate. Trust me, you will."

Even as his cock pulsed in response to that incredible dimple and the thought his tongue would soon be upon it, licking it the way he'd dreamt of doing since they'd met, he felt there was something off about her smile and the playful glint in her eyes. It wasn't something enough to stop him from removing the rest of his clothes. Sure as hell not enough to stop his fingers from itching with the need to reach out and touch when Kelsey disposed of her jeans a moment later to display a red lace thong that, like her bra, revealed more than it concealed.

The thin strip of material that covered her mound was damp and he could smell her excitement on the air. His thoughts roamed to earlier this day, to catching her in this tent fingering herself. To the glorious sight of her pussy parted and her fingers glistening with the juices of her arousal. He'd wanted to fuck her so damned bad then. He wanted to fuck her even more now.

His impatience heightened, Nate jerked off the spandex biker shorts and finally the cup that had cramped his cock in for way too long. He released a loud sigh of relief, and she laughed and rocked back on her heels once more to watch. He was naked while she still wore her panties and bra, but he didn't mind. Those scraps of lace would be coming off soon enough and he'd just as soon be the one to do the removing, preferably with his teeth.

Recalling he still wore the voice alteration device, he yanked the thin flap of plastic and wiring from his neck and then did the one thing he'd wanted to do since the moment they'd met. He tugged Kelsey into his arms.

Her laughter over his brisk move filled the tent as he settled her on a sleeping bag. He followed her down, reclining his knee between her legs so he could feel the dampness of her panties brushing against his upper thigh. Expectancy shone in her smoke-gray eyes, and she reached her arms to his neck and attempted to yank him down on top of her. Not about to give in that easily, he caught her hands in his and dragged them over her head. He held her hands there with one of his own and lowered to the hollow of her throat, breathing in the subtle earthy smell that had driven him to distraction from the moment they'd met. The same smell that back at the river had caused him to speak aloud in his feminine voice and send her running.

She wasn't running now, Nate thought as he ran his tongue over her warm flesh and was rewarded with a shiver and a husky moan. She wanted him every bit as much as he wanted her. How her feelings worked into the equation was another subject. She claimed she wasn't the too trusting, too easy to fall in love woman she had said she was at the campfire. He knew she was lying. She felt something for him. And as much as it pained him to admit it, he felt something for her too.

Something that had developed from his taking the time to get to know her, even if her answers to his questions were partial ones that had left him wanting more. Something he feared that would never pass in just one night. Something he should have examined before letting things get to this point, but now it was too late. He wasn't stopping. He would, however, take things slow, and give her the foreplay she said she didn't want or need. The leisurely lovemaking he so rarely took the time for.

He skimmed his tongue from the hollow of her neck to brush warm, wet kisses along her nape and over the sensitive flesh below her ear. She shuddered beneath him and squeezed her face to her neck, attempting to block his way. "What are you doing?"

He pushed her face away with the pressure of his own and nipped at her damp skin again, grinning when she writhed beneath him. "Kissing you."

She attempted to block him again, but he merely pushed her away once more and hooked his mouth onto her ear, suckling the tender lobe, blowing on her wet flesh. Her struggles to thwart him ceased and a throaty whimper escaped near his ear. "I can feel that, but why?"

He drew her ear into his mouth again and she squirmed beneath him. He worked his way down, laving his tongue back along her salty wet flesh to the top of her shoulder. He caught the thin strap of the electric red bra in his teeth and drew it down her arm until the pale rise of a breast was exposed. "Because I want to."

"I told you I don't need you to go slow."

He palmed her right breast with his free hand while his mouth latched onto the newly exposed flesh of her left. He pushed the lace farther down the supple mound until the deep, dusky pink of an areola came into sight. He licked at the dusky bud, then moved the lace away from her breast completely and drew her erect nipple into his mouth. He tugged at the hard nub and she bucked up, grinding her pussy against his thigh. He could feel the growing wetness of her panties on his leg and knew the slow, sensual route he was taking was exactly what she needed, even if she didn't think so.

Releasing her nipple, Nate looked up at her. Her eyes were darker now and hazy in the lantern light. Her hair, which he had always thought of as straight, dark and simple, surrounded her head in a wildly gleaming halo and her full lips were deep red and moist. She looked so beautiful, so damned sexy. His cock pulsed with the anticipation of plunging into her tight, wet body. He reined in his control, refusing to do that. He could give her the quick fuck she'd asked for and thoroughly enjoy it for the short time it lasted. He wouldn't because if she only wanted him once, he knew he'd live to regret not taking more time with her when he'd had the chance.

He brought his thumb to her lower lip and rubbed it. "You might not need to go slow, Kelsey, but I do."

Her eyes called him a liar and her words did much the same. "I don't think so. I don't think you're the type of man who even knows what slow is about."

He knew. He just didn't often take advantage of the knowledge. Never had he felt the desire to do so for the sake of keeping a woman in his arms as long as possible the way he wanted to do with Kelsey. "What type of man do you think I am?"

"You're like my brother. Always on the move, never staying in one place for long. Or maybe for you it's just about with the same woman for long. You're exactly the way you said. You make it clear from the get-go things are just about sex. No attachment. No strings. Just a round or two of sex and then you move on."

The assessment was right on, at least for the way he'd always behaved in the past, but he had no intention of admitting it. Instead, he brought his mouth to hers and sank his tongue between her lips. Her mouth was still for an instant as if she were surprised by the rapid entry, and then it came alive, tasting, licking, meeting him thrust for needy thrust. He pulled back slightly breathless, and her jagged gasps told him she was the same.

He caught her breast in his hand and idly caressed the aroused nipple. "If I am so cavalier about sex, then you should be happy, right? That's what you want from me, just a quick fuck and then for me to move on."

She paused an instant, then nodded. "Yes, it is."

No, it wasn't. She wanted more. She couldn't hide the truth when it burned so brightly in her eyes. It gave him hope that he'd never expected to feel. The hope that after this night they might be able to try again. That maybe if he apologized enough for not being honest from the start and leading her to believe things about herself that could be no further from the truth she might forgive him. Not that he wanted forever with her or was ready to have that with any woman, but he did want a chance. Time to think over the feelings she'd awakened in him that he never before realized he'd been without. The ones his brother had clearly known he was missing out on.

Nate wasn't going to waste his time thinking about Joe tonight, or how his brother was going to have a field day when he learned just how right he'd been. Tonight was about Kelsey and proving to her he wasn't the untrustworthy jerk she believed him to be. "If this is just about one night of sex, then why do you care if I take a few extra minutes?"

Another pause, longer, followed by more lies. "I don't. Take all the time you want. It doesn't matter to me either way."

"Then relax and let me take things slow."

Kelsey closed her eyes and drew in a long, calming breath. She didn't want slow, soulful sex. She wanted a quick, hasty fuck followed by revenge. It looked as though she didn't have a say in the matter. Nate wanted slow, soulful sex, and if she didn't agree to be a willing participant this night would never end the way she had planned. Being a willing participant really wasn't such an awful thing. Not such an awful thing at all, she thought on a breathy sigh as he latched his oh-so-capable mouth onto her nipple.

He released his hold on her arms and his hand started a slow journey down her torso. As his palm glided over her, he alternately flicked his warm, wet tongue over the hard bud of her nipple and bit into her puckered flesh. His fingers found her navel then, and he toyed with the ring at her belly for a few seconds before continuing further downward.

He moved back slightly and she felt the hard length of his cock rubbing along the inside of her thigh. The muscles of her pussy contracted with the thought of him burying his thick cock deep within her. She'd been wanting that since this morning, she realized now, aching to feel him impale her in whatever way he chose, as he had done in her dream. One that had been of Nate and her, not Natalie or Todd or anyone else, she now knew.

"I want your fingers inside me."

Nate lifted his head from her breast and eyed with her humor. "You really are impatient, aren't you?"

"You can go slow, but please just give me something."

He grinned, and her breath caught with the realization it was the first time he had smiled so honestly while she was looking upon him as a man. He had been an odd-looking woman, but he was one damned fine-looking man. One who seemed strangely familiar. But that couldn't be.

He nuzzled his rough upper lip against her breast and moved his hand beneath the edge of her thong. His fingers tangled in her damp pubic hair and, forgetting all about her wonder over his familiarity, she arched against his probing touch, struggling to draw his thick fingers deep inside her damp cunt. "C'mon, Nate! Now!"

He let go a husky laugh. "Okay. I'll give you something."

She sucked in a thankful breath. Now he would fill her with his big fingers. Only to her amazement, he didn't fill her at all, but pulled his hand away.

"What are you doing?" she demanded.

His eyes sparkled with mirth. "Giving you something."

"Well, what is it?"

He didn't answer in words, but actions. His fingers wrapped around the thin strap that held her panties in place and ripped. Juices pooled between her thighs with the unexpected action, then turned to an all-out river of need when he moved the torn panties aside. In one quick move, he buried his head between her thighs, cupped her ass in his large hands, and plunged his tongue deep inside her cunt.

"Oh, God!" she cried out at the forceful entry and latched onto his hair. She thought her dream had been good, that it had felt consuming when he'd tongued her then, but it was nothing compared to this.

His tongue moved rapidly, thrusting in and out of her slick pussy, lapping at her swollen cunt, driving her dizzy with desire. He pulled back and scraped his teeth over her clit and her entire body shivered. He repeated the action, moving his teeth back and forth over the inflamed nubbin. Her shivers turned to intense shudders that racked her frame and had her heaving breathy sighs while blistering need surged forth with the insistent chafing.

She was so wet, so achy. She could explode at any moment. And when his teeth stilled their relentless scraping to grab hold of her clit and tug, she did just that. Her nails dug into his skull and her hips bucked wildly against his face as the orgasm sliced through her. His teeth lifted away and his strong tongue lapped at her, feasting on her, eating at her sex until the last of the come drained from her body and she lay on the ground feeling as weak as a newborn kitten.

Nate's face appeared just above her half-opened eyes and Kelsey managed a breathy, "Wow."

His grin returned, splitting his face in a sexy smile that had his golden eyes dancing. "I take it you liked that something?"

It was a cocky question. One she shouldn't swell his head any more by answering. She might not have either if at that moment he didn't take her mouth in another long, wet, hot kiss filled with the salty taste of her essence.

"I liked that something," she admitted when he pulled back. "I liked that something a whole lot." Too much, but she would deal with that later.

He moved his big body between her legs and his jutting cock pressed against her wet sheath. "You ready for a little something more?"

She was definitely ready, but the something he was offering wasn't so little. It also wasn't wrapped up in a neat, little package. She was on the pill, but she didn't know Nate's track record and she wasn't taking any chances. Hell, she didn't really know the man at all. Outside of the fact he gave mindblowing oral sex and could tell lies that sounded so authentic she believed every word of them.

His shaft rubbed against her opening again and though she had just climaxed, a fresh course of arousal dampened her pussy lips and had her aching with want. "I'm more than ready, but do you have any protection?"

He brushed a kiss to her lips, then rolled off of her and reached for his duffel bag. He pulled out a box of condoms and grinned. "Never leave home without 'em."

Kelsey's belly tensed with the statement and the arrogance in his grin. It shouldn't matter he came prepared or that he could speak the words with such flippancy, but it did. She shook off the hurt that coursed through her and smiled. What was happening between them was all just part of her revenge plan, nothing more or less. She would not care if he carried condoms around with him on a daily basis or for that matter how often he restocked his supply. She couldn't afford to.

"Well, thank God for that," she said with as much sauciness as she could muster.

He quickly rolled a condom on and returned to her. His intense gaze roamed the length of her, and she forgot about his ready condom supply as desire licked through her, flaming an inferno of burning need deep within. She reached out her arms to welcome him back in.

He shook his head. "Turn around."

"What?"

"You have got the cutest little ass I've ever seen. It's the first thing I noticed about you. You stood up out of the mud and waved that thing at me and I've been hard and wanting you ever since."

The words should have startled her, worried her that he would want to take her from behind the way he had done in her dream. Instead, she laughed while a foolish tugging erupted in her heart. What he said hadn't even been close to a sentimental admission, nor had they been words that should increase her trust in him. Yet, that he'd wanted her well before she admitted her weakness for trusting and falling for men way too easily had her giving in to him all the same. Smiling, she turned onto her knees. Nate's large, warm body covered her from behind and the length and thickness of his erection rubbed along the seam of her ass as a strong arm wrapped around her middle.

Against her desire to do so she tensed, waiting for him to turn more aggressive, to fill her up from behind. Instead, his mouth claimed her ear in a teasing bite and his hot breath slid over her flesh, sending shivers of ecstasy rocketing through her. His hand moved from her belly to between her thighs. His long fingers dipped into her center, petting the swollen flesh of her pussy while his other hand cupped her ass, rimming the crack with his fingertips. "Oh, yeah. I love this ass. Nice, round and firm. I could definitely get used to looking at it."

The words hit Kelsey like a lightning bolt, shocking her into silence and making her forget all about her anxiety over the way he planned to take her. Her entire body went still and for an instant so did Nate's. She guessed from his reaction he hadn't meant to speak those words and he didn't give her time to respond. In one fluid move, he aligned his cockhead with her damp sheath and thrust hard inside. Her breath caught at the size of him, filling her inch by glorious inch, and she heard his gasp as well.

One of his hands returned to her waist and she came down on all fours, waiting to see if he would continue as they had begun. His hot mouth suckled at the back of her neck and his thrusts grew longer, harder, ensuring he had no plans to change position. The air around them thickened with the scent of sex. Their pace quickened. The slick sound of flesh slapping against flesh resounded in the night as his balls drummed against the rear of her pussy.

His fingers returned to tease at her clit, rubbing and stroking the swollen nubbin, and breathing became near impossible. Holding her eyes open any longer was beyond impossible so she let them fall closed and gave in to the tempo. The erratic pace of their slamming hearts, the heavy gasps and moans, and then her own loud cries as the muscles of her cunt clenched tight around him and she climaxed with a force that made her head spin. It also had Nate coming as well.

He shuddered around her as the orgasm overtook him, and the hand at her waist turned relentless in its grasp. She grabbed hold of that hand and focused on squeezing his cock with her muscles, milking every last drop of come from his body, until she knew his satisfaction was complete.

After several long seconds, his biting grip stilled and he slumped against her before rolling onto his back and pulling her along with him. He wrapped his arms around her and leaned forward to kiss her forehead. Neither of the actions was expected. They were far too intimate, as if he actually felt something for her. She knew he couldn't and she also knew she didn't dare open her mouth right now or look up and meet his eyes. After what had just occurred between them she was feeling incredibly stripped down and raw. In short, she was feeling emotional as hell and that was by no means a good thing.

"I liked that something," he said quietly near her ear. "I liked that something a whole lot."

"Yeah," she said as flippantly as possible, refusing to cave to the sensations swamping her with the honesty his voice seemed to hold. "For sex with a complete stranger, it was okay."

Nate stiffened beneath her and for a foolish few seconds she believed it was because her words had bothered him, then she met his gaze and saw only vacancy. Kelsey buried her face back against the muscled sinew of his chest and closed her eyes. She wasn't going to get teary-eyed or make anything more out of this than what it was. Revenge sex. Revenge sex that just happened to be some of the best of her life.

Great or not, it didn't change the cold, hard facts. He had admitted to coming here on a challenge. She didn't know what kind of challenge and she didn't care. The only thing that mattered was that he had lied to her, led her to believe things about herself that were nowhere close to true, and exploited her trust. And worse, far worse, made her fall in love with him.

She would get over it. Just as soon as she put her final plan into action and got the hell out of here, she would. And that had to happen soon. As much as she now longed for it, there was no way could she afford to stick around and live out this morning's dream.

Chapter Seven

Duane finished chewing the bite of pizza and gave his head a shake. "Oh, man, I can't believe she actually left you like that. That's too damned funny."

"A regular riot," Nate said dryly, cringing all over again at the memory of waking up naked to find an army of women glaring at him. It wasn't bad enough to wake up in the buff in a place he clearly wasn't wanted, but after hacking away at her tent until not much remained but the floor of it, Kelsey had spread pictures of him in his female form all around his nude body. Pictures and a note that had contained a three-word question that twisted his gut with guilt every time he thought about it. *How's it feel?*

He had known that night something was off about her smile, the glint in her eyes when she told him she would be sure he got as good as he gave. He now understood the look completely. He also understood that he had been right in his assumption her feelings had been involved every bit as much as his own had.

He'd been shaken when he'd woken up to find that she was gone, that what they'd shared had all just been a part of her getting back at him. It had worked. He'd never felt worse over anything in his whole life. He also had never wanted to track someone down and grovel at their feet so damned bad. Not that he was admitting that to anyone. He'd already had to fess up to Joe that he hadn't been able to handle a nonsexual relationship with an attractive woman. He didn't dare mention that the moment he'd started opening himself up to someone and learning about them in return, he'd started caring.

Joe smirked from across the restaurant table. "So, did Kelsey at least appreciate that you took the time to get in touch with your feminine side?"

Not about to respond to the smart-aleck question because he knew he couldn't do so with a level head, Nate stood. "I have to run. I have...things to do."

"That reminds me," Joe said, "I stopped by the *Wharf* on my way over. Jan said if I see you to tell you to come by after lunch."

Great. That's just what Nate needed to top off the week. He hadn't been in the headquarters store since last Friday and as Jan had been on vacation until this morning, he could just imagine the problems that had occurred in their absences. If nothing else, taking care of business might get his mind off his other problems for a while. "Thanks for letting me know. I'll run by right now."

Joe nodded. "You're still planning on coming out to Grandma's place tomorrow night for the party, right? It is being thrown in your honor, after all."

Nate grimaced at the unwanted reminder. The papers had gotten wind of his trip to the woman's weekend and had had a great time with it. He'd used the excuse he had planned before attending the woman's weekend—that he'd been there in disguise for the sake of research—to get the press off his back. That excuse hadn't worked for his grandmother. After reading about his weekend stunts, she was throwing a party in an attempt to find him a wife to tame his wild ways. She claimed that wasn't her purpose, but Nate had gotten it straight from his mother that it was.

He would attend the gathering solely because he loved his grandmother, but there was no way in hell he was going to consider it a wife-finding party. Or even a girlfriend-finding party. After his experience with Kelsey and the lasting effects it had on his guts, he had serious doubts he would be ready for either for some time.

"I'll be there," he assured Joe, then walked out of the restaurant before another topic he didn't feel like discussing could be brought up.

Duane waited until Nate was out of sight, then looked across the table at Joe who stared after his brother with a cocky smile. "Did you guys have some serious cash riding on this or what the hell's got you so happy, man?"

"No money, this is much better."

"What is?" Duane asked, not missing the satisfaction in his voice.

Joe looked at him. "My little brother's in love."

"You got that from the last half hour?" Duane asked skeptically, "because from where I'm sitting he sounded pretty damned miserable."

"Misery. Heartache. Same thing. Just watch sometime, the minute he hears Kelsey's name he gets this stupid look on his face." Joe's smile turned knowing. "It's a lot like the one you get whenever Candace comes up in conversation."

Duane's gut tightened. He'd done his damnedest to keep his feelings for Candace hidden. Obviously, he'd done a shitty job of it. At the very least, no one knew the extent of those feelings or how abnormal his need to be with her, to have her as his mate, truly was. "You're an evil man. And I'm not about to acknowledge the last half of that."

"You know she doesn't hate you. She just needs a little encouragement."

Right she did. If Joe, or any of her family for that matter, knew the real reason Candace avoided him they wouldn't be having this conversation at all. In fact, Duane would be lucky to still be associating with them. "About Nate. If he's in love, how can you be so sure he's gonna make a move and do something about it?"

"Let's just say he might not have a choice. He might be put into a situation where he has to deal with his feelings whether he wants to or not."

"You set him up?"

"I merely provided a little guidance."

Duane smirked. "Have I mentioned what an evil man you are?"

"Have I mentioned about Candace and how she just needs a little encouragement?"

Duane grunted his response, already seeing the wheels spinning in Joe's head. They could go right on spinning, because he didn't need help with his women, human or otherwise, least of all with the last woman in the world who wanted anything to do with him and for completely understandable reasons. Understandable and yet ones he had no intention of letting remain forever. He needed Candace, needed her as his mate if he was ever to have a complete life again, and it if was the last thing he did, he would prove both that and his feelings to her.

* * * * *

Nate parked his truck in *The Sports Wharf's* crowed lot, smiling automatically at the store's success. His smile fell flat at the sight of a red Jeep parked a few spaces from the front door. The parking space was for employees and not one single employee he knew drove a red Jeep. In fact, only one person he knew drove a vehicle like that one.

His gut knotted as he pushed open the store's front door and strode through the scattered customers in search of Jan. The odds the Jeep belonged to Kelsey were next to nil, but he still planned to speak with Jan and get out of here just as soon as possible. He wanted to talk to Kelsey. He wanted a chance to explain all the things he hadn't been able to tell her before. He wanted to try to make sense of the way he felt about her. He didn't want to do it in the *Wharf* on a crowded Saturday afternoon.

"Nate?"

He spun around at the familiar sound of Jan's voice, and the tall redhead smiled at him. "Oh, good, you must have gotten Joe's message."

"I did. What's going on?"

"Nothing." He frowned at the odd response and she added, "I mean nothing bad. I just knew you'd be around today and was hoping you would watch over things so I can take off early and spend some time with a visiting friend."

Nate groaned. He should have known Jan wanting to see him would lead to something like this. She'd always been one of his most valuable employees, but the last month she was gone more than she was here. "I wasn't really planning on staying."

Jan batted her lashes in a way that never worked on him and she knew it. "Please. I know I've only been back for a few hours, but she's leaving tomorrow and since she lives over an hour away, we don't get to see each other nearly enough. She's also still ticked off at me about ditching her last weekend."

"What was last weekend?" he asked, hoping to veer the subject away from her leaving long enough for him to get out of the store.

"The Wild Woman's Weekend."

The unexpected response had the hair on the back of Nate's neck standing up. He half expected a laugh to follow Jan's answer, but outside of a bright smile she was stoic. Obviously, she hadn't had time to read the paper. "I didn't realize you went to that."

"Normally every year, but this year Rex sprung Cancun on me at the last minute and I ended up having to cancel. And honestly I didn't have time to explain the reason to Kelsey before we had to leave and so I kinda lied and on top of the fact she had a crappy weekend—"

"Kelsey?" he repeated in shock.

"Did you want me?" The voice was Kelsey's all right and like a bad dream she appeared beside Jan. Her mouth fell open the second her gaze landed on Nate. Her eyes went in the other direction completely, narrowing into slits that reflected dark fury. "Nate." She made his name sound like a curse.

"Uh, hi."

She puffed out a hot breath. "I have to go."

Jan stared from Kelsey to Nate, her eyebrows drawn together in a way Nate guessed was supposed to convince him she was confused. The gleam in her eyes and the smile that tugged at her lips belied that fact. Remembering the way that Joe was grinning at him over lunch he had a good idea why. They had set him up.

"You two know each other?" Jan asked innocently.

Nate smirked at her. "What a coincidence, huh?"

Kelsey crossed her arms over her chest. The venom that continued to shoot from her eyes ensured she hadn't played a part in arranging this meeting. "Remember I told you I met another lying jerk last weekend, Jan? Well, you're looking at him."

"Nate is your jerk?" she asked, sounding more amused than surprised. "But he doesn't lie."

Typically Jan was right. He didn't lie. But he had this time and whether they'd been coerced into this reunion amidst a growing crowd of onlookers or not, it was time to set things right between Kelsey and him. "I did this time."

The words appeared to be all the catalyst that Kelsey needed as she took off for the entrance. Nate shot Jan a "thanks for the help, but no thanks" look, then hurried after her. He caught up with her and grabbed her arm, forcing her to swing around to face him. "Kelsey, wait. Please."

"So you can lie to me again? Or was it that you were hoping to make me feel like an idiot again? Maybe try and see if you could confuse me just a little bit more about my sexuality? On second thought, don't bother. I am officially done with men. You opened my eyes to the beauty of dating other women. From here on out I'm a lesbian." She glanced to a woman who stood in the aisle behind them. "Are you up for a date? If so, I'm single and obviously a sure thing that I'd sleep with someone as repulsive as this jerk."

Nate chuckled at the absurdity of the words and the woman's shocked expression. "You're not a lesbian, Kelsey, and you're also not easy. Now please do me a favor and quit scaring my customers."

"Fine, I'm not a lesbian. But I wish to hell I was."

"I'm glad you're not."

She wrenched the arm he still held free and fisted her hands at her hips. "Please don't even try to sugarcoat this."

His initial assessment of her had been that she was a pushover who would open her heart and home to anyone. How he could've made such a huge mistake was beyond him. She wasn't a pushover. No, she was all passion. Her eyes danced with anger and her lips were pressed so firmly together they were blood red. They looked the way they did after he kissed them and Nate found he wanted to do that now. Only attempting to do so now, while she shot daggers of pure fire his way, was liable to be the equivalent of placing his neck on the chopping block and waiting for her to set it into action. "I'm not sugarcoating this, Kelsey. I am honestly glad you're not a lesbian. I'm also sorry. I never wanted to lie to you and I sure as hell never wanted to hurt you."

"Oh, God, you are so arrogant! You didn't hurt me. I would have to care in order for you to hurt me and I don't."

She did. The tears that glistened at the back of her eyes guaranteed what he'd already known. Her wounded expression brought to the forefront the depths of his own feelings, making him realize while he might have failed at the challenge Joe had set before him, he wasn't the sex-crazed maniac he'd come to believe. At least, not for any woman but this one. His heart swelled with emotions he'd always done his best to avoid. Though he'd spent the last week telling himself he wasn't ready for a committed relationship, he knew now that he'd been wrong. He was ready for a commitment and for every one of the feelings that coursed through him, making him ache to reach out and grab hold of her. "What if I do?"

Her face registered shock, maybe even a trace of hope, while her words hung onto their cool veneer. "What if you care? I don't think so."

"Is that really such a hard to believe concept?"

"Yes. It is, Nate. I'll admit that for a millisecond I had hoped you might care, but that was before I knew who you were. You're exactly the guy that I guessed. You don't care about women. At least, not beyond a few days. And I don't do casual sex, so consider yourself lucky for that one time and move on."

"I'm sorry."

The torment in his voice, the regret in his expression, it all seemed authentic and Kelsey wanted to believe it. She wanted to believe that he cared about her the way he claimed, that the person she had come to know during their time in the woods was truly the person he was on the inside, if not the outside. She couldn't because not only had he lied to her, betrayed her trust, and taken advantage of her feelings, but because he was Nathan Anderson, multimillionaire, a paparazzi favorite, and a man with a bed partner count that topped the double digits.

Damn it, she had questioned why he'd looked so familiar that night in her tent. She'd passed the question off at the time. She shouldn't have. Just like she shouldn't have given in and agreed to meet Jan at the store today. She'd purposefully avoided telling Jan the name of the man she'd spent the weekend with, but clearly Jan had found out anyway. Her so-called friend had also clearly taken Nate's side on the whole thing and lured her into his store and his presence in the hopes of helping him out.

She should have ended their friendship last week when Jan had ditched her to spend time with Rex. Stupidly, she hadn't and now thanks to Jan she had to stand here and listen to the idiot who she hadn't stopped thinking about all week tell her more damned lies. Argghhh! What was it with her and lying jerks who disguised themselves as caring men just long enough to get into her pants? Only this jerk was going even farther than that. He wanted back into them. Well, it wasn't happening!

Kelsey turned on her heels, intent on leaving and never looking back. "Apology accepted. Have a nice life."

"You don't even know what I'm sorry for."

And I don't care. At least, she shouldn't. But still she stopped and turned back, cursing herself all the while. She was too damned nice of a person. It was the reason she had met Nate in the first place. She'd looked at him and seen a woman in need of a friend and she'd allowed herself to become that friend. Or sap in her case.

A pathetic sap who, even after hearing all his countless lies, had to give him a chance to speak his mind. "What are you sorry for?"

"For allowing you to think that what we shared was just casual sex. More importantly, that I didn't let you see the real me enough to know when I'm speaking the truth. I am speaking the truth right now, Kelsey. I do care about you. I won't lie to you. Most of what you've read or heard about me is true. *Was* true. I am not that person any more. I don't want to be. I just want to be with one woman."

He was a terrible, awful man for standing there and looking at her that way, with what appeared to be both genuine affection and truth shining in his eyes. He was even worse for making her heart squeeze with hope she didn't want to have. "And I suppose that woman is me?"

He nodded solemnly. "Yes."

Her heart gave another squeeze and then felt as though it turned over completely. She couldn't listen to it. Her heart had a track record of leading her down the wrong path and this path was the worst one she had ever come upon. This man had not only worked his way into her head and heart, but he'd made her want to open up and share her past. "No. I don't think so, Nate.

Even if we'd met under different circumstances it wouldn't matter. We're just too different."

His eyes lightened a little, as if he thought her answer had somehow given him hope. He stepped toward her. "No, we aren't, Kelsey. I thought the same thing at first, that we had nothing in common, that you weren't even close to my type. You are my type, exactly my type. And we have a ton in common."

They had a good deal in common, but not the things that mattered. "I don't lie and I sure as hell do not dress up as a man for the sake of winning any stupid challenge."

The regret that flashed through Nate's gaze ensured the remark hit home. "You heard Jan. I don't lie in general either, and for the record I lost the stupid challenge."

So he wasn't a pathological liar. So what? It still didn't change the facts. "Sorry to hear that, but I'm sure there will be another one just around the corner."

"You don't even want to know what the challenge was?"

"No. I want to leave." And yet she couldn't budge. She stood there, staring at him, waiting to hear what the stupid challenge was.

"It was to prove that I'm in touch with my feminine side by forming a nonsexual relationship with a woman I find attractive."

"I get it. I was that woman and you lost because we had sex." She snorted. "Geez, that's some rough loss."

"That was only part of it. The second part was not to care about that woman. Not to fall in love with her and want to spend not just a week but my whole life with her."

It was a direct hit, straight to Kelsey's pathetic little heart. It pounded madly against her ribs and she had to suck back a hard breath to still the emotions gathering in her throat. "You don't love me! You don't even know me."

"Yes, I do. Maybe not everything, but enough. More than enough to know I want to spend the rest of my life getting to know you. That I want to hear the things you won't tell anyone else. Don't tell me you don't have those things, because I know you do. I also know what they're about or at the very least who. I want to hear it all, Kelsey, and I want to help make things easier for you to deal with."

Why was he doing this? Why was he standing in the middle of his own store on a crowded Saturday afternoon, making fools out of both of them? Did he honestly mean the words? Could he care so much about her that making fools out of them didn't matter? Oh, God, did he honestly want to know the details surrounding her parents' death? Due to Andy's public profile, most of the men she'd dated had known her parents were deceased, but no one knew why and no one had bothered to ask. At least, not until now.

The emotions in her throat grew dense, and she swallowed them back and shook her head. "This is stupid."

"What?"

"Arguing in the middle of the kayak aisle with the entire store listening."

"We can go to my house."

"No!" His house was the last place she wanted to be. If they went there things would only go from bad to worse. Nate already had her teetering on an emotional edge. One step into his home and a few more words out of his mouth and she would be back in both his arms and in his bed. Bad idea. Very bad.

"Well, then you pick it, because I am not leaving until you listen to me. I love you Kelsey Stuart, much more than I have ever loved your brother."

It was the dumbest thing she had ever heard come out of a man's mouth and she had heard plenty of dumb things through the years. It was also probably the only thing he could have said right then to push her emotions past teetering and into the great wide open. Tears leaked down her cheeks even as laughter bubbled up in her throat. She hoped to God she didn't live to regret it, but she couldn't keep the words in any longer. Not when he was standing there with so much affection shining in his golden eyes. "You are such a jerk, Nate. And I swear I must be out of my mind, but I love you too."

His grin drew deeper, reflecting into his eyes. "Does that mean you forgive me?"

"That means it's a start," Kelsey said grudgingly, though she knew she'd already forgiven him long ago. The first time he opened his mouth and said he loved her to be exact.

"In that case, do you think I could talk you into attending a party at my grandmother's house tomorrow? She's throwing me a wife-finding party in an attempt to tame my wild ways, and I would just as soon bring my own candidate."

"Is this the grandmother you go shopping with and carry her bags?"

"And endure weekly sessions of gas-buffered bingo with? Yes, that would be her."

"So you weren't lying about that?"

"I didn't lie about anything but my gender, my occupation, and my name."

Those three things were some of the most pertinent details he could have lied about. Fortunately for him the pertinent detail that topped them all, that he loved her, he hadn't lied about. "Then yes, I'll go. And if you're lucky, I'll stay the night. And if you're even luckier, I'll stay longer."

Relief shone on Nate's face and Kelsey realized, up until this moment, he hadn't been sure how things would end between them. Now that he knew, he reached for her, pulling her into his arms. "How about forever?"

She tipped her head back and smiled up at him, loving just how incredible those words sounded. She'd been without anyone but Andy for so long, the thought of having someone else in her life was nearly too much to take in. She did so with laughter and teasing words. "How about you stop pushing your luck and give me a kiss?"

His lips brushed over hers for the briefest of seconds and then he pulled back to hug her. Needing much more than a surface kiss, she stood on tiptoe and claimed his mouth in a long, hot, wet kiss that had whistles going up around them.

Nate pulled back laughing. "I love you, Kelsey. I would never lie about that."

"I love you," she said, taking his arm as they started toward the store's entrance. "And if you ever lie to me again I will do much more than expose you to an army of female campers, I will personally see to your death."

"Via the chopping block."

"What?"

"Nothing." He chuckled once more, then shook his head and shot her a bemused look. "I was so wrong about you. I had you pegged as this sweet, clumsy pushover who would take in a big, ugly ogress and make her feel loved."

"What's so off about that?" she asked as they cleared the store's entrance and started toward his truck.

"I'm not ugly or female."

He wasn't ugly. Not by a long shot, but since he seemed so immensely aware of his good looks she wasn't about to point that out and inflate his ego any further. "Well, you're half right."

He stopped and gaped at her. "Are you saying that you think I'm ugly, Kelsey Stuart?"

"I'm saying the tabloids have a way of talking a guy's appeal up and I happen to know that your dick is nowhere near as long as your arm."

They both laughed as they continued on to his truck. He slid into the driver's side and grinned at her. "That's just another thing I love about you. You don't try to butter me up to get on my good side or at any other part of my body or bank account, and you don't have to. You're already welcome to everything I am and have simply because of who you are."

Her heart warmed each and every time that he said he loved her, and as she gazed at his mouth and remembered how effective it was at providing pleasure, so did the rest of her. "Enough talk about love, take me home and give me sex."

Nate's eyes lit with humor as he started the truck and backed out of the parking spot. "That's all you care about, isn't it? No feelings for you. You're just a big sex addict."

"Yep. You know me so well."

"Better than you'd ever guess, sweetheart, but you'll have plenty of chances to try over the next sixty years."

"If you're lucky and I decide that I like you enough to keep you."

"I'll be lucky. And if the worst happens and you decide that being a lesbian truly is what you want, then I'll just have to become Natalie permanently."

She laughed and shook her head. Natalie was a nice woman, but Nate was a far nicer man. "You honestly have to love me if you'd give up your manhood for me."

He passed her a pained look. "I do love you, but please don't make me prove it. At least, not that way."

"Well, you know what they say, use it or lose it."

"Oh, I'm going to use it. So much you'll forget you ever thought of me as being anything other than a man."

Heat pulsed through Kelsey's body and wetness tingled in her pussy with the promise in both his look and words. She couldn't stop herself from boldly reaching to his lap and stroking her hand over his cock through his jeans.

Nate raised an eyebrow her way and she smiled. "Now that is one challenge I look forward to you rising to."

The bulge of his shaft swelled beneath her palm and a grin claimed his face. "Well then, sweetheart, you'll be happy to know I've already started."

Epilogue

Kelsey snaked her foot under the crowded restaurant table, not quite able to check her triumphant smile when she met up with her destination of Nate's lap and he responded with a gasp. The sound died away and the look in his eyes went from wide with surprise to dark with lust. He sank down in his seat and widened his thighs, wordlessly encouraging her wandering foot to move higher and stroke over the swelling bulge of his cock through his slacks. Not about to let the invitation pass, she curled her bare toes against the growing thickness of his shaft and was rewarded with a telltale twitching of his penis that had desire flaming to life deep within her sex.

Reveling in the warm wetness that moistened her panties, she licked her lips and sank lower in her chair. Hanging onto the seat of the chair for support, she slid the shoe off her other foot and lifted it to his lap as well.

They'd come to the prestigious Clarion Heights Supper Club for their engagement dinner, and while dinner had been superb it couldn't begin to compare with the promise of dessert in Nate's eyes. Or the secret thrill that coiled deep within her belly, tightening the muscles of her pussy when one of his hands disappeared beneath the table and unzipped his pants. Her toes touched down on the hot, hard flesh of his cock and her cunt filled with the juices of her anticipation.

Three short months ago, she never would have been caught dead doing anything this daring in mixed company, particularly company that included Nate's family and her and Nate's mixed group of friends, but then three short months ago she hadn't known Nate, or the limits of her own confidence.

She knew both well now, knew that when he looked into her eyes and told her how much he loved her that he meant every word. She also knew he'd make good on every one of his promises, including the one about helping her find answers to her parents' death. The reality was they would probably never learn anything more, but that he was willing to help out however he could spoke to her heart in a way no man ever had.

The way he lifted his own foot and moved it beneath her skirt to brush over her damp panties with his sock-covered toes, spoke to every other part of her. The desire licking through her burned higher with the slow, sensual strokes and when he dipped beneath the edge of her panties and chafed his toe over the distended nubbin of her clit, that desire threatened to flame out of control.

Kelsey bit down hard on her lower lip, fighting back the squeaks that seemed determined to make their way out of her mouth and focused on driving him just as wild, to make him be the first to either lift her foot away or cry uncle.

The seconds of fondling turned to minutes and the need to explode built within her so intensely that her fingers hurt from where they bit into the chair's seat. Her pussy ached for release and the heat that filled her cheeks had to be evident for all to see. She should stop. She should move his foot away. But all she wanted to do was sink even farther down and let him bury his toe deep into her burning flesh.

She slid lower in her chair and parted her thighs wider. The sweet reward of his big toe pressing against her cunt with heightened pressure nearly pushed her over the edge. She couldn't allow that to happen, couldn't climax here for all to hear and smell, but yet as much as she knew that, she also couldn't stop herself from sliding her hand beneath the table and re-angling his foot to rub even harder against her mound. His toe grated against her clit with remarkably forceful pressure and she bit back a moan as a wave of sheer pleasure washed over, making her feel boneless and weary.

She had to stop this, had to stop him. Had to—

"Might I interest anyone in dessert?"

Kelsey jumped at the server's soft voice so near to her ear and shot upward in her seat. Her cheeks aflame, she knocked Nate's foot away and retracted hers from his lap while passing him a guilty look across the table.

He laughed shortly, then looked to the woman waiting for their answers and grinned. "Thanks, but I'm already having mine."

Puzzlement crossed the server's face and Kelsey felt as if everyone at the table was staring at her in wait of an explanation. She bit back a groan and felt the heat in her cheeks blaze to a shade that had to be somewhere between crimson and blood red.

"What about you, Kelsey?" Darla Anderson, Nate's mother, questioned from several seats down. "You really should start eating more. You never know when you'll need to be doing so for more than just yourself."

Nate's brother Joe laughed while their younger sister Carrie rolled her eyes. "Geez, Mom, give her a break. She just accepted Nate's proposal last night."

Darla flashed Kelsey a warm smile that helped to ease the stinging in Kelsey's cheeks. "Well, you know what they say, dear. It's never too early to start."

Nate nodded, as if he couldn't agree more. He returned his attention to Kelsey then and his grin turned mischievous. "Which is why we've been practicing so much, right sweetheart? As a matter of fact, I think Kelsey's about to crawl under the table and—"

"Oh, God," Nate's sister Candace blurted, effectively masking Kelsey's mortified gasp, "would you two get a room already?"

"No kidding, man," Duane put in. "You don't see any of us attacking each other in the middle of a restaurant."

Nate glanced at him then Candace and smirked. "No, but I'd bet I'm not alone when I say I wish to hell the two of you would attack each other and get it over with already. It's obvious to anyone who sees you together that you have this almost animalistic attraction. Well, anyone but the two of you apparently."

Duane made a strangled sound while Candace glared at him. She redirected her dark look at Nate then quickly turned her attention to her plate. Only it hadn't been quickly enough. There was something about his sister's look, something that Nate wasn't sure he liked. Candy had looked almost scared by the idea of being with Duane. Why? It was a question he would get to the bottom of, just not tonight.

Tonight he planned to spend teasing his adorable fiancée.

He refocused on Kelsey and noted the striking shade of red had left her cheeks. Unfortunately for her he had every intention of putting it right back. She'd loosened up a lot in the last three months, had learned to take more stock in her convictions whether she was around friends or complete strangers, but she still could stand to loosen up just a bit more. Particularly, since she was the one who had provoked him into his current aroused state.

Nate discreetly readjusted his cock and zipped his pants. He stood and went around the table to her side. "You know on second thought that room idea does have some very good potential." He held out his hand and sent Kelsey a knowing grin. "What do you say, ready to go for a ride, sweetheart?"

Her eyes widened and the red streamed back into her face, making it clear she hadn't missed the implications in his words. The rapid beat of her pulse visible at her neck also made it clear she couldn't say no to the question because she was more than ready to go for the kind of wet, wild and slightly wicked ride he had in mind.

Guiding her to her feet, he took her hand and ran his thumb along the sensitized skin of her palm, stroking her flesh with the same featherlight touch he used on the back of her knees and elbows and at the rim of her mound. The touch he knew drove her crazy at the same time it made her wet and needy.

The breath whooshed from her mouth in a hot, hazy stream and she jerked in his arms, then tugged away with a frantically whispered, "Would you behave!"

Nate laughed, but let her go, aware she'd be back in his arms and succumbing to his subtle caresses soon enough. To think that he'd actually believed he would never find a woman like her, that if he did find a woman who loved him in spite of his money, not because of it, he would eventually become bored. There wasn't a single thing boring about Kelsey—mentally or physically—and he knew deep down there never would be.

More than ready to claim the dessert he'd been interrupted in the middle of savoring, he waited restlessly while Kelsey said her goodbyes and hugged everyone. He took his turn hugging his mother and grandmother, then gathered up the handful of engagement gifts they'd received and guided Kelsey toward the door.

The early September air was warm, muggy even, but the humidity had nothing on the heat Kelsey stirred in his body with her mere presence. Now more than a little anxious to get her in his truck and act on her unspoken offer of dessert, he rounded to the tailgate and loaded the gifts while she climbed inside the cab. He was about to get in as well when he spotted Duane leaving the restaurant.

He'd told himself he'd wait until tomorrow to ask the man about Candy, but between the odd look in his sister's eyes and his own curiosity, the question was eating at Nate beyond tolerability. It would only take a minute to either get an answer or a "Go to hell" out of Duane and certainly Kelsey could wait that long.

His mind made up, Nate crossed back to the restaurant's entrance and rounded the side of the building where he'd seen Duane go moments before. The side lot was empty save for a handful of cars and, for a long moment, Nate saw no real sign of life, then a flicker of blue caught his attention. He glanced out in the distance where the twilight of late evening settled and the breath stilled in his throat even as his heart took off at breakneck speed.

A man stood in the distance, a man with Duane's build, Duane's clothes, Duane's everything, but this man wasn't Duane. This man was hunched over and quickly moving away. This man's blue shirt and jeans seemed to evaporate into nothingness and his flesh soon followed suit as the dark covering of what looked to be hair encased his frame. His limbs lengthened and his movements grew faster, his jog ascending to an all-out run, and then in a flash he was gone.

"Nate?"

Nate shook his head and blinked furiously at the sound of Kelsey's voice just behind him. He had to be losing his damned mind to believe he'd seen what he just thought he'd seen. Either that or lack of sleep thanks to one very sexy bed partner was to blame for his odd hallucination. Whichever the case, he wasn't about to say anything to Kelsey. At least, nothing more than he had to in order to placate her.

He turned back and she looked at him through concerned eyes. "Is something the matter? You look like you saw a ghost."

"I don't know," he answered automatically, then corrected himself, "I mean, I thought I saw Duane coming out of the restaurant and I came over to ask him something, but when I got here, he wasn't here."

She shrugged. "It probably wasn't him."

"Maybe not." But if it wasn't him then who the hell was it? Or what? Just his imagination. It had to be. Any other answer was unthinkable.

"But?"

He frowned. "But what?"

"You look like you wanted to say something else."

"Oh." He should know better than to try to hide things from her. After his initial lie, the mammoth one he had to thank for having her in his life, she could read him better than anyone else he knew. Right now she clearly could see he was holding something back. Still, he couldn't tell her the whole truth, if there was any truth to it at all.

Nate wrapped his arm around her shoulders and nodded toward the truck. They fell into step as he considered his response. "I just thought I saw…a wolf, I guess."

"Well, that's sort of strange, but not unfeasible. People spot them up in the mountains from time to time and that's only about twenty-five miles from here. Or it might have just been a dog. Some of the larger breeds are huge."

A dog? Was that possible? A dog that wore clothes and walked on its hind legs until it wasn't convenient to do so. No, it couldn't have been a dog. His earlier reasoning had to be the answer. He was losing his damned mind. Or maybe he was delirious. It wouldn't be the first time Kelsey's handling had had that effect on him. With her impromptu cock-tease, she'd successfully managed to drain all the blood and therefore judgment from his brain and send it directly to his balls.

Nate's temporarily forgotten erection jerked to life with the memory of her bold moves. He stopped their slow stride to his truck, turned her in his arms and captured her mouth in a hot, hungry kiss meant to rejuvenate every bit of the longing she'd lost in his brief absence. Kelsey surprised him when instead of responding tenuously, as the very open setting would seem to indicate she would do, she tugged him closer yet and rubbed her breasts against his chest while she met his tongue thrust for needy thrust.

She pulled back after several long seconds, her breasts rising and falling rapidly and the edge of her hard nipples abrading his chest. "Unless you plan to run in and ask Duane that question, I suggest we see about getting to that dessert."

Nate forgot about his odd sighting completely with the joint forces of humor and promise that filled her dark eyes. "What you're saying is you're ready for your ride?"

"I'd say the answer's pretty obvious, but if you need a clearer picture, just keep standing there and you'll find out up close and personal along with your entire family."

"You wouldn't dare."

She dropped her hands to the waistband of his slacks and the glint of humor in her eyes faded to raw appetite. "Get moving. If you're lucky you'll make it inside the truck before I start molesting you."

Chuckling at her audacious behavior, he hefted her in his arms and hustled to the truck. He lifted her through the driver's door then closed it and came down on top of her on the bench seat. She wriggled against him, breathing out in shallow gasps and cries when her mound contacted with the hard muscles of his thigh. Her fingernails urgently nipped past the thin material of his shirt and she whimpered her impatience.

A husky rumble of laughter drifting from his lips, he snagged her wrists in his hands and pinned them near the armrest on the passenger's side door. "Always my little aggressor, after me for sex and nothing more," he teased.

"Oh, yeah, you know me so well, Nate."

He grinned with the truth in her words, even if they had been spoken sarcastically. He did know her so well, in a way Joe had been so sure he'd never accomplish, in a way Nate himself had nearly been convinced he was incapable of knowing a woman. His heart swelled with pride and awe as he looked into her smoky eyes and the infinite trust that shone there, at the knowledge of how much she knew him in return.

Kelsey yanked at her bound arms and squirmed harder then, the hard ridge of her mound hitting his cock in just the right spot to have the few brain cells that remained above his waist zipping downward. He laughed once more at her futile attempts and held tight to her wrists with one hand while he popped open the buttons of her shirt with his other. The thin lace of her pink bra was the style she favored, the style he'd quickly learned to favor as well. The kind that revealed more than it concealed.

His tongue moved against his mouth in anticipation of taking the aroused nipple that winked at him from beneath the pale material into his mouth and sucking and biting at it until she begged for him to stop. He bent his head slowly, savoring the shudders of her body beneath his, the spasms of air that slipped from her slightly parted lips. Then just when he was about to touch down on the aroused dusky bud, he looked up at her flushed face and the expectancy and love that filled her eyes, and smiled. "Yes, sweetheart, I do know you so well. Know you and love you like no one else in the world. Now be a good girl and lie still while I enjoy my dessert."

One Wild Weekend

Dedication

To the five little angels that tiptoed through my life during the writing of this story. Four of you were only here for a very short while but I loved you all the same and still think of you every day of my life. Every one of you touched my life and my heart in a very special way and, for that, I will never forget you.

To Paige Burns, Wicked West and Valentine Dorr, because, no matter how much I complain or go for days without having the time to say so much as hello, you're still there for me and I know you will be forever. Thank you. I love you all.

To the vixens. Every day you brighten my life with your smiles and happy thoughts or broaden it with your sorrows and times of trouble. I am blessed to have you all in my life and I hope to keep you there always.

And last, but never least, to my husband Bill. Though it doesn't seem possible when I already love you so much, each day I spend with you, whether in times of happiness or those of sorrow, I love you even more. Thank you for being you. I can't imagine what my life would be like without you in it and pray that I never have to find out.

Trademarks Acknowledgement

The author acknowledges the trademarked status and trademark owners of the following wordmarks mentioned in this work of fiction:

Technicolor: Technicolor Videocassette B.V.

The Clapper: JOSEPH ENTERPRISES, INC

Chapter One

"You've got to be kidding me!" Candace Anderson glared at her older brother from across his kitchen table. "How could you do this to me, Nate?"

Leaning against the low counter several feet away, he shrugged. "How could I not? I've been asking you for damned near a year now what's going on between you and Duane. Every time, you say nothing. If that's the case, I don't see why your being paired up with him in the wedding is such a big deal."

And she couldn't tell him either. She couldn't tell another living soul why it was she went out of her way to avoid the man who'd been like a part of her family nearly all of his thirty-three years. Even if she could tell someone why she avoided Duane, they wouldn't believe her. Why should they, when most days she still refused to accept the truth?

"I just want to be with someone else. Including yourselves, you and Kelsey are having five stand up on each side. Why can't I be with one of the other four men?"

"Because they're either married and standing up with their wives or content with the person we placed them with. The plans are firm, Candy. And even if they weren't, there's no way in hell we'd make changes this late in the game. The rehearsal is tomorrow night."

Like he needed to tell her that!

Candace's belly tightened with the idea she'd be seeing Duane tomorrow. She couldn't get around it this time any more than she could get around being close to him. She'd be expected to stand centimeters away, arms intertwined much the same way she'd once foolishly allowed their bodies to be.

It hadn't seemed foolish at the time.

Duane had been living in Braxton, positioning his newest sport equipment rental store amidst the bustling city's main strip. Candy had visited Braxton three times in the year, plus he had called the place home and it seemed that the third time really was a charm.

The night before she was set to return to Clarion Heights, she'd chanced upon Duane in one of the area's upscale bars. He'd been there with a handful of other men and, by the time she'd spotted him, she'd had more than enough liquid courage worked up to approach him. Whether it was the fact that they were several hours from their hometown and her overly well-meaning family and friends or just that the time for action had finally come, Candy hadn't held herself back that night.

She'd grabbed his hand, led him onto the dance floor and made known what she wanted in seconds. She'd relished the fact Duane clearly wanted that same thing by the intensity of the hunger in his smoldering dark eyes and the impressive erection that rubbed against her belly and flamed her arousal a notch higher each time they moved.

It had been a night of dreams and decade-old fantasies come to life in wild, magical, breathtaking Technicolor. And then it had all changed. Duane had changed, become something she never could have imagined. And her dreams, her fantasies, the foolish desires she'd harbored for the two of them for years had morphed into a stinging awareness that was caught somewhere between fiction and reality.

The memory of the time Candace had spent in Duane's arms raced through her mind and brought an icy shiver coursing down her spine. She wasn't one to be easily shaken, had seen just about everything there was to see through her nursing position with the emergency care section of Mount Mercy Hospital. Yet, he'd managed to scare the hell out of her that night. Terrified her and hurt her in a way she could never forget.

Shaking off the unwelcome thoughts, Candace stood and grabbed her car keys from the table. She passed Nate a last glare as she moved to the kitchen door. She wished to God she hadn't stopped by his house on her way home from work. Not that the news could have been delayed forever but even a few more hours would've been nice.

Since it hadn't been delayed... "I'd be careful if I were you. If this thing turns out half as bad as I think it will, you're going to regret ever having me for a sister."

His gaze narrowed, curiosity clear in the vivid auburn eyes shared by all five of the Anderson siblings, and then he let go a boisterous laugh. "Just imagine if there actually *was* something going on between you two. I wouldn't be able to sleep at night for fear my life was in jeopardy."

Candy laughed dryly while her insides tightened further into painful knots. If the words she'd spoken only half in jest did keep her brother awake at night out of phobia, then at least he would be in good company. Because that's exactly what she'd been dealing with for almost a year now, since Duane's return to their hometown. More, since he'd made it clear he wasn't ready to put to rest what happened that night in Braxton. Regardless of the way things had ended, he still wanted her. Deep down, she still wanted him as well and that's what made sleep damned near impossible.

Every night she lay awake for hours, staring at the ceiling, fearing if she closed her eyes for so much as a second, she'd wake to find him prowling through her room, rounding her bedside, then throwing himself over her and latching onto her flesh. If he did that, she'd never be able to resist. Duane and the changes that had come over him during the time he'd spent in Braxton frightened her, but he also held something over her. Some kind of power, a magical pull. One she knew she couldn't deny.

The moment he laid his hands — or possibly his paws — on her she would lose the battle she'd waged for over ten months. She would succumb to the demanding strength of his arms, the hard, lean lines of his body, the drugging sting of his bites. And she couldn't do that. She wouldn't risk him hurting her again, wouldn't risk suffering any more injuries like those that remained as faded scars on her breasts.

She'd cared about Duane once, had believed that he felt the same way. But that had been before she'd learned the truth about him, long before he turned violent on her. And sure as hell before he shifted into his half-human/half-wolf form and barked out demands that were anything but tender.

"See you tomorrow, sis."

In the process of exiting through the kitchen door, Candace broke from her reverie and glanced back at Nate. As much as she wanted to stay angry with him, and likely would in at least some part of her mind, she couldn't leave him with a glare. She flashed a smile and said with as much as levity as she could muster, "If you're lucky."

And if she was lucky, the ground would open up and swallow her whole. She'd much prefer falling straight to Hell and having to endure the Devil's wrath, than find out if she had the strength to contend with the warring needs that filled her whenever Duane came within thirty feet. The need to run, the need to fight and, most disconcerting of all, the need to fling herself into his arms and never let go.

* * * * *

The citrusy smell of orange blossoms wrapped around Duane Livery's heightened senses and brought his body jerking to attention. The blood surged through his veins and his heartbeat stampeded, while his cock responded with an anxious twitch and lengthening that spoke to both his human half and his wilder side. He didn't have to turn from his conversation with his long-time friend Nathan Anderson and the man's father, Tom, to know who the owner of that baiting scent was. There was only one person who could affect him this way. Only one woman. *His* woman.

Candy.

He turned toward the chapel entrance and locked gazes with Candace. As the owner of a handful of "Sporties" outdoor rental stores, which catered to winter and summer sports enthusiasts, Duane typically had the off seasons to relax and enjoy life. This year hadn't been typical. He'd been forced to spend the better half of March and the first week of April back in Braxton, overseeing the design completion of his most recent store. More specifically, he'd been forced to spend it away from Candace and his goal of making her see what they were meant to be.

The last time he'd even been able to think about that cause and see the woman herself had been three Sundays ago when he'd been invited to share dinner with Tom and Darla Anderson and their grown children. Candace hadn't found out about his taking part until it was too late for her to bow out. She'd spent the night snarling across the table at him, her nostrils flaring in open hostility. They were doing the same thing now and, between that and her short denim skirt and breast-hugging gold sweater, his blood pitched toward the boiling point while his cock thickened further yet.

Did she have any idea how appealing it was when she twitched her nose that way? How animalistic a move, like she was scenting him the same way he was her. Like she knew how badly he ached to bound across this room, toss her to the floor and fuck her here and now, for all to see.

Okay, so maybe that was a bit drastic but he still wanted it. The werewolf in him demanded it. The human half grabbed firmly to control. He had waited months for her to come around and accept that they were meant to be, that she was his intended mate and no other female—human or otherwise—could ever fill that role. If he counted the time before he'd changed, back when he'd cared about her far more than as a friend or sibling figure, then he'd been waiting for her to come around and accept his attraction to her for years. A few more days wouldn't hurt anything. If his body behaved, it wouldn't.

Before the change, he'd wanted her, cared for her, but after the change, now, his hunger for her was like a living thing. An animal that silently yelped to be freed and take what was rightfully his. The woman who would give him the one thing he'd never known. A real family and not just one he pretended was his.

Duane excused himself from the conversation with the two men and started toward Candy. The remainder of the wedding party had yet to arrive for rehearsal and she stood alone at the back of the church. For her sake, he was glad. As much as he liked the Anderson family and felt gratitude for everything they had given him through the years, his need for Candace still overshadowed it. He wasn't above making a scene to prove she was his. She hadn't yet reached that level of understanding and would have no qualms about overtly rejecting him in the hopes it would dissuade him.

It wouldn't, of course.

It had taken some time to adjust to the lifestyle that had been set upon him one night last year, when he'd been too shit-faced drunk to acknowledge that the woman who'd picked him up and proceeded to take him home and make him her late night snack wasn't exactly normal. But he had adjusted and he knew what was meant to be.

Duane came to a standstill two feet from Candace and reached out a hand to sweep a strand of long, golden blonde hair behind her ear. She flinched at his touch and his body responded with a pang of raw hunger. "You look incredible. Good enough to eat."

Pulling away from his hand, Candy rolled her eyes and snorted. "I bet you wouldn't have any reservations about doing just that either, would you? Or are four-legged animals more your choice of entrée these days?"

He was surprised she'd spoken so candidly, even if they were beyond her father and brother's hearing range. Not that Candace wasn't frank. She was to the extreme, but in the past that frankness never extended to comments on his wilder side. Did that mean she was ready to face the truth between them? That she was at least ready to talk about it? "I wouldn't turn down a nice juicy steak but you know my favorite will always be extra-thick-crust pizza from Angelou's. Have you eaten yet? We could go there after this is over and talk."

She flashed a "yeah, right" look and took a step back. "Damn. I'll have to take a rain check. I promised Nate and Kelsey I would go over the last minute details with them. You know how stressed out the bride and groom get the night before the wedding."

He didn't doubt that some couples did but he'd spoken with both Nate and Kelsey several times today and neither appeared the least bit frazzled. Which meant Candace was digging for a way out. Why? Normally she would tell him, point-blank, no or possibly to go to hell.

Could it be his closeness bothered her? Was she as aware of the electric heat that sizzled between them as he was and doing her damnedest to deny it?

Warming to the thought and the many ways he might bother her further until she owned up to the way he affected her, Duane closed the short distance she'd put between them. Candace's eyes widened and the breath left her mouth as sharp pants as he reached for her once again.

"Actually, you didn't say anything like that, Candy."

The sound of Nate's voice just behind him had Duane taking a step back and his hand dropping away before it could make contact.

The alarm left Candace's expression and she looked at her brother tight-lipped. "Yes, I did," she grated out. "Remember yesterday when I was at your house? Remember what I said right before I left? I meant what I said then. Every word of it."

Nate came to a stop next to Duane and looked thoughtful for a few seconds before nodding. "Come to think of it, I do remember you saying something. That still doesn't change the fact we don't need help. Mom and Dad are watching over things so closely not so much as a hymn book is out of place."

Malice filled her eyes as she mouthed an, "Oh," then turned her attention back on Duane. "I still can't have dinner with you.

I already said no to dinner with my family because I have too much to do to get myself ready for tomorrow."

"Yeah, and I still don't get that." Nate cut into the conversation once more. "The dresses have been ready for weeks, your hair appointments are all set and you're having your nails and makeup done at the salon. You took four days off from the hospital, Candace. Take advantage of that time for a change. If you don't want to have dinner with the family, then have it with Duane. It won't kill you."

"It might even be fun," Duane put in, relieved to have Nate on his side. Up until last summer, they'd been best friends— Nate had been the one to bring him into the Anderson home and make him feel welcome in the first place—and in most ways they still were. Just lately, Nate was asking questions, acting as though he wasn't sure if he trusted him any more.

Nate glanced over and his brow furrowed. "I said she should go out with you. That's all I said she should do."

And that backed up Duane's theory that Nate didn't trust him any longer. "What the hell do you think I'm going to do her, man? Get her drunk and convince her to come home with me?"

"The thought had crossed my mind," Nate said too somberly for Duane's liking.

Nate had known about Duane's desire for Candace since they were hormone-driven teenagers but what he didn't seem to understand is that Duane cared for her as much as he wanted her. He knew her too well, her fears, her childhood secrets. Her most forbidden thoughts. He would never get her into bed by coercion. Smooth words, even dirty ones, possibly. Hypnotic suggestions and whispered thoughts, for sure. But never would he take her until she was good and ready to submit to both him and her own carefully concealed feelings about the two of them.

"So what if he did?" Candy bit out, her glare once more focused on Nate. "I'm twenty-seven—in other words, a grown woman. As I've told both you and Joe a million times, I don't need any overprotective brothers watching over me, getting in the way just when things are starting to get good."

"And you're saying they're starting to get good with us?" Duane asked, latching onto the unexpected words as hope cruised through his body as restless longing. Had his instincts been on before? Was she ready to talk, to own up to things?

"I didn't say that," she retorted. Only, her thoughts weren't falling in line.

Telepathy was an ability he rarely used, hadn't even fully gotten a handle on yet, but with Candace it was like second nature. Whenever she was worked up, the way she was quickly becoming now, her thoughts bulldozed straight into his head. Now they were making it clear just how much she'd believed things had been about to get good before Nate had interrupted them.

"Maybe not, but are they?" he pressed.

She looked at him for a long moment, her mind racing almost too fast for him to follow, then turned her attention on her brother. "Are you sure you don't need any help? Anything? Anything at all?"

"If you're that desperate, there is something you can do," Nate said. "I was going to have Dad help me with it later but there's no reason it can't be done now, when we're waiting for everyone else to get here. I want to add another row of chairs behind the pews just in case we end up with a bigger turnout than what we're expecting. They're in the storage room down the hall on the left. The wiring's messed up, so you won't have much in the way of light but, so long as you leave the door open, it should be okay. Actually, the door sticks, so you'll want to be sure to brace—"

"I'll be fine," Candace cut him off in a rush then, before either of the men could say another word, headed for the hallway that adjoined the rear of the church.

"I'm sure you will," Nate uttered to her retreating back. He turned to Duane. "Do me a favor and go with her. There are at least three dozen chairs there and, knowing her, unless someone steps in, she'll try to get them all at once."

Yeah, that sounded like Candy all right. Headstrong. Stubborn. Always thought she had to be outdoing herself. This also sounded like the Nate he used to know. The one who trusted him alone with his younger sister. True, their solitude would only stretch about twenty yards but that was more than enough distance to cause the kind of trouble Nate should fear. Not that Duane would, but it didn't change the facts.

He nodded. "You got it, man."

Duane moved out of the chapel's main room and down the hall. Blistering curses singed the air as he approached the storage room. He grinned. Candy might have attended this church with her parents as a child but she wouldn't make it here very long as an adult, that was for damned sure.

Tucking back his smirk, because he knew if she saw it she'd throw a fit that was nowhere close to holy, he rounded the half-open door. His shoulder brushed against it as he passed and it closed behind him, flooding the area with darkness. His eyes adjusted quickly, night lenses extending to cover human lenses. He could see perfectly. Candy bent over, jerking at a chair that was stuck in a pile. The short denim skirt hitching up on her shapely thighs. The very edge of her pink panties peeking out from beneath. The pale flesh of her butt cheeks exposed on either side.

She jerked upright suddenly and rounded on him. Her eyes glowed a golden yellow as if they were lit by the sun. "What the fuck did you just do?"

"Your brother thought you might need a hand."

"The door, idiot. You closed the door!"

"So."

"So, Nate said it sticks." She pushed past him to the door and jerked on the handle. The door remained firmly shut and she swiveled back on him. He'd never told her he had night vision and obviously she hadn't spent the last months reading up on werewolves to learn it for herself, so she did the one thing she never allowed herself to do around him. She let the panic she was feeling show on her face.

Damn, he'd known he worried her but he'd never realized how badly. It should have been a given. He would have been scared shitless in the same situation, not this one but the one he'd put her in the last time they'd been alone in the dark together. That night things had gotten seriously out of control. It hadn't been his fault. It had been mere weeks after the change and he'd had no idea the limits of his strength, of how rough and demanding he would become when he coupled with his intended mate.

He hadn't meant to hurt her, hadn't even known he had it in him to do so. He'd honest to god believed her cries toward the end of their lovemaking had been the same throaty moans from the beginning. He thought he'd been giving her the same pleasure she gave him. The blood and tears visible when he'd reached his climax and moved off from her, then tried to pull her back into his arms, made it clear she hadn't been experiencing ecstasy at all. The way she scurried off the bed and shrank back in the corner of his room, sobs jerking her body as she hugged her knees to her chest, had made him feel like the worst kind of monster.

That had been then and this was now. He had control of himself and he would never harm her again. He cared about her too much, the amazing woman she'd become and the headstrong little girl she'd once been. Somehow he had to convince her of that. To soothe her and make her understand what was to be.

Duane reached to her face and idly stroked a thumb over the rise of her cheek. "Don't be scared, Candy, sweetie. They know we're in here. They'll come for us soon."

She shuddered beneath his touch, her pupils dilating, and he cursed under his breath. He *could* control himself now but that didn't mean he *wanted* to. Just the gentle heat of her breath and the feel of her soft, smooth flesh beneath his fingertips made him ache to move his hands lower, along the tender column of her throat, down to cup her lush breasts, then further still to fill with the sweetly rounded globes of her ass.

His cock throbbed in response to the thought, the idea of tearing the pink panties away and plunging into her from behind. Of taking her the way every wolf before him had taken his mate. Of hearing her answering howls as he brought her to orgasm and filled her buttocks with his hot seed.

Candace jerked from his touch and backed up against the door. "I'm not scared!"

Loathing filled her eyes where before there had been fear. The fear he could abide by, the hatred he could deal with, the lying he couldn't tolerate for an instant. Having spent the first fourteen years of his life shuffled from one set of foster parents to another, all of whom swore they would keep him around and yet never did, made him despise dishonesty above all else. Her lies now called up a temper he never used to possess.

He advanced on her in a flash, pinning her tightly between the door and his body as he took her face in his hands. "Like hell you aren't. You don't have to be brave for me, Candy. You can give in, submit to your fears." *Submit to me.*

He didn't voice those last words but conveyed them in thought as he allowed his hands to journey the course they itched to follow. His fingers chafed along her neck where her pulse thrummed chaotically and then moved down her shoulders to the insides of her arms. She sucked in a hard breath when his palms met with the outer swell of her breasts. Slowly, he worked his way inward, until his hands covered her breasts through her sweater.

Her nipples beaded against his palms and the breath rushed from her mouth on a heated wave. "I want out of here, now!"

"No, you don't." Moments ago, Duane had thought she was afraid and, in some ways, he recognized she still was. He also recognized her thoughts, how they conveyed her excitement and the equally appealing way her scent did the same. She was hot for him. Hot and wet. She needed him every bit as much as he needed her. In mind, heart. Body. "You want my mouth on you, my hands cupping your breasts, buried under your skirt, dipping into your soaked pussy. And it is soaked. I can smell your arousal, Candy. Sticky sweet. You want me, just as I want you. It won't be rough like last time. It was all too new to me then; I had no idea what would happen. I couldn't control it. I can now. I will. Let me show you. Let me make you mine, the way you're supposed to be. You are mine, Candy. You have to know that. We've always belonged together."

The scent of her arousal heightened even as she attempted to move away from him. Clearly aware her efforts were futile, she stilled and narrowed her eyes. "I am not a goddamned possession. Yours or any man's."

The words were spoken low, acidic, in a pitch that called to every fiber of his soul. She pushed at him, at his composure; she always had, and it made him want to push back. Made him want to lock his mouth on hers, thrust his tongue deep inside and demand she respond in kind. Instead, he kept his hold on her breasts firm and said calmly, "I'll be yours too, just tell me the truth. Tell me you want me. That you always have. A single 'yes' is all it takes."

Her gaze narrowed further still, but it was her body's response that mattered. The way she shifted against him, moved her legs just enough to have them straddling his thigh and brushing inches from his swollen shaft. She was trying to rub against him, to ease the need that burned deep in her womb and, even if the action was only instinctual, it was the opening Duane had been looking for.

Rubbing the pads of his thumbs over her erect nipples through her sweater, he bent his knees slightly and leaned into her, rocked his groin against her mound. The subtle bite of his zipper against his cock registered but then was forgotten as he watched rapture take over Candace's face and turn her cheeks pink and her eyes the same brilliant gold shade as her sweater.

He moved one hand to her back, providing support as he

rocked harder, pressing his cock against her cunt, silently demanding she give in. "Tell me you want me, Candy," he ordered. "Say the words."

She bit down on her lower lip and shook her head. He waited for denial to follow that shake, to enter her thoughts and tumble from her lips but all that filled her mind was hunger and all that came out of her mouth was a desperate sounding, "Please..."

It was a please he couldn't resist even when he knew now wasn't the time or place to give in to it. He pulled her flush to him, trapping her breasts between their bodies, and crushed his mouth against hers. He swept his tongue inside, brushed over the flat tops of her teeth, then dipped into her heat. She was still for an instant then her hands were on his shoulders, her nails digging into his flesh through his thin shirt, her tongue crashing against his with violent need. The blood surged to his cock and his need to possess, despite time and place, stole over him in pounding waves.

He'd waited so long for this. Months. Years. Decades. And he couldn't accept it. Because, regardless of the way she might be acting now, she wasn't ready to take the next step, to submit to him and become all that he'd craved for so long. And even if she were, he would never take her here, in the storage room of a church with her family just down the hall. That didn't mean he couldn't give her pleasure.

Duane relaxed his hold on her just enough to ease her back from his chest. He moved his hand between them and fisted the material of her skirt in his hand, then pushed past that barrier in search of her panties. She squeezed her legs together, halting his progress and making the first real sign of resistance.

Still, it wasn't real resistance. Not when her nails continued to bite into his flesh and her tongue to lap at his with urgent demand. She needed reassurance. A reminder of what it was she would get once she gave in to him. Of what they would both get.

Moving his hand up the underside of her skirt, he met with the softness of her panties. His fingers slipped beneath the top edge of the cotton and dipped down to the treasure of heated curls below. He coaxed the stimulated flesh beneath the wet, wispy hair and she released a throaty cry that had one of his own tunneling up inside him.

Duane pulled free of her mouth and pressed a wet kiss to her throat as his fingers continued to pet her damp curls. "You can feel it, can't you? Feel the way we belong together. Feel that you are the only one for me, that we are meant to be. Don't tell me you can't feel it, Candy. Open your body to me, your mind!"

"I don't...want to...feel...this way," she admitted on a jagged breath but then let the tension leak from her thighs. She parted her legs and opened to him and he moved his fingers lower to rim the lips of her pussy.

He could smell her heat before, knew she was aroused but he hadn't been able to tell the extent of how wet she was. She was dripping for him and that knowledge pulled at the wolf within him, made him ache to give in and satiate it, to take her hard and fast and completely until she was his in every way, shape and form. "You test me, Candy," he growled, sliding his fingers along her drenched slit, slipping them in just far enough to fondle her inflamed clitoris. "You make me want to lose control."

"You will *not* lose control!" Candace's nails left Duane's shoulders and tension returned to her thighs. Once more she tried to clamp them together.

He pushed into her sheath with two fingers and silenced her urge. She was right, he wouldn't lose control but he also wouldn't stop now that he'd begun, not until she found her satisfaction. "I won't, but you will."

He added a third finger and circled her clit with his thumb, coaxing the nubbin until her breathing grew sporadic and she wriggled in his arms. She squeaked out a curse even as her eyes widened in a sensual haze. He worked his fingers in and out, in and out of her slick sex. Her breathing came faster, raggedly, and her hands returned to his shoulders, her nails nipping with painful pleasure into his skin.

Her feminine muscles shuddered around his fingers, pulling at them, trying to bury them further inside. He quickened his pace, pressing harder against her cunt, fingering her clit with more insistent strokes. The contractions of her pussy pulsed forth and trembles sliced through her, shudders that had his own body standing on end with the need to unleash, to let go. The trembles grew and she swayed toward him, leaning against him as her legs went weak and her body began to give itself over to pleasure.

"I won't come for you!" she ground out.

Chuckling, Duane took her mouth and teased her lips with nipping kisses as her sex contracted one last time and then leaked her juices onto his fingers in wet, hot, streaming waves. "You already are, sweetie. And you'll do it again, many times."

While he hadn't planned on those many times happening tonight, in this storage closet, he couldn't stop himself from pulling his fingers from her still-spasming pussy and going down on his knees. He wouldn't lose control, wouldn't take her the way he yearned to do but he needed to taste her, to savor her hot essence on his tongue.

"What the hell are you doing?" Candace rasped out.

Gripping her thighs, he buried his nose in the sodden crotch of her panties and inhaled her sultry sweet scent. "Smelling you. Tasting you." He pulled his nose back and gathered the wet material in his hand, gave it one fierce tug that had it falling to the ground unheeded. He brushed his coarse chin hair against her swollen pussy lips once, twice, and then buried his tongue deep into her dripping center.

Candace bucked against his mouth and a low cry tore from her lips. A cry that was followed by a strangled gasp. She jerked from his touch too quickly for him to stop her and hurried the short distance to the other side of the closet, feeling her way around brooms, buckets and other obstacles as she went. Her back pressed against a stack of chairs, she stared at him wide-eyed, her face suffused with passion and yet something more. Something that looked like the fear she'd shown when they'd first been trapped in here. He followed the direction of her frantic look to his hands, to the claws that protruded from his fingertips. She couldn't see them in the dark but that didn't change the fact she had obviously felt them. It also didn't change the fact he hadn't been able to maintain control the way he'd all but promised he would do.

Son of a bitch, he'd wanted to bring her closer to him, to show her he could be gentle, not scare her more than what she'd already been.

"I want out," she said in a quiet, uneven voice, then, when he didn't immediately respond, added much more loudly and forcefully, "Now!"

He couldn't blame her for her alarm or her fury. And he also knew he wouldn't get any farther with her tonight by keeping her here. She needed distance and he needed the same, before more of him shifted than just his nails.

Duane stood and moved to the door and, calling on superhuman strength, forced it open. He stepped back into the darkness, giving her a wide berth and, at the same time, shielding himself from anyone who might be nearby. She moved past him in a flash, only looking back when he said, "We aren't done here, Candy. Not by a long shot."

She narrowed her gaze and flared her nostrils. His cock throbbed with the action and his cells tingled with heat and need, signaling how close he was to shifting further. "Yes, we are," she spat, "We've been done for a long time. A very long time," and then turned back and hurried down the hall without a single chair in her possession.

Chapter Two

"Something the matter?"

Was that Nate's idea of a joke? Candace wondered as she came to a stop near the back row of church pews where her brother stood. She noted the rest of their family and Nate's fiancée, Kelsey, and her friend Jan had arrived during her absence and were gathered near the front of the church. She then shot Nate a disgruntled look.

Was something the matter? Well, let's see, she'd just been going at it with a wereman, or what ever the hell you'd call what Duane had been back there, in the pitch-black storage closet of a church. Yeah, that qualified as something seriously awry. A big damned something.

If it hadn't been for the judgment-awakening feel of his long claws digging into the soft flesh of her thighs, they would still be in that closet. He probably wouldn't be on his knees, rubbing the wondrously rough hair of his goatee over her pussy or tonguing her any longer, though. He would probably be buried hilt-deep inside her and…furry.

She shuddered at that last thought.

How could she even consider getting that turned on by a man who had the power to grow a silky pelt of chestnut brown hair any canine would be jealous of? Worse, to lose herself and her control to him? She couldn't let it happen again. Couldn't allow them to be left alone with only her fleeting judgment for a bodyguard. He hadn't hurt her this time but that had a lot to do with the fact she hadn't let him. The moment she'd seen the animal in him start to emerge, she had done what she should have done the instant he'd entered the closet. Demanded he let her out and not stopped demanding until he did just that.

"Earth to Candace. You feeling okay, sis? You look... flustered."

More like recently fucked. Maybe Duane had only managed to get his hands and mouth on her but she'd still been breathing hard, still felt the sizzling heat of orgasm slicing through her and tingeing her face with red. She'd still climaxed because of him.

Refusing to reflect on the mind-numbing orgasm or the way his long, strong tongue felt lapping at her cunt, Candace lifted her shoulder in a careless shrug. "I'm fine and nothing is the matter." She nodded toward the front of the church, then looked back at Nate. "Why aren't you with the rest of them?"

"Because I was coming to find you two and make sure everything was okay. It shouldn't take over ten minutes just to grab a few chairs." He glanced at her hands and frowned. "Where are they are anyway?"

The chairs, right. She'd gone to get chairs, not have a closet quickie. One that left her nether regions hanging out beneath her short skirt and a cool lick of air caressing her aroused flesh. She grunted at the reality of how turned on she still was. She wanted to be back in that closet, seeing just how far Duane would take things. She wanted to take things further herself. And that just wasn't right, damn it!

She had to get a grip on her body. Had to learn to ignore whatever hold it was he had over her, one that made her give in when she knew damned well she should be running the other way. "They are...the door was stuck. You said it does that sometimes; well, it's doing it again. Duane's still trying to get it to loosen up."

He frowned. "It sticks from the inside, not the outside."

She rolled her eyes with his rapid response. Wasn't that just her luck? She came up with an answer that was halfway reasonable and he had to go and prove it wrong. Not that she had any intention of letting him know it was wrong. She narrowed her gaze, silently daring him to dispute her. "This time it happened from the outside. The damned thing won't budge."

Nate looked past her and his frown grew for just an instant before disappearing. "Guess it must've finally decided to budge."

Though her suddenly pounding heart told her it was the last thing she wanted to do, Candace turned to follow the direction of her brother's gaze. Duane walked toward them, his arms laden with folding chairs. He nodded at Nate, then shot Candy a grin.

Her heart sped faster and her clit tingled with awareness. Why the hell did he have to have such a sexy smile?

Determined to avoid that smile and the masterful tongue hidden just behind it, she dropped her attention to his hands. They were free of claws now, thank God. Or maybe not thank God. She hated having to bear the burden of knowing what Duane was all on her own and yet she didn't dare tell any of her family members for fear they would think she was due for a visit to the loony bin. If they found out on their own, then they would have to believe her. But what if they found out and shunned Duane? He scared her at times, yes, but she didn't want her family to cast him out. He'd been a part of it for too long and didn't have one of his own to fall back on.

As much as her family could be a real pain in the ass at times, she couldn't imagine them not being there for her, just as she couldn't imagine what life would have been like growing up without her fourth brother, Duane. The one who teased and goaded her along with all the rest and yet wasn't a real brother at all. Considering her current feelings would be knee-deep in incest if he was a true sibling, it was a damned good thing he wasn't. Feelings aside, she had to keep his secret and therefore her family's close regard for him intact, and that meant making things seem normal between them.

She returned to his smile and, urging back the heat that consumed her with that simple look, put on one of her own. "Oh, good. You got the door fixed."

Duane nodded, then looked to Nate. "I suggest you have your mom tell them they need to put a new lock on that thing, man. If I hadn't moved Candace out of the way so I could give the door a yank, she'd still be there, trying to get into the damned room."

The calm she'd pushed into place frayed a bit as her temper threatened to spurn forth. She mentally forced it back. Somehow Duane had figured out what she'd told Nate as an excuse for their absence and, unless she wanted her brother thinking any differently, she'd best keep her mouth shut.

Nate glanced at her, his expression one of expectancy, as if he thought she would comment on Duane's remark. Not trusting her mouth, she nodded her agreement. Her brother's earlier frown returned as he glanced at Duane then back to her again. The wariness in his expression said he knew something was off. Thankfully he didn't ask on it any further but said, "Yeah, okay. I'll make sure she knows," then looked back to where everyone else was gathered at the front of church. "Forget about the chairs for now. We need to get the rehearsal started."

Candace waited for Nate to get halfway across the room before she asked in a low voice, "How did you know what I told him?"

"The same way I knew what you wanted back in that closet." The heat returned to Duane's eyes with the words, rendering their typically hazel shade a surreal yellowish-green. "Hate to break it to you, sweetie, but your thoughts are like an open book."

Candy snapped out of the daze of his eyes as the meaning of his words settled in and curled her belly with anxiety. "My thoughts... You can read my mind?"

"Only when you're anxious."

Which is what she became every single time he walked into a room.

Damn it. She had enough trouble convincing herself she didn't want him; if he knew for a second the mixed feelings she had toward him, he'd never be persuaded into keeping his distance.

"Then remind me not to get that way again any time soon," she snapped, then turned on her heel with the intention of joining the safety of her family. At least she hoped their proximity would act as a safety net. Duane wouldn't let on what he was to them any more than what she herself would do. Would he?

No. If he'd intended to do that, then he would have long before this.

"You're still that way right now, Candy. Just my standing here, a foot away from you, thinking the things I'm thinking, has you so nervous, your mind and heart are both racing. Then there's what's happening south of your heart. You're still wet, still hot. Still wishing we were back in that closet so we could finish things the right way."

She shouldn't succumb to his taunting. She shouldn't turn back and taunt him in return. She shouldn't but it wasn't in her nature to walk away. She pivoted back around, stopping short to fist her hands at her hips and glare at him. "You wish!"

"Yeah, I do. I wish you'd accept what's happening between us and give in to it already. It's going to happen, we're going to happen, so why fight it?"

"It's *not* going to happen and I'm *not* fighting a damned thing. I don't want you, not now and sure as hell not forever."

"Candy, honey, is something the matter?" her mother asked from the front of the church.

No. Nothing was the matter and why did people have to keep asking her that? If they wouldn't keep asking, she wouldn't have to keep lying to them or to herself.

Candace eased her hands off her hips and back at her sides. She looked to her family, all of whom stood gaping at her, and smiled. "Everything's fine, Mom. We're just talking about...stuff."

"Having a lover's spat's more like it."

"Corey!" Carrie, Candace's younger sister and Corey's twin, swatted their brother on the arm. "Don't be such a jerk."

A cocky grin turned up Corey's lips. "Well, that's what it sounds like from here."

"First off, we're not lovers," Candy bit out, "and secondly, what would you even know about the word? The only thing you love in this life is your own reflection."

His grinned deepened and he made a show of dusting his knuckles on his chest. "It is rather impressive, isn't it?"

"Oh, God—"

"If you two are done, can we get this thing moving along sometime tonight?" Joe, the oldest of the five siblings cut Candace off. "Candy might not want to take advantage of time off and spend the night out unwinding but most of the rest of us have dinner plans. Duane, you're invited to join us, of course. That is, unless Candy changes her mind and takes you up on your offer."

She stared at him in disbelief. What the hell was this, gang up on Candy night And who told him she'd turned down Duane's dinner offer, anyway? Not that it should really surprise her—Joe had this uncanny ability to know everything about everyone and an opinion to go with that knowledge—but lately his time and thoughts had been wrapped up almost completely in his wife, Gracie, and the impending birth of their son.

"I have things to do," Candace said in her defense. "I have to get myself ready."

"What do you all have to get ready, Candy?" Kelsey asked. "Is there anything I can help you with? It is my and Nate's wedding after all."

"No kidding, what do you have to get ready," Duane asked, pulling her attention back to him and the sensual smile that had overtaken his lips, "because from where I'm standing, you look pretty amazing right now."

Between the promise that seemed to fill that smile and the compliment, warmth charged through Candace's body too fast to stop it. She blushed before she even realized what she was about to do. Obviously the color stinging her cheeks was apparent from fifteen yards away, because Corey's cocky look returned and he said, "See, told ya, lover's spat."

Candace bit back a groan and focused on the only sane person in the room—at least it seemed that way at the moment—the minister, who stood off to the side of her family, looking like he'd lost track of the conversation long ago. "Can we please do this already," she pleaded. "I want to go home and..." *Pout.* Or something very close to it.

He gave her a grateful look. "Yes. Let's begin. Everyone will start at the back of the church. Nate, you'll be seating your parents. Since Kelsey's brother isn't here yet..."

Candace moved to the back corner of the church and sat down on a pew as she waited for the minister to finish explaining how things would proceed. Much to her relief and her surprise, Duane left her alone. At least until he didn't have any choice but to come for her, to escort her down the aisle.

She stiffened at the feel of his arm twined through hers, recalled the thought she'd had yesterday, about the way they'd once been twined together bodily. The same way she'd almost allowed them to become a very short while ago.

What was it about him? Did he truly hold some kind of magic over her the way she'd told herself on several occasions? Was that magic and the way he used it to enchant her to blame for her reeling senses and chaotic heartbeat? Was it the culprit behind her sudden desire to forget everything that had happened between them and start tearing his clothes off here and now to unveil the long, lean frame beneath?

Her mouth watered at the vivid image that formed in her mind. There was definitely an upside to his wolfishness and that was the effect it had on his physique. Maybe it was from the time he spent scrounging the fields at night for field mice or trotting along the highway looking for road kill but the man had a dynamite body and a killer tight ass just made for gripping.

Duane chuckled beside her as they started to advance down the aisle. She glanced over at his amused expression and mouthed a "What?"

"You're in serious need of an education if you honestly think that's the kind of stuff I eat, let alone how I spend my nights. I spend them just like you do, Candy, lying in bed, thinking of what would be happening if we were together right then, the way we're destined to be."

Candace's thought slammed to a halt and she bit her lip to keep inside the squeak that welled up with his too-knowing words. She tried to concentrate on the fact he read her mind as clearly as if she'd voiced her thoughts aloud, tried to consider what else she might have unknowingly admitted when she hadn't known he was listening in. All that was happening instead was that her body was responding to the implication in his words. Thoughts of what they would do if they were in bed together filled her mind in vibrant detail and had her pussy swelling with a fresh course of desire.

The humor in Duane's eyes turned to hunger. His nose twitched and he leaned closer, inhaled audibly and whispered near her ear. "I like this no underwear thing. Normally I can smell your arousal even when you have them on but off, it's so strong, it makes my cock hard with just one sniff. Then there's what it does to the rest of me."

Her gaze fell to his groin out of instinct. The bulge of his erection wasn't so obvious everyone else would notice but the way it twitched against his jeans as she stared upon it made it clear it was definitely there and large. Her sex pulsed with the memory of just how large and her inner thighs grew damp as juices seeped from her crotch. Her clit tingled, flamed, and it was all she could do not to reach down and rub her hand against it in the hopes of bringing some much needed relief.

Good God, she wanted to fondle herself because of the idiot and the thoughts he'd planted in her head. And in front of her family and in a house of God, no less!

Magical or not, it was seriously wrong, this hold he had

over her. It had to stop. Now. "Walk, Duane," she gritted out, doing her best to shut out the wetness that leaked from her thighs and the heat that poured through her veins. "And if you want to live to see tomorrow, don't say another damned word to me tonight but 'goodbye'."

* * * * *

Candace awoke with a start. Her pulse raced in her throat and fear wrapped around her limbs, locking them in place. Someone was in her bedroom. One sniff told her that the someone wasn't her sister Carrie, who lived with her. Rather, it was a man. Or maybe the better word was beast.

She couldn't describe Duane's scent if someone asked her to and yet, it called to her, made her limbs suddenly loosen and her body heat with awareness.

She sat in bed and whispered, "Duane."

Silence was her only answer. A deafening silence that brought the tension careening back into her body. She bit down on her lower lip and let the covers fall away from the death grip she had on them. She would not cave to her panic. She wasn't afraid of him. And even if she were, she would never let him see that.

Candace released her lip and drew in a calming breath. She waited for her eyes to adjust to the pale light of the moon bleeding in through her windows, then called his name a second time, louder, "Dua…"

She trailed off as a flash of movement snagged her attention. She looked toward the set of windows she kept cracked open, even during the cooler months, and her heart stopped for an instant, only to take off in a pounding rage.

She didn't want Duane to see her fear but, damn it, how could she stop it when he was in her room, mere feet from her bed, hunched down in his full wolf form and preparing to attack?

He's not preparing to attack, Candy. You can't even see any of him other than his outline and the glint of his eyes.

Okay, so she couldn't see him well but that didn't change the fact he was in her bedroom at one-thirty in the morning. If he wasn't here to attack her with logic-altering kisses and strokes, then why had he invaded her home in the middle of the night?

Anger burst forth with the realization he truly had invaded her home. As much as she'd worried about him doing just this for months, deep down she'd honestly thought that her concern was nothing more than the result of an overactive imagination. She hadn't believed he would really break into her room and pounce on her. For reasons that were now beyond her, she'd trusted him to leave her home as her sanctuary.

Well, he might have destroyed her trust and entered her home without her permission but there was no way in hell she was letting things go any farther. Whatever he had come here for, he was going to tell her and he was going to do it now.

Pushing away her fear, Candace let her growing frustration seep into her voice. "I can see you, you idiot, so there's no point in keeping your silence a second longer. Say what you came to say, then get the hell out of here."

She'd expected at least a snort of humor, or maybe a laugh — or whatever sound it was a werewolf made when it was amused — but once again only silence answered her. Silence and his strangely overpowering scent.

The odd aroma had grown stronger in the last few seconds, almost as if he'd come closer to her. In truth, he hadn't moved an inch. He was still hidden in the shadows of night, only his outline visible. She couldn't make out his eyes well enough to know if they were on her and, for that reason if no other, she shouldn't be feeling aroused. Only she *was* feeling aroused, unbearably so.

Once more her tension slipped away as his luring scent filtered through her senses and into her mind. Her heartbeat slowed to a rhythm of desire and her inner thighs heated while her pussy flooded with the juices of expectancy. Back in the church, Duane had worked his magic on her, made her ache to touch herself, to stroke her clit and ease the restless burning in her sex. It had to be magic making her feel those same things now, because, before she could even consider what she was doing, her hand was beneath the covers and touching a heavy, naked breast.

She stroked her fingers over an erect nipple and the breath caught in her throat as an answering pool of wetness seeped from between her thighs. Tugging at her swollen nipple, she kicked back the covers and moved her free hand lower, to the edge of her slit and the damp curls that concealed it. One finger moved inside the slick, open valley of her cunt, piercing her core with a pumping thrust and she nearly came off the bed at the exquisite sensations that coiled through her.

My God, she felt ready to come, and all from a simple stroke. But, no, it wasn't from a stroke. It was from Duane. From the heat of his potent gaze, from the knowledge that he watched her fingering herself. From the magic he worked over her senses.

Damn it, she would not succumb to that magic!

No matter how good it felt to touch herself under his watchful gaze, no matter how wickedly naughty, and yet somehow so very right, she couldn't give in to his sexy goading smile anymore than her own forbidden desires.

Cursing her moment of weakness, Candace jerked her hands from her body and narrowed her eyes toward Duane. "You have two seconds to speak your mind and after that I am coming over there and hurting you."

One. Two. More silence.

Maybe he was working on the right words and needed a few extra seconds.

Three. Four. Five. Still more silence.

Damn him! Why was he acting this way? He had to know by now his magic had failed, that, as much as she ached to reach down and finger fuck herself into mind-numbing climax, she wasn't going to do it. So what was his game plan then? Was he angry that his efforts at seducing her with his mind alone had fallen through and was trying to frighten her? If that were the case, then why had he told her not to be afraid of him less than eight hours ago? He'd never been the kind of man to say something like that and not mean it. But then she'd also thought he wasn't the kind to hurt her or break into her home when he knew damned well he wasn't wanted.

Son of a bitch, something had to be done. She wasn't going to spend the night stuck in a limbo of wanting to fuck herself and wanting to kill the man responsible for getting her in that mindset in the first place. Or better yet, fucking that man himself.

But, no. She didn't want to do that. She just wanted him out of her room.

What if she went over there and he used it to his advantage? What if he said she'd come to him voluntarily and therefore she was his to do with as he pleased? Once he started, she'd never be able to stop him. She wouldn't even want to, no matter how logical it might be.

Shit. She couldn't go over there. Her only hope of getting him to go away without causing any more havoc on either her mind or body was to ignore him, pretend as if she couldn't care less if he watched her sleep. Pretend like her pussy wasn't on fire with the need for just one more thrust. Oh, hell, for a whole lot of them.

"Fine!" she snapped, her body's state of arousal fueling her words with passion. "You don't want to talk, then stay there all night and watch me sleep. I'll warn you though, I snore like a banshee."

Flopping back to the mattress and onto her stomach, Candace burrowed against her pillow and closed her eyes. She opened them immediately, knowing how pointless it was to even bother with trying to sleep. She would never sleep with him here, not when she felt his gaze boring into her back, his scent threatening to overtake her logic. Not when she couldn't stop thinking about the fact she was naked beneath the covers, naked and stimulated and burning to do something about it.

It was a pity she hadn't installed a Clapper. She'd always wanted one of the automatic light sensors when she'd been a kid. If she had one, she could just clap her hands, turn on the lights and take care of the situation. Not that she really thought a little light would sway Duane into leaving but it sure couldn't hurt. It might even—

A rustling sound brought her rambling thoughts up short and she drew in a sharp breath and rolled back over, half expecting to find a werewolf lying in the bed next to her. Much to her relief and maybe just a bit to her sorrow, there was no one in her bed and Duane was still in the corner, still watching her. Still driving her nuts and making her feel wet and achy.

"Can you smell me?"

Candace closed her eyes and swore under her breath. Why the hell had she asked that? It had to be because of his comment at the wedding rehearsal, about how he knew she'd been wet and wanting him in that closest long before he'd touched her, about how he could smell her arousal even as they were walking down the aisle.

Once more Duane remained silent. If he was going to respond to any of her questions, then it should have been that one because, in its own way, it sounded like she might be interested in whatever it was he'd come over here to offer. So what was up with his silence? Had he grown tired of her lack of action and fallen asleep?

The idea eased her some, enough to have her opening her eyes and moving to the side of the bed. Gripping the top cover around her, she stood and, with held breath, moved to the light switch next to the door. She might be feeling a bit bolder but she still wasn't about to go over there and confront him in the dark.

Turning her back on him long enough to flip the switch, she swiveled back, blinked at the suddenly intense light...and laughed out a disbelieving groan.

There was a wolf in her bedroom all right but that wolf wasn't a werewolf or a living creature of any kind. It was an almost life-sized stuffed animal.

Candace crossed to the window and the wolf that sat beneath it, staring at her through yellowish-green glass eyes. This fuzzy, lifeless, almost cute stuffed animal is what had scared her? Even worse, what had turned her on until she couldn't stop from fingering herself?

Okay, so maybe there hadn't been any magic ruling her actions, maybe she'd just been horny since leaving Duane at the church and had used the idea that he was behind her behavior as an excuse to touch herself.

That still didn't explain the smell. She had smelled Duane. It had been his scent that had first stimulated her. Hadn't it? Was it possible she'd seen the wolf's outline and allowed herself to make up the scent? But no, she'd smelled it before she'd seen the stuffed animal. There had to be some other excuse. Some excuse that explained how the animal had arrived in her bedroom in the first place.

She did have a few cherished stuffed animals left over from her childhood and even a few more recently given to her by hospital patients but none of them were wolves. It could be Carrie's but, if it were her sister's, that still didn't explain what it was doing in her room. Why it would appear tonight of all nights and why it would have to remind her so damned much of the one man she was determined to forget—sexually, if physically wasn't a possibility. Whatever the reason, it would have to wait for tomorrow. Maybe Carrie could tell her something then or, at the very least, get the animal out of her sight.

* * * * *

The moment Candace's bedroom light came on, Duane had darted out of view of her windows and into the shadows that surrounded the outer city limits house. He knew better than to come around here this time of night, this time of the month, when the moon was almost full and his longing to barge into her bedroom and make her his nearly painful.

He hadn't been able to stop himself. He had to see her. Had to know if she'd accepted the gift he'd asked Carrie to give her. He'd spotted the wolf in a department store window next to the restaurant where he'd shared dinner with the rest of the wedding party. Everyone but Candy, that is. He'd thought the animal appropriate for a number of reasons — one of which was to offer her comfort from her many bad dreams and sleepless nights and another was to get her used to the idea of having a wolf in her life full-time.

Aware Candace wasn't the type to be swayed by gifts or, for that matter, even accept them, particularly from him, he'd asked Carrie to give it to her under the pretense it was from her. Thankfully the younger sister wasn't half as obstinate as the older and had quickly agreed.

The wolf was now in Candace's bedroom. Not in her bed the way he craved to be, but in her room at all was a step and, if what he'd just witnessed through her window were any sign, a big one at that. His cock expanded further, throbbed as the image of Candy fondling first her large, rigid nipple then her sweet, dripping pussy filled his mind. He'd never expected her to respond so overtly to the wolf and he'd never expected himself to have such a mind over body struggle to turn away from her actions.

Tonight he had no choice but to do just that, turn away and return home alone.

Tomorrow was another day though. Tomorrow he'd take the next step in ensuring his loneliness would soon come to a permanent end. Tomorrow he'd infiltrate himself into her thoughts throughout the wedding and reception, convince her to dance with him many more times than just that first obligatory dance of the wedding party and soon, very soon, replace that stuffed wolf with a much larger, warmer, responsive one.

Chapter Three

"It's all about resolve."

After pulling on her robe, Candace tossed open her bedroom door and started toward the kitchen, chanting the words to herself.

That stupid wolf might have made her panic and then get turned on but that was last night when she'd been tired and out of sorts. This morning she was relatively alert and ready to face the day ahead, no matter how bad the latter half of it might be.

"Morning, sunshine."

It was all about resolve, Candy repeated the words silently, this time in regards to her younger sister's cheerful morning attitude. Morning people had serious issues but she wasn't in the mood to point them out to Carrie right now. Instead, she forced a not-quite-sincere smile and made her way to the cupboard. She grabbed a mug, filled it from the pot of coffee on the counter and sat at the table across from her sister.

The coffee was steaming hot but the scintillating aroma was too much to ignore, particularly in her quickly returning irritable state. She took a long swig, almost enjoying the way it scalded over her tongue and down her throat. After taking a second tastebud-numbing drink, she set the mug on the table and looked to Carrie. "Did you put a wolf in my bedroom?"

In the midst of bringing a spoon laden with oatmeal to her mouth, Carrie halted her arm's progress and shot Candace an odd look. "Ah, no. Did you find one?"

"I woke up last night and it was watching me."

"A real wolf was in your bedroom last night, watching you?"

"I don't mean watching me, watching me. I mean…" What, that a stuffed animal was spying on her as she slept, making her hot and horny with its supposed magic and stimulating scent? Yeah, that sounded rational. "No, not a real wolf. It's stuffed. It's a big stuffed wolf and it isn't mine. I don't like it and I don't want it."

"Well, it isn't mine, either."

"It is now."

The hasty retort pulled a frown from her sister followed by a shudder. "A big stuffed wolf magically arrives in your bedroom in the middle of the night and you want to give it to me? Very sweet, sis, but no thanks. That's just a little too creepy for my taste."

Carrie returned to her oatmeal and Candace watched her eat in silence. Her sister's reaction seemed to speak to the fact she had no connection with the wolf but if she didn't, then it meant someone else had been in her room last night. Someone or something had planted the wolf there in the hopes of gaining Candy's attention, in the hopes of making her react to its commanding presence and intensely knowing eyes by fondling herself. In the hopes that, when she thought back on it this morning, she would grow warm, wet and wanting all over again.

Right, they had. And she was officially losing it.

Candace straightened in her seat and forced herself not to rub her thighs together against the wet heat gathering between them. She was not turned on by the idea it really had been Duane watching her, just as she hadn't been aroused for that reason last night. She was merely…in need of a topic change. "Fine. Since you don't want it or know where it came from, I'll throw it out."

Carrie's attention snapped from the oatmeal bowl to Candace's face. "No!"

So much for changing the subject. How could she when it was obvious by the passion in her sister's response that she had everything to do with the wolf? At least, its presence. Where Carrie had come by the animal was another question and one that Candy could well guess the answer to. What she couldn't guess is why her sister was covering for Duane. Carrie liked Duane, of course, but Candy was family by blood and that should be worth something, damn it. "Why not? You said you didn't want it."

"I don't but that's no reason to throw it out. What if it's important?"

"To whom?"

Carrie lifted a slim shoulder in a shrug and focused back on her bowl and making oatmeal hills with her spoon. "I don't know. I guess whoever put it there."

Candace bit back a groan at her sister's continual avoidance of an honest answer. Since when had she gotten so good at keeping a secret anyway? It used to be, she'd overhear something and the rest of the family and most of the city would know it by nightfall. The Carrie of old couldn't be so far gone.

Perhaps it was a simple matter of throwing out a little reverse logic. "No one put it there, Care."

Carrie looked up, eyes narrowed, and tilted her head to the side, sending the blonde ponytail that had seemed a permanent fixture on her head since puberty swinging. "So you think it just got there all by itself?"

"Yes. No. I don't know. I just don't want it. If you want it, fine, go into my room and get it. Otherwise it's going out with the garbage on Monday morning."

"What are you going to do with it 'til then?"

"I thought I'd bring it to the wedding with me as my date. What do you think I'm going to do? I'm leaving it where it is."

For an instant, Carrie's eyes lit with relief and then that look passed and she scooped a spoonful of oatmeal into her mouth, muttering an "Oh," in the process.

Between the momentary flash of thankfulness and the same relief that seemed to fill her sister's mumbled response, Candace immediately regretted her hasty words. She didn't want that animal in her room until Monday. Only now she could hardly remove it without risking her sister's wrath in the form of twenty knowing questions; starting with if she was moving it because it bothered her and ending with if that concern had something to do with who she thought its presenter might be.

Maybe that was Carrie's whole point—trying to get Candy to admit it bothered her because it came from Duane and brought all those thoughts of him she tried to push away to the forefront of her mind. The idea made sense and fit with her sister's persona perfectly.

At twenty-three, Carrie still managed to hang on to a spark of youthfulness and energy. She also hung on to a penchant for getting bored too easily and constantly trying new things. It was the reason she was still in college with no real direction after five and a half years and, Candy was willing to bet, the reason for her behavior now. In typical Carrie fashion, she'd gotten bored yet again and decided to take up matchmaking as her latest endeavor. Candy could guarantee this endeavor was doomed to fail. As she'd told her older brothers numerous times through the years, she didn't need help with her love life or lack thereof. She for damned sure didn't need anyone pushing her in Duane's direction.

Candace opened her mouth to tell her sister to stop with the matchmaking attempts. Before she could do so, Carrie stood and said, "You'd best get in the shower soon. Mom and Gracie said they'd be here a little before ten to pick us up and, knowing you, you'll need at least an hour of shower time before you'll be nice enough to associate with anyone." Then, before Candace could so much as respond, Carrie placed her bowl in the kitchen sink and left the room.

* * * * *

Idle chitchat had never been her thing. As Candace sat in the day salon, waiting for the beautician to finish her hair, she remembered why. Because between women that chitchat typically turned to one of two things. Men or shopping. The latter she could handle. The former, however, was the current topic and she feared at any moment the conversation was going to come around to her and Duane.

"I still can't believe he's going through with it," Jan, Kelsey's best friend, said in regards to Nate and the fact that up, until a year ago, he'd been all but a sworn bachelor.

"I can." Sitting next to Kelsey, Darla Anderson sniffed. She swiped at her misty eyes and smiled. "When he was a boy all he ever talked about was how he was going to grow up some day and have a big family of his own. I'm just thankful he found the right woman to give it to him."

Kelsey looked past the nail technician, who was coating a second layer of polish on her nails, and laughed. "In my case, I'm just glad I found the right *man*."

The women fell into laughter over the way she'd emphasized 'man'. Even Candy had to give in to a quick chuckle recalling how Nate and Kelsey had met. He'd been operating under the guise of a woman and, because of the way her body reacted every time they'd touched, had managed to convince Kelsey she was a lesbian or at least bisexual.

If only her own problems were so simple, Candace thought. She could handle being attracted to another woman far easier than being attracted to another species. Needing to get her mind off thoughts of Duane, she said to Kelsey, "I'd tell you that was a fluke and my brother's the sweetest guy you'd ever meet but then you already know him better than that."

Carrie rolled her eyes. "Yeah, don't we all. Talk about a pain in the butt to grow up with." She looked at Candy. "But then again, you weren't much better."

"Nonsense!" Darla scolded her girls' teasing words. "All of you kids were a joy. I can only hope that your own children turn out to be as wonderful. " She turned a meaningful look on Kelsey. "And the sooner the better."

"Hey, don't look at me," Kelsey tossed back. "I love kids

and Nate and I definitely want them but we're not even married yet. Besides, you already have one grandbaby on the way."

"Yes, I do." Darla smiled the short distance to where Joe's wife, Gracie, sat. Her hair had already been finished and, since she was foregoing nail polish, she'd taken up residence in a nearby chair. Apparently, seven months of pregnancy had started to weigh on her, as her eyes were closed and she appeared to be asleep. Darla looked back to the rest of the women and added, "But there's nothing wrong with a couple dozen more."

"A couple dozen?" Kelsey squeaked out.

"They don't all have to come from you and Nate, dear," Darla assured, "or even you two and Joe and Gracie. I have two other perfectly lovely daughters."

At her mother's pointed look, the tension that had subsided from Candace's belly during the casual banter returned full force. "Don't even think about it, Mom."

"Of course, I'll think about it. I'm your mother, it's my job. Besides, you're not getting any younger, honey, and from what I hear you're also not going to find any better catch than what you already have." Candy was barely aware of her mouth falling open and a gasp slipping out, when her mother continued, "Don't act so surprised; I'm not blind. We don't need to talk about it now—it's Kelsey's day—but whenever you're ready, I'm here."

"Uh, thanks," Candy managed.

"You're welcome and that goes for you too, Carrie." This time it was Carrie's gasp that filled the room. Their mother seemed oblivious to both it and her horrified look, as she turned back to Kelsey and smiled. "Now about this boy of mine. He's a keeper and I think you already know that."

"He has his moments, I'll give him that." Kelsey's smile slipped into a full-fledged grin that revealed a dimple in her left cheek. "Okay, so he has more than a few of them." Her grin faded and she said solemnly to Darla, "Thanks for raising for him for me; I can't imagine my life without him. Without any of you. Andy was all I had for so long." Her voice cracked on the last words and her eyes filled with tears.

Darla let loose her own tears and stood to take Kelsey's free hand, giving it a reassuring squeeze. "Oh, honey, we're the ones that are thankful. You've made our family even bigger and better. And pretty soon—" she swiveled back and her gaze once more landed on Candace, "—it will be even bigger and better yet."

Candy fought off the urge to shed her own unexpected and highly unwanted tears. As much as her mother might want to see her and Duane together, as much she might want it herself in some very deep and dark recess of her heart, it could never happen.

* * * * *

The dress had shrunk.

Kelsey had picked hunter green A-line dresses for her bridesmaids to wear. The last time Candace had tried hers on, a few short weeks ago, the dress had hung to the floor, hugging her body gently. Today it fit like a second skin and made her breasts stick out like beach balls.

"You look gorgeous."

Candace shifted her attention to Jan, who stood next to her in the side room of the church. If anyone here looked gorgeous it was Jan, with her deep red hair done up in a French twist and spirals framing her flawless face. Her dress didn't hug her body like it was painted on either. Candace moved her attention lower, to where the woman's breasts all but plunged over the neckline of the gown, and groaned. Okay, so maybe her dress fit that way too but she swore that hadn't been the case a few weeks ago.

"I feel like I've gained twenty pounds this month." *All in the chest.*

She couldn't walk down the aisle dressed like this. No, she

couldn't walk down the aisle next to Duane dressed like this. His attention was going to be on one place and it wasn't her Cinderella pumps.

"Oh, please," Gracie put in from several feet away. "If anyone here gets to complain about feeling fat, it's me." She glanced meaningfully at her rounded belly, then back at Candace. "You look amazing, so stop worrying." She looked to each of the other women and smiled. "All of you do. And considering all of you, but Kelsey obviously, are single, I'd say there's going to be a reception full of men, begging for dances tonight."

"I dance alone," Carrie said, scowling at her mirrored reflection. She patted the French twist of blonde curls atop her head. "And I still don't see what was wrong with wearing my hair in a ponytail. I look—"

"Beautiful." Kelsey's smile turned sympathetic. "You know, I don't like getting dressed up this much either. As soon as the cake is cut and the first few dances over, I promise we can all change into jeans and T-shirts and put our hair back in ponytails."

Carrie groaned but then nodded. "Okay. I guess I can handle it that long." She looked at Candace and opened her mouth as if she were about to say something but then stopped short and walked over to her. Her gaze fell to her chest and she frowned. "Not that I make a habit of checking out your chest but I don't remember ever seeing marks on it before. When did you get scars on your breasts or are they wolf scratches?"

Disbelief shot through Candace and she slapped her hands to her chest and squeaked out, "*What?*"

Carrie's eyes danced with humor and she laughed. "I thought maybe your stuffed friend from last night was to blame."

Oh. *That* wolf. Not that the inference was made any better because it was meant as a joke. Carrie had still noted her scars, which meant at least part of them was visible above the dress's low-cut bodice. Which meant not only would others be noticing them as well but that Duane was going to spend the night with his attention focused on her breasts for certain.

But maybe his seeing them was a good thing. Those first few seconds trapped in the storage closet yesterday, he'd seemed genuinely concerned about her fear of him. He'd sounded almost apologetic about the way he'd handled her that first time they'd been together. In truth, he had made numerous comments over the last year to that same effect.

If he truly was sorry about his behavior that night, then putting her scars out there, right in front of his face, might just be the thing to finally convince him to keep his distance. It was about the only thing she had in the way of hope right now, and so, as the music started up, playing a trumpet voluntary, and the women filed toward the door, she clung to it.

* * * * *

With his first look at Candace in a dark green, body-hugging gown, her plentiful breasts rising tauntingly above its scooped neckline and her citrusy scent wrapping around his senses, Duane felt like a real wolf. And while that might not be saying much, it still said something. Namely that, if he wasn't careful and watch himself tonight, he was liable to lose control and become a *real* wolf right before everyone's eyes.

Candace reached him and, smiling at her, he took her arm, slid it through his crooked one and started down the aisle. He could feel the tension radiating off her as they walked and was tempted to lean over and say something to ease it. Only doing that wasn't liable to go unnoticed. Leaking a few thoughts into her head, however, wouldn't leave anyone but Candace the wiser.

You look too amazing to be so tense.

She tensed even further and her next step faltered slightly. She didn't look at him but he could sense her scowl in the sharpness of her thoughts. *Stop it, you idiot! Get the hell out of my head!*

Quit frowning and relax before people start to think something's wrong.

Something is *wrong. At least, something is going to be if you don't knock it off, because I'm going to kill you.*

You don't really want to do that, Candy. You want something far different from me and we both know it. Before this night is over, you're going to admit it, too. You will because it's meant to be, sweetie. We're meant to be.

"We are not!"

Candace jerked to a halt and breathed out a gasp with the loudly spoken words. Duane bit back a chuckle and pulled her into motion, tugging her along beside him until they reached the end of the aisle where the minister and part of the wedding party, including her brother Nate, already stood.

Nate glanced from Duane to Candy with an irritated look but then let it go and turned an expectant smile back down the aisle. With a squeeze of her arm, Duane released Candy to the women's side of the aisle. She was barely in place when her thoughts reached him.

I swear to God if you don't stay out of my head, I will personally see to your death.

Promises, promises, Candy. Now be quiet and watch your soon-to-be sister-in-law walk down the aisle. I don't want to have deal with Nate later if you have another outburst and I am sure he'll find some way to blame it on me.

That was *your fault and don't tell me what to do!*

Shh...

Grr...

Candy, sweetie, growling is not the best way to turn me off. Neither is flaring your nostrils at me. In fact, both are really good ways to get me to make a scene like you don't even want to think about. Shall I explain?

No, you shall not. Now be quiet and watch Kelsey walk down the aisle.

Candace's thoughts died away and she turned her attention

solely on the entrance of the church as *Here Comes The Bride* started up and an overjoyed-looking Kelsey appeared. Duane laughed to himself. That was his Candy, turning his order around on him, so that it looked like she was the one who'd voiced it to begin with. She wasn't, of course, but it did give him some ideas on how he might use that particular trait of hers to his advantage.

Half-listening to the ceremony, Duane grinned as thoughts of Candy naked beneath him, crying out his name, smiling up into his face and begging for more, filled his mind, and his anticipation for the night ahead grew with each one. He had promised her before this night was over she would see things his way. And she would do just that; even if getting her to that point meant coercing the truth out of her by way of his hands, mouth and a number of highly salacious thoughts.

* * * * *

"And now for the bridal party dance."

Candace's belly did a slow roll and anxiety skittered along her spine. She had been dreading this moment since walking into the reception hall over an hour ago. And Duane, judging by the taunting smile that curved his too damned scrumptious mouth as he approached her, had been waiting for it with baited breath.

He reached the table where she sat chatting with cousins she hadn't seen in over a year and extended his hand. "I believe that would be us."

And she believed now would be the opportune time for a trip to the ladies room.

Duane's smile kicked higher and he took her hand and tugged her to her feet. "You can do that in a few minutes; first, you're mine."

Candy blew out a hard breath, not sure if it bothered her more that he had read her mind yet again or called her his among mixed company, then proceeded to tug her onto the dance floor like a rag doll. Deciding on the latter, she stopped

169

short, jerked her hand free of his grip and started back off the dance floor. She'd taken two steps when she spotted Nate glaring at her from where he slow-danced with Kelsey.

Damn it. She owed Nate for sticking her in this situation to begin with but she couldn't retaliate by ruining even a few minutes of his wedding. She had to dance with Duane. Resigned, she swiveled back and collided with the hard wall of Duane's chest. His hands came around her waist, pulling her flush against him and trapping her hands between their bodies in the process. Then, before she could say a word or attempt to remove them, he picked her up and swung her around in a circle that left her mind spinning and her breath wheezing out as pants.

He set on her feet and brought his arms back around her waist, swaying with her the way the slow song dictated. With laughing eyes that seemed to almost glow in the darkened reception center, he smiled down at her. "Are you having a good time?"

"I was," she said, purposefully adding bite to her tone.

He chuckled and pulled her closer still, far too close for propriety's sake. She'd felt his hard body beneath her hands moments ago when she'd run into him but that had been only for an instant, not nearly long enough to cause her mind to wander. This time his long, lean frame was molded against hers and her breasts were all but squished between them and he was showing no sign that he planned to release his hold on her any time soon.

His odd scent—slightly tangy, slightly woodsy, totally entrancing—seeped into her senses and curled warmth in her belly. She tipped back her head and eyed his mouth. Thanks to the added height of her pumps, his full, succulent lips were entirely too close to her own. If she rose on tiptoe even the tiniest bit, she could brush up against them, bury her tongue between and caress his, remembering just how hot he made her when he stroked hers in return.

Duane's lips lifted in a knowing grin and Candace jerked

her attention away and swore under her breath. She wasn't rising on tiptoe and she also wasn't going to consider how incredible he looked in the black and green tuxedo. She was going to focus on the same thing too damned many others had been focusing on tonight. Her breasts. She'd come up with an excuse to explain the scars to everyone else. With Duane there would be no excuses, only the cold, hard truth.

She glanced down at her chest. "I never realized how low cut these dresses were when we were being fitted." She flitted her gaze back to his and looked at him meaningfully. "People keep commenting on my scars."

The sexy grin left his mouth in an instant. He cursed just loud enough for her to hear while his eyes filled with what looked to be remorse. "I'm sorry about that, Candy. I've told you so a hundred times. I also told you it will never happen again and I meant it. I can control myself now. I *will* control myself."

Right, like he had last night in the closet? She wasn't going to voice that thought and she also wasn't going to give him the chance to pick into her mind and respond to it. She forced a smile. "Good. I'm sure whoever you sleep with next will be relieved to know that."

The remorse in Duane's eyes was overtaken with frustration. He tightened his grip on her and bent his head, growled low near her ear, "The only woman I'll be sleeping with, tonight or ever, is you. You're mine, Candy. You know it."

Candace shivered against the heat of his breath, the commanding way he tried to get her to give in to him. She'd always hated men who tried to take control, despised the ones who thought they should have the upper hand over a woman. That was exactly how Duane had been acting around her lately and she should hate him for it. And maybe the sensible portions of her did but the not-so-sensible portions were feeling something entirely different. They were becoming more and more stimulated with each slow grind of his groin against hers.

As if he knew her thoughts and, knowing him he probably did, he shifted his pelvis slightly, enough for her to feel the long, hard press of his aroused cock against her belly and yet not make a glaring public display. Her eyes widened with that first subtle brush and her heart sped while her sex responded with an insistent heating. Wetness gathered in her panties and her pussy throbbed with a stab of desperate need. She bit back the urge to press her thighs together and squirm, to lean closer to his ear and beg for him to rub harder, to move his hand from her neck and use it to stroke her burning flesh through her gown.

The slow song was replaced by another and the DJ announced the dance floor was open to everyone. Couples filed onto the floor, surrounding Candy and Duane, taking away the security that came from knowing their actions could be seen by all. In the throng of swaying bodies and darkness broken only by twinkling white lights and sporadically placed candles, no one would be able to detect their movements. That left way too much room for temptation.

Candace attempted to break free of Duane's arms. He held tight. "One more song."

"One." She could last through just one more. If she could get her thoughts off his pants and how badly she ached to get in them, that is. In dire need of a topic change, she asked the first question that came to her. "Did you ask Carrie to give me a wolf?"

Duane stopped moving and frowned at her. "What?"

She shrugged, hoping to somehow make light of the situation. "I woke up last night and thought I smelled you in my bedroom. Then I thought I saw you. It wasn't you but it was a wolf. A big stuffed one that wasn't in my room when I fell asleep. Carrie tried to deny putting it there but I know she's lying."

He looked thoughtful for a few seconds, then gave a shrug of his own and resumed his slow, sinuous moves. "Sounds like you have a secret admirer."

Candace gritted her teeth and locked her body in place. Maybe they weren't in plain view anymore but she still wasn't about to stand here and let him rub up against her. "The only admirer I have is you and you're not a secret or wanted, so I suggest you quit with both the moves and the presents before I take my earlier threats seriously."

"You plan to kill me?" he asked, looking more amused than worried.

"The thought has some real appeal."

Duane laughed, the sound deep and throaty and somehow directly connected to her pussy, as it let loose with a flood of juices that had her clit tingling and her fingers itching to grab hold of his clothes and rip them off one piece at a time.

She cursed herself for the thought. It was his damned magic. It had to be. She honestly could not want him this badly. It wasn't even in her physical makeup to do so. She wasn't asexual exactly but men just didn't leave her weak-kneed and wet. They certainly didn't rub against her and have her burning with the need to tear off their clothes and toss them back on the dance floor to ravage in front of her entire family. Annoyed with how badly she ached to do just that, Candy snapped, "Why is the thought of my killing you so funny? You never would've laughed about something like that before."

"In case you haven't noticed, I'm not the man I used to be. Time and circumstance have a way of changing a person, showing them those things that matter most."

"Trust me, I've noticed." And what exactly did he mean by 'those things that matter most'? Was he talking about her? Them? It wasn't important because he had changed and he'd never again be the man he was, just as her lust for him could never be naive. "If you were that same man, then you might have a chance."

"But since I'm not, I'm just shit outta luck?"

"Amazing, you do understand. For a while there I was beginning to think that, along with the rest of your changes, you'd become dense."

Duane laughed again; this time the sound was dry. He

sobered and peered down at her with burning intent in his eyes. "I'm not dense, Candy. I'm also not taking no for an answer. I know you, I know what you want."

His hips started up again, moving against hers in a slow, rolling grind. She caught her tongue in her teeth to stop herself from moaning out a growl of acquiescence. Reining in her haywire libido, she bit out, "You don't know a damned thing about me."

His eyes sparked, seemed to come alive with glowing light and a smug grin settled on his mouth. "No? Then tell me this doesn't make you feel something."

His mouth was on hers in an instant; his kiss firm, commanding, impossible not to sink into and feel a whole range of sensations because of. And yet Candace knew she had to stop herself from doing just that. Pressing at his chest, she struggled to push away but he held her firm to him, his arms as rigid and unmoving as dead weight. She attempted to cry out, to scream at him to stop but her words came out as muffled gasps barely audible to even her own ears above the music and conversations of others.

Damn it, let me go!

Let yourself go. You want this. I know you do, have for years. Give in to it. Give in

to me.

No. I won't!

But, whether it was the influence of his magic or just the truth in his thoughts that she'd been wanting this very thing for years, she already was giving in.

Duane's hands slid from her waist to move along her sides. His palms grazed the outer swell of her breasts and her nipples peaked and throbbed as if he'd pulled them between his lips and sucked. His tongue pushed past her mouth, rubbing against hers in a slow move that held barely any pressure at all. Had there been pressure she would have been able to find the strength to pull away — somehow she would have — but where there was no force she was powerless to do anything more than respond.

Aware she'd already lost this fight, Candace did the one thing she'd been aching to do since he'd pulled her onto the dance floor and rubbed her body against his. Grinding her pelvis in the same teasing way he'd done to her, she stabbed her tongue deep into his mouth, loving the way his unique scent exploded as tantalizing flavor onto her tongue and danced across every one of her taste buds. She retreated then sank in again, stroking and suckling at his tongue with each sure thrust of her own. Her senses reeling, her mind spinning, she moved her hands from where they lay dormant at his back to knead his firm ass beneath the tails of his tux jacket and through his thin slacks.

God, how she ached for so much more. Her pussy felt afire with the need to feel his hot, hard flesh pumping into her, mimicking the action of their tongues. She wanted his hands on her everywhere, beneath the dress, fondling her bare breasts, burying into her cream-drenched slit and making her come undone completely. She wanted him to make her moan, groan and howl. She wanted to submit.

"As much as I hate to interrupt, the music's stopped."

Candace's recklessly speeding thoughts came to a jerking halt with her sister's words. She released her hold on Duane's butt and pulled free of his mouth, struggling to attain normal breathing as she concentrated on the sounds and sights around them. The mass of bodies that had before encompassed them was gone. Chattering voices still carried on but otherwise the hall was distressingly silent.

Heat consuming her cheeks, Candy wrenched herself from the grip Duane still had on her and shot her sister a guilt-ridden look. "Uh, right. Thanks."

Carrie laughed softly, then narrowed her eyes in speculation. "You okay, sis? You look a little…overheated."

Wasn't that the understatement of the decade? She was aflame, scorching with the need to let go, to return to Duane's arms and admit that everything he said about her was accurate. That she did want him, had for years. That it wasn't magic to blame for her behavior tonight or the visceral way she'd responded to the stuffed wolf last night. It wasn't the naïve lust she used to harbor for him either. It was raw, unadulterated desire. Decade old longing that refused to be extinguished no matter how hard she tried. The truth was that she wanted him and in a way she'd never wanted another man. In a way she feared went well past the physical and that she could she never feel with another.

Duane's murmur of acknowledgement brought her attention zinging back to his face and she realized he was reading her mind again. Not about to consider what he'd just learned from her thoughts, because it was more than even she was ready to deal with, she turned to Carrie. "I'm fine. I just need something cold."

"In that case, I was about to go change. If you want to go with me, we can grab a couple beers on the way." She glanced at Duane and grinned. "Don't worry, loverboy, I'll have your woman back in no time."

"His *what?*" Candace's blood ran cold with the accusation, one heard by a good deal of the reception attendants thanks to the lack of music. "I am *not* his woman!"

Carrie shot her a "yeah, right" look. "Mmm hmm. Looked that way ten seconds ago when you were lip-locked and groping his ass." Candy gasped, realizing just how bad and completely accurate it had looked, and her sister laughed and grabbed her arm. "Let's get moving before Mom tracks you down for details."

Oh, God. Their mother had made it clear at the salon she knew something was going on with Candy and Duane. Now she would believe there was more than a little something and, as Carrie had suggested, want all the details. Ones along the line of when they were planning to take things to the next level in the form of wedding bells. And since the answer to that was a big fat never… "Good idea. Let's."

* * * * *

"So, dish," Carrie said the moment she stepped into the women's bathroom. She'd remembered her duffel bag was still in the car halfway to the bathroom and had left Candace to wait for her while she went and grabbed it.

Candy had had no plans to wait where the wolves could get her and had come promptly to the bathroom to start changing. Only she hadn't gotten around to it yet. She'd taken one look at her flushed face and kiss-swollen lips and realized cooling efforts came far before comfortable clothes.

She dabbed at her newly washed face with paper towels from the nearby dispenser, then tossed the damp towels into the wastebasket and looked at her sister. "About what?"

Carrie pulled a brush and ponytail holder from her duffel bag. She set them on the double sink basin and snorted as she started to remove the bobby pins securing her hair in place. "Right, sis, like you don't know. What's going on with you and Duane? You were practically mauling each other on the dance floor."

"We were not!"

Why did everyone have to describe the attraction between her and Duane in such primal terms anyway? The few times Nate had actually come out and suggested there was something going on with them, he'd said the way they acted toward each other was animalistic. Corey had jumped on the bandwagon in an instant. Joe didn't put things in quite those terms but he certainly took his fair shots at making it known he thought they belonged together. At least he had before Gracie had gotten pregnant. Thank God for that blessed event. One less sibling with a matchmaking agenda was exactly what she needed here. Okay, so four would be even better.

"Oh, please—" Carrie finished with the pin removal and caught Candy's gaze in the mirror as she started brushing her hair, "—I have eyes, so does everyone else and, after the way you two were going at it, I can guarantee you I won't be the only one to ask what's up."

"Nothing is up." No matter what she wanted, what she had to admit if only to herself she craved, nothing could be up. Because…just because. "It was a slip of judgment, heat of the moment kind of thing. It didn't mean anything and it isn't going to happen again."

Carrie stopped brushing her hair to level a direct gaze on her. "Duane's okay with this?"

What, was she kidding? Like her sister actually thought she would ask him. "Duane doesn't have a choice. Besides, he's not even my type." Admittedly, she wasn't sure what her type was but she was pretty danged certain it wasn't four-legged.

Carrie's gaze went from direct to joyful. Smiling, she turned back to the mirror and twisted her hair into the ponytail holder. "Then I guess you won't care if I ask him out."

Candace was in the process of opening the locker where she'd stored her casual clothes when the words reached her. She swiveled back, stunned. "*What?*"

In the mirror, Carrie's smile blossomed into a dreamy grin. "He might not be your type, whatever that is, but he is mine. He's been like part of the family for so many years, I guess I never really took a good look at him until recently. He's changed somehow, become more…passionate. I like it."

She couldn't be serious. Carrie *never* dated. Not to mention this was Duane they were talking about. Duane! He had changed but not for the better. Only if that were the case, why did the thought of her sister dating him twist her belly with loathing?

"He's ten years older than you," Candace blurted, hating the jealousy she heard in her tone.

Carrie closed her eyes on a wistful sigh and shrugged. "I happen to know someone who's in love with a man almost twice her age. Eleven years is nothing."

"It's ten years! An entire decade."

"So?"

"So..." So she couldn't really be this upset over her sister wanting to be with Duane. Not when she'd spent the last ten months plus trying to convince him to move on. Not even if she could finally admit to herself she still wanted him. She wasn't about to act on that desire and that meant it had to be more than jealousy eating at her gut. Maybe the frosting on the wedding cake was spoiled. "So I don't think it's a good idea," she finally snapped.

Carrie opened her eyes and turned back. The dreamy look was gone and in its place was a knowing that cut directly to Candace's soul. She held her breath, torn between awe and disgust. No way, that did *not* just happen. Her little conniving bitch of a sister had just set her up. But she had and, like the idiot she was, Candy had fallen for it.

"Because you want him to yourself," Carrie said. "Admit it, sis. You want his bod."

Oh, hell. What point was there in denying it, when she'd all but come out and made it clear with her resentful tone? "I shouldn't."

"Why not? You are so overdue for some fun, Candy. You work almost non-stop. When you aren't at the hospital, you're doing stuff around our house or at Mom and Dad's place. I say let yourself go for once. Take Duane up on his offer."

She narrowed her gaze at her sister and the knowing way she'd voiced those last words. "I never said anything about an offer."

"I'm just guessing there had to be one by the way he looks at you—" she wiggled her eyebrows, "—like he wants to find a dark corner and play doctor."

Candace laughed despite herself, then tacked on a "Carrie!" for good measure.

"What? He does. I think it's hot. I also think you need to say 'yes'."

Candy sobered in an instant. God, how she wanted to do just that, say a loud and long 'yes' and throw herself into his arms, but... "I shouldn't."

"You already said that but you never said why."

Fear. But no, she'd told herself on numerous occasions she wasn't afraid of him. Duane himself had told her she had nothing to worry over. But if it wasn't fear, what was holding her back? Just the idea of what he was? What he could become? A glance in the mirror revealed the answer in the form of pale scars just visible above the neckline of her dress. It wasn't fear exactly but it was damned close. "It's complicated."

Carrie dropped her brush into her duffel bag and sank a hip against the sink basin. "But you admit you do want him, even if you shouldn't?"

What she shouldn't do was answer her sister, the woman who, up until this morning, had always had looser lips than a gossip columnist and yet the need to tell someone had been driving her crazy for ages. If she couldn't count on that someone being her sister, then who could she?

"Only the better part of my life," she finally admitted.

"That long, and you've never done anything about it?"

Carrie sounded aghast, her probing gaze one of amazement, and, for some reason, that brought a sting of heat rushing into Candace's cheeks. One that apparently wasn't missed by her sister, as her mouth gaped for just an instant, then she said, "Candace? You two didn't... Oh my gosh, you did! When?"

Why bother stopping now? She'd already laid the bulk of it out there. Not that she planned to go into details, like the part about Duane turning feral on her, but she might as well speak the rest. "Last winter and it was a one time thing."

"He was *that* bad?"

"No, it wasn't like that. It was just...not important." But even as she said it, she knew it was a lie. The truth was, as much as she remembered the bad moments of that night, she remembered the good far better. Things had been going really well up until the point where he'd actually entered her. It was like the moment he was inside, he'd gone wild. But before that...before that it had been incredible, like the joining of two souls that had always been meant to be together. Like nothing she ever could've fully imagined and everything she'd always wanted. Perfect.

Candy sighed. She wasn't the type to think in terms of perfect and yet she couldn't stop herself from wishing for that very thing now, at least the perfection she'd found in Duane's arms, as temporary as it might have been.

Was it even possible that he meant it when he said he could control himself now? What about when he said she was the only one for him, his life mate? Did that stupid stuffed wolf somehow factor into things? Oh, God, was she out of her mind to be having these thoughts? "Truth time, Care, did you put the wolf in my room?"

"Why are you so hung up on that thing?"

Because she'd smelled Duane last night and for a while there she'd been so sure he was nearby, watching her. If her sister hadn't put the wolf there, then maybe Duane had. Maybe he really had been in her room last night, watching her while she slept. Not waiting for his chance to attack or working his magic over her mind and soul but simply watching over her, the way he thought a good wolf should watch over its mate. "I just need to know."

Carrie pushed off the sink basin and eyed her for a long moment before responding. "If I answer you truthfully, will you answer me the same?"

"I wasn't offering a barter." And yet she was suddenly desperate to know.

"No, but I am. Take it or leave it. I can live with it either way."

Candace laughed at her no-holds-barred tone. "When did you get to be so conniving?"

Carrie smiled. "It's just a little something I picked up living with my big sister."

She laughed again, not doubting that for an instant. "Okay, I agree." *Even if I do live to regret it.* "Now spill, where the hell did that thing come from?"

"I put it in your room. I know you've been having trouble sleeping and I thought it might make you feel more secure."

"Oh." Well that explained that. However, it still didn't explain the smell.

She'd scented Duane, damn it. That hadn't been her imagination. Unless Carrie was lying to her again, the way she had this morning. "If that's the truth, then why didn't you just tell me this morning?"

"Because you seemed upset by it and I thought my putting it there had done more harm than good." Sympathy passed through her eyes. "I'm sorry that it's been bothering you so much. I guess I should've told you the truth when you first asked."

Yes, she should have, because it would have saved Candace from considering the reasons Duane might have given it to her, from imagining he'd spent the night watching over her as a protector and someone who might care about her enough to curb his inner beast the way he claimed he could. From thinking even for a second maybe the two of them had a chance at something real and lasting.

That hadn't been the case and she was fine with it. Better than fine, because this way she didn't have to worry about softening where Duane was concerned. She didn't have to think for a second on the way he would behave if she were to take a chance and give into him. She was so much better off. Really, she was, even if the sudden constricting pressure in the vicinity of her heart would seem to speak to the contrary.

"Forget about it." Candy turned back to the locker. "We should get changed and back out there before someone starts wondering where we are."

"Not so fast. You still owe me one," Carrie said, the sympathy of a moment ago replaced with a commanding tone.

Candace blew out a breath, resigned to the fact her sister hadn't forgotten the latter half of their agreement. "Right. I forgot," she said but kept her back to her sister and continued to open the locker and grab her clothes bag.

"Truthfully, if you had the chance to be here alone with Duane right now and were able to put aside those complications you mentioned, even temporarily, would you take advantage of the situation?"

Candy set her bag on the floor and squatted to dig through it, frowning over the question in the process. It was absurd, since it would never happen, and therefore she decided to answer with candor. "Sure, I would. I'd push him up against that sink basin you were sitting on before, tear off his clothes and proceed to rock his world. Since Duane isn't any too likely to come into the ladies' room, I won't waste my time waiting for any of that to happen."

"I wouldn't be so sure about that, Candy, sweetie." A voice too deep and masculine to be Carrie's responded from somewhere behind her. One quick inhale, which had both her heart and her hormones hammering into action, told her just who the owner of that husky voice was.

Chapter Four

In one swift move, Candace shot to her feet and spun around to glare at Duane. Her eyes were alive with aversion and his blood sizzled in response. He'd had second thoughts about taking Carrie up on her offer to get him alone with Candace and then to watch the bathroom door for as long as he wanted privacy. Now that he was standing here, about to be alone with Candace, those doubts were long gone.

"What the hell are you doing in here?" she snapped.

He tried not to smile, knew it would anger her all the more, and yet he couldn't help it. She was just too damned appealing when she was riled up. Always had been. "Carrie invited me."

"She *what*?" Candace looked from Duane to Carrie and her glare turned deadly.

Carrie grabbed onto the handle of her duffel bag, and darted for the door. She flashed an innocent look as she pulled it open. "Oops… I just remembered I promised to bring Mom a fresh glass of wine. Gotta go."

The door closed behind her and Candace turned back to Duane, nostrils flaring. "She's going to die."

So was he, of an explosively hard cock, if she didn't stop with the nose thing. It took her level of appeal and turned it into a thing of danger, one that called forth all of his baser urges and made him want to forget about talking things through first and getting down to action. He wouldn't risk that, not now that he had her alone where she'd be forced to listen.

He moved his gaze higher, to the simmering heat that filled her auburn eyes, and tried for levity. "Good to know I'm not the only one you plan to do in tonight."

"What do you want, Duane?"

Easy. He wanted everything he'd never had before—a family of his own, a place to call home, someone to love and who would love him in return—and all with her. She wanted it, too. She might have had those things before, might still have them, but the way she'd acted toward him at the club that night in Braxton told him she wanted more. That night her feelings, her hunger for him had been clear for all to see, in her eyes, her face, the carnal way she'd danced against him. While she might not be letting those feelings, that hunger for him show so overtly these days, it was still very much alive in her thoughts, in the words she'd spoken to her sister.

Duane took a single step closer when he burned to take so many more than just that one. Five would put him directly in front of her. Six would have him buried inside. He'd get to six eventually but first he had to get her admission that those things he'd overheard in her thoughts and just now in this bathroom were true. "What I want, Candy, sweetie, is the same thing you do. The same thing we've both wanted for years." Emotion flickered in her eyes and he allowed a small smile. "Yes, years. I've wanted you since you were old enough for it to be legal. I'd always hoped you felt the same; sometimes I felt like you wanted to say something or do something to let me know for sure, but you never did and, until last winter, I was never certain of your feelings. I am now, just as I'm certain about my own."

Her anxiety level shot up with those words; he knew it did because her warring thoughts of what to deny and what to confess pummeled into his mind like a freight train. She clearly decided to deny it all, as her gaze narrowed and she said, "I told Carrie that I *wanted* you, note the past tense."

"That's not what you said, sweetie, and it wasn't meant in the past tense either."

"I am *not* your goddamned sweetie and it should have been." With a last cutting look, Candace turned her back on him and squatted down to her gym bag. Jeans and a sweater tucked in the crook of her arm, she stood, turned back and nodded toward the door. "Now if you don't mind, I need to change."

Duane shrugged, not about to let the venom in her tone deter him. He knew just how insincere her hard attitude really was. As much as she liked to pretend to be callous, she was a big softie at heart and, if he voiced that aloud, she was liable to knock him on his ass. "Go right on ahead. It's not like I've never seen you naked before. Besides, I have X-ray vision. I can see through your clothes any time I want."

Her hard look relented as her eyes went wide and her mouth fell open. She shut it to breathe, "No way."

Yeah, there was no way and it also seemed there was no end to the things he could tell her about himself and have her believe. He laughed shortly and risked another step toward her while she was distracted with her thoughts.

"I was joking, Candy. I don't have X-ray vision." He let his gaze drift to the fullness of her lips then farther to her chest. The pale scars visible on the rise of her breasts momentarily tightened his gut. He forced himself to move past that area, to take in the rest of her wondrously curvy body in the snug gown. He'd seen her dressed in everything from her hospital scrubs to a tiny string bikini, yet something about this dress called to him more than anything else, aside from her birthday suit, ever had.

He'd told her she looked amazing earlier. What she really looked was edible. His tongue moved by itself with the thought, licked across his teeth and over the sharpening points of his incisors. Just being this close to her, watching her expressive face, inhaling her intoxicating scent had the wolf in him attempting to emerge.

He shouldn't move any closer, shouldn't even stay in this room for fear more than his teeth would begin to transform. He didn't want her to think for an instant this thing between them, his need to take things to the next level, had anything to do with his being a werewolf. It didn't, at least not beyond the way that change had opened his eyes, made it clear that if he was ever going to have those things he wanted most he needed to act on them. The change had helped to set his priorities straight, gave him the strength to follow through on feelings he'd had for years, but that's all it had done.

And that was why he should leave now, because he wasn't thinking with feelings, at least not completely. He was letting his inner nature pull at him, letting the throbbing ache of his cock rule him. He should leave, walk out the door and let her ponder what he'd said so far, but he couldn't. Instead, he took three more steps forward and caught her chin in his hand.

Candace's wide-eyed look returned in an instant. She attempted to take a step back only to run into the lockers behind her and whisper out a curse. Duane smiled, aware of just how trapped he had her. Even more aware of just how much she wanted to be there, forced to put her fears aside and own up to the truth. The reality of that was in the way her eyes darkened to gold, the way her breath came out as anxious puffs of air, in the subtle tremble of her lips.

He set her chin free to stroke his thumb along her cheek. "I might not have X-ray vision but I remember perfectly what you look like naked. I remember just how long and smooth and silky your legs are. How you have that tiny pear-shaped birthmark on your inner thigh. How when I run my tongue over that same spot, it makes your head tip to the side and the rest of you quiver."

He moved closer still, until her breasts rubbed against his chest, and allowed his hunger for her to be reflected in his voice as a needful rasp. "I like it when you quiver, Candy. I like the throaty sounds you make when I stick my tongue deep inside you. I love the way you growl and dig your nails into my shoulders when I suck on your clit."

The anxious puffs turned to ragged breaths and her tongue slipped out, dabbing at her lips. Duane grunted in the back of his throat and swallowed down the raw burst of need that coursed through him, pulling at his control with her artless move.

Struggling to continue in a voice that wasn't half as commanding as he suddenly felt like being, he rubbed his thumb over her soft, moist lips. Her nostrils flared. He flared his own back, inhaling her cloying scent. It was laced with far more than a citrusy perfume now. It was thick with arousal.

He grinned at the knowledge, at how hot she already was for him. "But you know what I really love, sweetie? I really love how you can stand there and try to deny your feelings for me and yet be so wet and needy all you can think about is pushing me to the floor so you can fuck me. Or maybe you want to have me up against the sink the way you told your sister you would do if we were in here alone. I dare you to go ahead and do that. I promise I won't stop you."

Turning her face away from his touch, Candace wet her lips again and glanced past him to the sink. She looked back and her throat worked visibly. "I might want that," she admitted in a breathy voice. "I might even wish for that in some very remote part of my mind but I won't act on it. Tonight or ever."

"Because you're afraid of me."

"Because we don't belong together."

"No, because you're afraid of me. Because you think I can't control myself whenever things start to get intense." That truth was alive in her eyes, just past the glow of awareness was fear. Duane had seen it yesterday but believed he could get past it by way of his hands and mouth and a few carefully chosen words and thoughts, by revealing his own long-time feelings for her. He knew better now.

There was only one way she was going to get past her worries and accept that deep down he was the same man she'd cared about for years, only a wiser version. It wasn't by coercing her into having sex with him the way he ached to do. It was by shelving his restless need for her another few days and using the time between now and then to convince her how harmless he truly was.

Duane returned the pad of his thumb to her shimmering lips, allowed himself one last touch, then dropped his hand at his side and took three steps back. He pushed his hands into the pockets of his tuxedo jacket, not trusting them to behave on their own, let alone remain in their human state. "I'm going to prove you wrong, Candy. I'm going to take you out tomorrow night and show you that I'm exactly the man you remember from a few years ago. Then I'm going to take you home and show you just how intense things can get and how gentle I can still be."

Candace nodded then shook her head. Her thoughts were just as at odds. He wanted to reach into her mind, to help her along a little, but he wouldn't do that. She had to come to terms with things on her own. He wanted her love more than his next breath but only when she was ready to give it her heart and soul.

She shook her head once more and said in a voice too calm for her roaming thoughts, "Sorry to disappoint you but I already have a date."

The unexpected words brought a laugh into the back of Duane's throat. Candy didn't date. She hadn't in ages, just as he hadn't and, whether she knew it or not, they shared the reason for not doing so. Because long ago they'd met their match and mate in each other. "I might have been gone these last few weeks but I have it on good authority you weren't dating anyone during that time. You haven't dated once since I moved back to Clarion Heights and, as I remember, you didn't date for years before I left. I find it awfully damned hard to believe you would suddenly have one now."

The façade of calm that had come over Candace faded in a blink. She fisted her hands at her hips and narrowed her gaze. "Well, I do. So believe it."

"With whom?"

"That's none of your business."

"I'm making it my business. I don't want you going out with just anyone." Just the idea of her going out with another man made Duane want to find the guy and tear him apart with his teeth. He could never admit that aloud. Relying on a half-truth, he said softly, "I've known you for too damned long to see you get hurt."

Her cool look faded as surprise replaced it. She schooled her features and shrugged. "If you must know, it's with Andy."

The composure he'd only just managed to attain shattered into a million pieces.

Bullshit. She was making it up. Kelsey's sports mogul brother might be every woman's fantasy to look at and maybe even imagine what he'd be like in the sack but he wasn't the type to date. He also wasn't the type Candace would be caught dead with. He was every bit as dominating as Duane had become as of late but he was also the kind to jump from one bed to another with careless ease. "When did you even talk to him? He didn't show up until a few minutes before the ceremony started."

"After the ceremony, when the pictures were being taken. The attraction was instant and, from there, it only took a few minutes to realize how much we had in common outside of the desire to get physical."

Duane's growing temper shot up a notch with her surefire tone. His hands curled into fists inside his jacket pockets, lengthening claws nipping into his palms. She was lying, goddammit! She had no longing to get physical with anyone but him. She also had nothing in common with Andy, sure as hell nothing more than what she had in common with Duane. "And what the fuck exactly would that be?"

The words had been snapped out and apparently the harsh tone was enough to set Candace's anxiety on edge, as her eyes narrowed once more and she scooted along the short row of lockers until she stood a good ten feet away. "Plenty. None of which I need to explain to you." Her gaze shot to the door then back on him and she ground out, "Do yourself a favor and leave before I call someone in here to make you."

He snorted at the absurdity of the words. "Who do you think I would be scared of enough to let them toss me out? And don't even think about saying Andy. He might get your panties wet but that's all he's capable of doing."

She flinched but then retorted with a hasty, "Nate."

"I'm not scared of Nate."

"No, but you are worried about him finding out your secret and how it might affect your friendship. If you make me call him in here, I promise I'll tell him every sordid detail."

"Right, and ruin his and Kelsey's wedding in the process."

"I wouldn't be the one ruining a thing. You would. You will be if you don't leave immediately."

It was panic talking, Duane knew, making her say or do whatever it took to get him out of this bathroom without touching her again. The odds she would really call Nate in here were slim to none. Still, for the sake of setting her anxiety at ease and potentially keeping a lifelong friendship intact, he'd go. "I'm leaving but don't think for a second I'm through. We will get our date, Candy. And once we do, you'll never be able to tell me we don't belong together again. At least, not do so and mean it. We do belong together and one day soon you're going to admit it."

* * * * *

He was in her room.

And this time it wasn't just a figment of her imagination.

Duane wasn't a stuffed wolf sticking to one corner of her bedroom and not making a sound. He was a real, live werewolf advancing on her bed with malicious intent burning in his yellowish-green eyes.

Candace had experienced fear around him before but, until this moment, she'd never realized how frightening he truly could be. He looked like he wanted to attack her and this time not with pleasure in mind, but brutality.

"You will *not* go out with him!" he snarled as he leapt onto the end of her bed.

Her belly crimped with terror at the threat behind his words and she pulled her knees up and shrank back against her pillows. She tugged the covers tightly around her neck, then immediately tossed them back.

Damn it, she would not be scared of him!

Let him snap at her, let him even come so close as to try and harm her. She wouldn't let it happen. Never again would he cause her pain.

Candace pushed up on her elbows and glared into Duane's glowing wolf eyes mere feet from her own. She gritted out, "I'll do whatever the hell I want."

He bit out a sound that was somewhere between a laugh and a howl, then crept up further in the bed, his big paws falling on either side of her legs. "If you were doing what you wanted, then you would be doing me."

Even if his odd scent was filtering into her senses and working its magic on her hormones—spiraling warmth into her womb and seeping the juices of arousal from her pussy—she would never have sex with him in his wolf form. She would never have sex with him *period*. "Sorry, but I gave up doing it doggie style years ago."

He let out another bark of almost laugher and stalked closer. His eyes lit further, brightened so intensely they hurt to look at, and then he looked away, down at something she could only guess at. "No you haven't, Candy, sweetie. In fact, I think that's exactly what you're hoping for."

He moved too fast for her to acknowledge what was happening. The covers were thrown back and his cold, wet nose brushed against her naked thigh. His intention settled in then and her breath drew in sharply, snagged in her throat and left her gasping. His rough tongue pressed down, made its way up her inner thigh to centimeters from the swollen lips of her sex, and that gasp turned to a moan.

"You want this," he taunted. "You know you do. Say it. Say 'yes'."

"No-ooo…" Her protest died on a fresh moan as his tongue moved upward, inward, taking advantage of her naked state and probing at her bared cunt.

His paws came to her thighs, pushing her legs up and out, while his long claws bit into her flesh and shot shards of ache rioting through her. Then, just when she thought she couldn't spread her legs any wider, couldn't stand the bite of his nails any longer, his paws moved away and the dampness of his nose brushed over her clit.

His wide shoulders pressed against her legs, tickling her with his fur. The coarseness of his canine tongue lapped at her pussy, caressing her most sensitive spots with an abrasiveness that had tremors surging forth in an instant. Heat unfurled in her belly, licked its way through her limbs and deep into her womb.

The press of his shoulders grew and he buried his head further between her legs and sank his tongue deep into her sheath. He licked at the cream of arousal that slickened her core and then turned those licks to demanding stabs.

Pressure sizzled through Candace's body, brought flashes of dazzling light to her eyes and had her mind spinning out of control. Her lungs ached, burned. Her pussy felt much the same. Duane's tongue moved faster, deeper, fucking her cunt with a fierceness that stole her energy and her breath. Still, she managed to arch up, lift her hips and growl out a scream of urgency.

She fell back to the bed and fisted her hands in the sheets, panted out hasty breaths over the inebriating affect he had on her. She'd told herself it wasn't magic he held over her but, damn it, it had to be. He made her feel drunk with uncontrollable lust, with the savage hunger to give in, to let go and give him the answer he demanded…

Shit. She was losing perspective here fast.

Concentrate! You have to concentrate.

Through hazed eyes, she glanced down and her efforts to concentrate were forgotten as the sight before her brought a shiver coursing down her spine and a fresh wave of arousal pooling in her sex.

A wolf was between her legs. A big, furry wolf with a beautiful coat of chestnut brown hair, and his tongue... His ungodly long, marvelously talented tongue was buried in her cunt, lapping at her, eating her, driving her slowly out of her mind.

The harsh stabs of his tongue ceased, and Duane pulled back and bared his pointed fangs. The tips of his incisors snagged the moonlight, glinting with wetness she knew to be her own juices. "Say it, Candy," he ordered. "Say 'yes'. Say you will be mine. Say you will succumb."

Yes — but no! You cannot give in!

No matter how much her pussy throbbed. No matter how badly she yearned to feel his long, hard cock—she knew well in his wolf form it was a cock to rival all others—pumping inside her, she could never give in.

She had to stop this, had to make him go away.

"Succumb," he snarled again and bent his head back to her sex. He lapped at her clit, flicking back the hood and scraping his rough tongue over the inflated nubbin beneath, then moved to her dripping slit and drove hard inside her.

Oh, God... The lights that before had been dazzling were now brilliant and moving before Candace's eyes in a seductively mesmerizing dance. Tension pulled at her from her toes to her fingertips. She dug her nails into the mattress and bit her lip to keep from crying out. She had to stop this, had to make him go away.

But she couldn't.

She couldn't say or do anything when he was thrusting into her this way, when his cold nose and soft fur were brushing up against her pussy lips and racking shudders of pleasure from deep within her soul. Hell, she didn't even want to send him away any longer. She just wanted... Just wanted to...

She just wanted to say... "Yes! Oh, God, ye-esss..."

Her hips shot up in the bed and she reached for Duane's head and buried her fingers into his silky fur. His tongue continued its relentless assault, lapping at her, fondling her with sensual delight, and the tension that pulled at her released itself.

She purred her exultation as cum flowed freely from her quivering sex and coated his rough, gifted tongue. An answering growl of fulfillment rumbled up from deep within his chest and the reverberations against her pussy brought another round of tremors surging forth. He continued to lap at her until the last of the juices was gone, then took one last long, slow lick and pulled back to smile up at her.

Candace shouldn't have known what a wolf smile looked like but this one she could read well. It was a smile of victory. He thought he'd won. He thought her "yes" had been for his sake. It hadn't been. But that he thought it had took her moment of bliss and turned it into a thing of terror.

"I knew you'd see things my way," he said smoothly, smugly and bounded onto her chest with his front paws. The air cruised from her lungs on a painful wheeze and eyes that an instant before had been fogged with pleasure now filled with salty, stinging tears. "Lay still, sweetie, because things are about to get good."

Duane shifted his weight, adding more pressure to his forearms and digging into her breasts with his long claws. Her heart ached. Her lungs screamed for air. She couldn't breathe when he stood on her this way, couldn't even move. She couldn't—

His head bucked down and the sharp points of his fangs sank into her breast. Pain welled in her joints, through her limbs. Horror seized her as his teeth dug in, gnashing into her flesh, tearing at her skin, ripping into her bones.

Oh, God, it hurt. It hurt so bad. "Stop! Please...stop..."

"Candy?"

Candace silenced her pleading at her sister's voice. Carrie was so close. If Duane heard her, saw her, he would go after her, too. He couldn't hurt Carrie. She would die before that happened. "Please don't—"

"Candy?"

No! She couldn't get any closer. "Go away! Before he hurts you, too."

A hand connected with her arm. A hand that was cool and soft to the touch and free of fur. A hand that was her sister's. Damn it, she hadn't listened. She'd—

"Hey, sis, wake up."

The hand shook her and the wolf at her breast snarled. *You want me. You know you do. You are mine, Candy. Mine!* He flashed his fangs, sticky now and crimson with her blood, in a conquering smile. Then he was gone.

The hand shook her once more. "Wake up already, Candy. It's just a dream."

Just...a...dream...

The words reached Candace in a slow motion daze and then took effect in an instant. Her heart stampeding in her chest, she opened her eyes and blinked at the harsh light above her, illuminating her bedroom against the darkness of night. Then blinked again at Carrie's worried face. "What are you doing in here?"

"You were dreaming or having a nightmare by the sounds of things. You were screaming so loudly, you woke me up from three rooms away. You okay?"

Her breathing coming out unsteadily, she glanced at the tangle of sheets wrapped around her and the sweat that clung to her flesh. No, she wasn't okay. She was losing her mind, letting a fear she claimed not to have enter her sleep and attack her. She couldn't tell that to her sister. "I'm fine," she lied. "I don't even remember what it was about."

"Oh, well in that case—" Carrie looked to the stuffed animal still taking up residence in the corner of Candace's room, then smiled back at her, "—maybe the wolf's helping at least a little." She moved to the door and turned off the light. "Good night. And this time do us both a favor and have sweet dreams."

"Night." Candace waited for her sister to close her door,

then reached to her spare pillow and chucked it at the corner of her room and, more notably, the evil creature standing there that reminded her too damned much of another. One who had her so haunted she couldn't even function normally any longer. "Goddamn, fucking wolves! I don't care if you're to blame or not, tomorrow you are so out of here."

* * * * *

"I can't believe you're going out with him or that you're wearing *that*." Carrie took a long look at Candace's attire of a hip-hugging leather miniskirt, all but see-through cream-colored top and strappy spiked heels, and shook her head. "You're just lucky Nate didn't find out before he and Kelsey left for their honeymoon. He thinks Andy's great, awesome from an athletic standpoint, but he would never approve of either of us dating him in a million years."

Candace grabbed her calf-length jacket from the living room closet. She pulled it on and buttoned it up, trying to make it look like she was preparing for the moment when Andy arrived and not that she was hiding her body. She couldn't believe what she'd worn either. She was going to freeze her ass off in it, not to mention get plenty of disapproving looks from passersby. Wearing the tacky, off-season outfit had been an act of pure desperation.

After several assurances to Andy that she and Duane weren't an item, she'd been able to make good on what she'd told Duane and get Andy to go out with her tonight. What she hadn't been able to attain was the slightest bit of attraction for the man beyond agreeing he was decent to look at. And she needed to.

Andy might be an adrenaline junkie, might even be the kind of aggressive male with a bed hopping reputation that she generally loathed, but he was also human. She needed to connect with, to physically want a nice, normal human being. They were safe, maybe not with her emotions for certain, but in many other ways. Ways that wolves were not safe.

She wasn't going to think about wolves tonight. She wasn't even going to think about humans that could shift into the wily creatures. She was going to go out with Andy and spend the evening proving to herself she could both want and care for another man.

Who knew, it could even work.

She'd come to the conclusion, as she lay awake last night following that horrific dream, that Andy might just be her answer to moving past Duane, because they shared a similar background. Neither of them had parents and that called to the sympathetic nature she tried her best to ignore outside of at the hospital and, in doing so, opened her feelings to them. It had to work. It had to be because she was desperate. If she could just get another man into her head and want that same man in her pants, she might be able to forget the one who currently took up residence in both, at least in her thoughts and dreams if not reality.

Candace focused back on Carrie. Her sister stood in front of the living room couch, hands on her hips and looking as though she expected a response. Candace could waste her breath explaining just how little she cared about what Nate or anyone else thought of the men she dated, or for that matter all the ones she hadn't dated through the years, but why bother? She'd done it a hundred times before and no one listened anyway. "Don't you have class to attend or something?"

"It's Sunday," Carrie said dryly, "and Spring Break."

Oh. She should have known that, given that weddings typically took place on Saturday, but her erratic work schedule always had her so mixed up it could be Wednesday as easily as Sunday. "In that case, why aren't you using the time off to find your own man? You're so gung-ho on getting involved in my love life and yet I can't even remember the last time you went on a date."

Carrie scrunched up her nose and made a face. "I have my reasons for being selective when it comes to men." Her nose relaxed and a smile tugged at her lips. "If it makes you feel better, then you'll be happy to know I have a date lined up very soon. As a matter of fact, I'm really looking forward to it."

"Oh. That's…shocking." *In a big way.* Carrie dated even less than she did. That she had a date now and with a guy, the mere thought of whom made her smile, was nothing short of a miracle. "It's good shocking though," Candy clarified. "Hopefully things will work out for you two."

Carrie sank onto the couch and her smile turned reflective. "Hopefully. There are too few good men out there to let them slip through your fingers when you finally find one." She glanced up at Candace. "Know what I mean?"

The question was rhetorical, the knowing look in her sister's eyes wasn't. Her happiness over Carrie's mystery man faded to red-hot temper. "Damn it, Care, I told you last night to knock it off with trying to push me at Duane. Maybe I admitted to wanting him but I am *not* going out with him. He is a *friend* of the family. That's it. All he will ever be. End of story."

Carrie's calculating look faded and she shrugged. "I never said a word about Duane, though I won't argue with you over his being a good man. He definitely is. Better than ever. He's really changed this past year."

Candace bit back a groan and flexed her fingers so they wouldn't be tempted to do anything unforgivable, like cross the room and strangle her sister. Why in the hell were they even still talking about Duane, and, for that matter, having the same conversation they'd had last night? "So you've said."

"He wants you. You want him."

Yep, same damned conversation as last night. Candace flexed her fingers a second time, then crossed her arms and glared. "Get it through your head already, *I don't care.*" She let her arms fall back at her sides and strode toward the door. "Andy should be here any minute; I'm waiting outside." *Where I don't have to deal with idiot little sisters.*

"You might not care but Duane does. Enough that the moment he found out about your sleeping problems, he gave you a guard wolf in the hopes it might help things."

The breath caught in Candace's throat and she swiveled back around to gape at her sister. "He *what*?"

Carrie lifted a shoulder in a shrug. She tipped her head to the side and fingered the ends of her long blonde ponytail as if she was bored. "You wanted the truth, there it is. It was from him. He knew you would never accept a gift from him, so he asked me to give it to you." She stopped twirling her hair to give Candace a pointed look. "Since you didn't want it and made it quite clear you didn't want him either, he's moved on."

"'Moved on'? When the hell would that have been? Last night he was —" The buzz of the doorbell cut her off. She jerked back around to glare at the large, dark outline just past the beveled glass. "Shit. Andy's here."

"I thought you wanted to go out with him," Carrie said from behind her.

"I did. Do. I do." Even if the idea of spending the night with the man suddenly sounded about as much fun as pulling her hair out one strand at a time.

Damn it, why did Carrie have to spring the truth on her now? And even worse, why did her belly have to tighten with a sensation somewhere between jealousy and animosity, as if she actually cared that Duane hadn't lived up to his feelings any more than he had his words about her being the only one for him? Or maybe she was still his only one, maybe he was only pretending to go out with someone else in the hopes it would lure Candace in. That had to be it.

Well, it wasn't working. He could pretend to date someone else all he wanted, she wasn't giving into him. No way in hell.

The doorbell rang again and Carrie said, "Put your happy face on and go get the door. Andy's a great catch. I'm sure you guys will have a wonderful time together."

Candace rolled her eyes and moved to the door. She gave her sister a glance as she reached for the knob. "Five minutes ago you thought Andy was all wrong for me."

"Hey, what do I know? I can't even decide what I want to do with my own life, why should I know what you should do with yours?"

Shaking her head, Candace turned back to the door. Carrie used to make such sense, used to be so easy to read and even easier to get information out of. Now she was a frigging walking enigma. One that Candy had no time to try and figure out.

Determined to forget about her sister's odd behavior as of late, she put on a wide smile and pulled open the door. "Hi, Andy. Sorry to keep you wait-ing." Her heart lodged into her throat as the all too familiar form of the man before her materialized against the backdrop of the porch lighting and the blackness of night.

Andy's hair was black like Kelsey's. This man's hair wasn't black. No, it was chestnut brown, the same damned shade as the silky pelt of the wolf from her dreams. The same damned man that wolf was supposed to represent.

Duane stood with his back to her and she swore his ass had never looked so tight and graspable as it did in faded and well-worn jeans. Her cheeks heating, she dragged her gaze past his leather bomber to the back of his head and cleared her throat. He turned and his eyes lit when they landed on her. He flashed a sexy smile.

Candace bit her tongue to keep from sighing. She didn't have as much luck with the rest of her body. Her nose went to work, drawing in one hasty breath of his too tempting scent and her blood heated while her pussy swelled. Wetness seeped into her panties and her nerves stood on end with awareness.

Fuck. That smile was going to be the death of her yet.

She forced her own smile to turn to one of antipathy when what she really wanted to do was drag him out into the night, strip away his clothes and lick him from head to toe. Nostrils flaring, she bit out, "What the hell are you doing here?"

Duane's gaze fell to her mouth, or maybe it was her nose, she couldn't be certain. His eyes darkened and he stayed still, staring for several long, torturous seconds, then he shouldered his way past her and into the house. "Going out with your sister. Didn't she tell you we have a date?"

Chapter Five

"Kitchen. Now!"

Duane just managed to hold in his laugh over Candace's order to her sister. He hadn't been sure about taking Carrie up on her offer to continue to help him with Candy—not only did he not want to pit sister against sister but he wasn't convinced that pretending to go out with Carrie would upset Candace. At least, not in a jealousy kind of way. In a fury kind of way, because she feared for her sister's safety around him, that he was sure he could bring about. He was also sure it was fury shooting from her eyes right this moment.

Carrie stood from the couch and looked from Candy to Duane, then back at Candy. "Sorry, sis, no can do. We have a dinner reservation at eight-fifteen and, unless we get out of here now, we're not going to make it."

"I don't care," Candy growled, already moving toward the kitchen. "We need to talk. Now!"

"We've already talked plenty." With a dismissive wave of her hand, Carrie grabbed her coat from the closet and joined Duane near the door. She called back over her shoulder, "Enjoy your date." She wiggled her eyebrows at Duane. "I certainly plan to enjoy mine, maybe even all night long."

"Carrie!" Candace gasped. She looked to Duane, fear and loathing flowing from her gaze like a living thing. *Please, if you care about me at all, don't do this.*

The desperation of her thoughts was almost too much for Duane to ignore. The reality that taking Carrie out and bringing her back home again safe, sound and unhandled, might be the best way to convince Candace he meant no harm to either of them was even harder to overlook. "Don't worry, I'll take care of her."

The plea left Candy's gaze and she bit out, "That's exactly what I'm afraid of."

Carrie let out a huff and reached for the doorknob. She pulled the door open, then took Duane's hand and sent her sister a parting look. "Relax already. You said yourself that Duane's like part of the family, that he has been for years. I'll be perfectly fine."

Candace hustled to the door and her eyes narrowed on Duane while her nostrils flared with open hostility. "If you so much as lay a paw on her, I swear I will—"

"Kill me," Duane finished with a knowing grin while doing his best to avoid the temptation of her twitching nostrils. Even without focusing on her nose, the damned thing was having an affect on his body, heating his blood and hardening his cock. They needed to get the hell out of here before it had an affect on the rest of him and he totally blew the cover on this date. "I got that you were into bodily harm yesterday."

He gave Carrie's hand a squeeze and, seeming to understand he wanted to leave immediately, she tugged back on his and moved out the door, saying as she went, "He's not going to lay a paw—hand—on me unless I want him to, which I very well might, so knock it off and try to enjoy your own date. And, since we all know that isn't any too likely to happen, when you do come home alone, don't even think about waiting up for me."

* * * * *

They weren't really on a date. It was too coincidental that Carrie and Duane would have reservations at the same restaurant and almost the same time as she and Andy had. No, this wasn't a date. They were just trying to make her jealous so she would give in to both her feelings and the longing Duane stirred in her.

But if it wasn't a date, if it really was just make believe, Candace asked herself as she glared over the top of her menu to where Duane and Carrie sat at a candlelit corner table, why did they keep touching? They'd even kissed! Right in front of her. Okay, so not in front of her, but sitting less than a hundred feet away and, damn it, they had to know that. Had to know how disgusted it had made her feel. How much she'd wanted to go over there and wrap her hands around both of their no-good necks.

"You sure you're okay with them eating here?"

"It's fine," Candy snapped.

That she was on a date with a man that, less than an hour ago, she'd been praying was her answer to forgetting Duane, came back in a flash. She put her menu down and fixed a smile on Andy. He looked at her through eyes the same rich shade of blue-green as the ocean. Set beneath thick, black lashes, they were mesmerizing. At least that's what she'd recently read about them. Frankly, they didn't mesmerize her even a little bit. All they did was look sort of nice. All he was doing was looking across the table at her like he regretted ever agreeing to this date.

Shit. She had to focus. Had to remember her reasons for asking Andy out. Had to forget that Duane had been the one to give her that stupid wolf, because he really and truly cared and wanted to see her watched over during her fitful nights.

That was such a load of crap. He didn't really care about her. If he did, he wouldn't have stuck his tongue down her sister's throat.

Candace's belly knotted as the revolting image of them rubbing mouths replayed in her mind. She forced herself to stay focused on Andy, to smile even wider, to act like she was having the time of her life. Who knew, if she could just give the man a chance, she might. "Sorry if I snapped at you, I'm just feeling edgy. Probably has to do with not working in so long. I go back on Tuesday." *Thank God.*

Just another two days and she would be back to spending ten to twelve hour shifts at the hospital and, even better, away from Duane.

"You're an ER nurse, right?"

She rarely let her softer side be known, hardly ever talked about her passion for her job; doing so with Andy was bound to go a long way toward cementing something solid with him.

Candace relaxed in her seat and pushed her menu aside, flashed him a real smile for the first time since he'd picked her up a half hour ago. "I do. It's a great job. Not seeing all those people injured or sick, but the helping out factor. Knowing I'm doing something that matters. That's not to say someone with a job like yours isn't helping out or making people better. I know a lot of people worship you for what you do."

"But not you," Andy asked, a black eyebrow raised in introspection.

Worship a man who made his living by partaking in daredevil stunts? Respected his valor, maybe, but 'worship' was a bit much. "I've never seen you in action."

He winced. "Ouch. With Nate owning an outdoor superstore chain and attending numerous sporting events for publicity's sake, I figured your knowing the playing field would be a given."

Nate *and* Duane. The thought popped into Candy's head without any forewarning. It wasn't her fault; she'd been grouping the two men together for as long as she could remember. They were alike in so many ways, including the fact they both owned outdoor stores. So many ways, but the one that mattered most.

Her brother was not a werewolf. Duane was and, if her conniving bitch of a little sister found that out the hard way, then she would get exactly what was coming to her.

Guilt tightened her stomach and she bit back a curse of self-reprisal. Carrie did not deserve to get hurt for wanting Duane. And she probably didn't even want him anyway. More than likely it was a rouse, kiss and all. Truthfully, Candace hadn't seen any tongue involved in that kiss. It had just looked really hot and wet from her vantage and so she'd stupidly let her mind drift with thoughts of what might be happening.

"That could be fixed, you know."

She jerked her attention from where it had been creeping back to get a peek at Duane and Carrie to Andy's face. "What's that?"

His lips curved into a smile and his eyes carried an invitation so dark and carnal she couldn't have missed it if she'd tried. "Having not seen me in action."

She hadn't missed his hot look and yet she also wasn't feeling it. No heat cruised through her body and into her limbs. Her heart wasn't beating even a little fast. She didn't want him. God, why couldn't she want him? Maybe what he was offering up didn't revolve around feelings but it could still be the answer she needed. Had to be the answer she needed.

Determined to want him as much as he seemed to want her, Candace flicked her tongue out and over her lips, purposefully drawing his attention to the way she knew the flickering candlelight made them glisten. She allowed her mouth to tug into the sort of seductive smile she generally loathed. "I'd like that. Later."

Andy reached an arm across the short expanse of the table and stroked his fingers over the back of her hand. "Later's good, but so is right now."

Now? Like now, now? And why the hell was he touching her?

Because that's what you want him to do, dumbass.

Right. What she wanted.

She resisted pulling her hand back and struggled to keep her smile warm, enticing. "Now, I'm hungry. And I can be a real bear if I don't get my food."

Andy's smile slipped away and she half-expected him to pull back his hand and leave. Instead, he tipped back his head and chuckled. He looked back at her, his grin huge and his eyes so vivid they almost glowed in the soft lighting. "You're out with the right man then, because I certainly understand animalistic behavior." His grin seemed to grow even bigger still, the white of his teeth to flash. Sharp points glinted.

Fangs.

Fangs?

Tension mounted the length of Candace's spine and she jerked her hand from beneath his to dig her nails into the cushioned seat on either side of her thighs. Her heart pummeled against her ribs. She sucked back air, chanting reassurances to herself. It had just been her imagination, images conjured up by bad dreams from last night. She hadn't really seen fangs. They were teeth. Just teeth. Not fangs.

"What do you mean?" she asked, intent on keeping the anxiety from her voice.

Andy looked to the table, to the spot where her hand had been, to where his own lay still. His grin was gone and in the place of the humor he'd exhibited moments ago was alarm. The look faded and he shook his head and pulled back his hand. He picked up his menu and, concentrating on reading it, muttered, "Nothing important."

Then why was he suddenly acting so strange, like he was guilty of something? Or maybe trying to hide something. Something like—

"You're not..." *Don't even think about finishing that question, you idiot!*

He is *not* a werewolf. He does *not* have fangs. He's just confused about the way you jerked your hand away so fast. He's thinking you don't want him and, given his reputation, that's probably never happened to him before.

Andy glanced up from the menu, the sudden lack of interest in his eyes all but tangible. "I'm not what?"

Damn it. She'd been right. He thought she'd thrown up a red light. He couldn't think that. She might not want him quite now, but she would soon. It was imperative she do so. Even more imperative that she make him realize there was some major chemistry between them. Enough to start an all-alarm fire. Enough to vanquish thoughts of another man, beast or whatever the hell you wanted to call Duane, from her mind permanently.

Candace slipped her tongue back out of her mouth and again wet her lips in the disgustingly tawdry way she loathed. Taking it a step farther, she crossed her arms tightly and leaned forward, letting her cleavage press against the low-cut front of her too-summery shirt. "I meant you haven't. As in, you haven't already eaten, have you?"

He looked from her eyes to her lips to her breasts and the glint of hunger returned to his expression full force. Setting his menu aside, he extended his hand. She quickly slid hers into it. He grinned in exchange, a grin she knew would have any other woman wetting her seat. All Candy felt was the subtle urge to smile back.

"No, I haven't," Andy said. "Even if I had, I always have room for more. I have a killer appetite. Particularly when it comes to red meat."

Killer. Appetite. Red. Meat.

Candace gulped down a hard breath and forced her fingers to remain within his, teasing, caressing, while her thoughts raced with possibilities she didn't want to consider and yet they sprang through her mind all the same.

He wasn't a werewolf who lost control in the height of passion, goddammit. And before this night was over, she would prove it, too.

* * * * *

"What's the matter?" Carrie asked Duane from where he sat beside her at the candlelit table.

"I don't know." Just that, for a moment there, Candace's thoughts had come skidding into his mind and they hadn't been close to pleasant ones. They also hadn't lasted more than a few seconds. Whatever she'd been anxious over, her panic had passed. Now he couldn't get a read off of her for anything and he burned to do just that. He couldn't turn in his seat without making it obvious where his attention was centered, but Carrie could certainly fill him in.

"What's she doing now?" he asked, hating how desperate his voice sounded. He shouldn't be using Carrie as a pawn, even if she did seem eager to help. He should be relying on his own prowess, on the —

"Getting ready to crawl across the table and into Andy's lap."

The words squeezed at his gut like a leaden fist and he wrenched around to focus on Candace and Andy's table. Rage made his heart beat faster, a growl to rumble up from deep in his throat. The bastard was holding her hand and looking like he planned to do a whole lot more than that before the night was through. As for Candy, she was licking her lips like she couldn't get them wrapped around Andy's dick fast enough.

"Nice," Carrie said dryly. "Very smooth move."

Duane shifted his attention back to Carrie, aware just how collected his move hadn't been. She passed him a sympathetic smile, then reached across the table to pat his hand. "Maybe we should try another kiss. That seemed to work well the first time."

That kiss *had* seemed to tick Candy off, made her stare at them so lividly he could feel her glare from across the room. It had also made him feel like a complete lecher. He'd told Candy he would take care of her sister tonight and he damned well meant it. But what if Carrie didn't want to be taken care of, at least not in a hands-off manner? It was something he'd never considered before — that maybe Carrie had agreed to help him not for the sake of getting him closer to Candy, but to Carrie herself.

"For you or Candace?" he asked, only half-jokingly.

She pulled back her hand and stuck out her tongue. "Funny, Livery, but you're like a brother to me and I am *so* not into the whole incest thing."

"You didn't like that kiss even a little?"

She lifted a slim shoulder in a shrug and reached for her beer bottle. "If not for that whole aforementioned brother complex, then yeah, it was pretty hot—at least as hot as a no-tongue kiss can be. And before you suggest it, no, I am not implying that I want to find out what a tongue kiss would feel like." She held up a hand, palm toward him. "Please, save those for Candy."

Duane grinned. He might not know why it was that Carrie was helping him out with Candace but at least he knew her reasons were altruistic. His grin fell flat with his next thought. "The last thing your sister wants is my tongue. At least, it's the last thing she's admitting to. You heard how long she's wanted me. She knows damned well I feel the same. I wish to hell she'd quit putting up a fight and give in to her desires already."

Carrie took a drink of her beer, then sat it back on the table and shrewdly narrowed her gaze. "No, you don't. You like that she's hard to get. Maybe not all the time but, if she were a pushover, you wouldn't want her half so much. It's not in your blood."

She was right. If Candace wasn't the hot-tempered yet compassionate to strangers who chanced by during her hospital shifts woman she was, he would never feel the way for her that he did. He'd always been decently strong-willed but, since the change, he'd become incredibly so. Just as Candy was. Between her strong state of mind and her bend toward humanity, she was his perfect offset, his perfect mate, and it had everything to do with his blood.

How the hell did Carrie know that?

"Has Candy ever mentioned anything about me?"

She made another face, scrunching her nose up and sending her blonde ponytail swinging. "I've known you most of my life; what's she gonna mention?"

And that would be a 'no', which meant her too-close-to-home comment about his longing for Candy being tied to his blood was nothing more than a coincidence. "Good point. Forget I said anything."

Her nose uncrinkled and understanding filled her eyes. "Oh… You mean about the two of you hooking up last winter?"

In the midst of reaching for his beer, Duane stopped short. Maybe her comment hadn't been a coincidence. But if Carrie knew his secret, knew what had happened that night with her sister, wouldn't she be acting differently than what she was? Like reaching across the table with her fist? "Yeah, that. What did she tell you?"

"Nothing really. I just guessed on it last night. She admitted to it but then said it wasn't a big deal and changed the subject. It was pretty obvious it *was* a big deal."

"Why?"

"Because she got all flustered looking, like she wanted to hunt you down and run off to a dark corner together and not for conversation, either. Actually, that was right before you came into the bathroom."

Came in and heard how badly Candy wanted him, that she'd been wanting him for years. Then she'd proceeded to turn him down for a date because she'd already had one planned with Andy. The man she was about to crawl across the table and jump on.

Duane's blood boiled with the thought, with the visual that remained in his mind from when he'd turned back to glance at Candace and Andy. His hands curled into fists and he moved them under the tablecloth and forced his tone to come across calmly, his temper to stop from exploding. He had to remain collected here, in control, and keep leashed the wolf that was clawing to be let free to do bodily harm to Candy's date. "So, she didn't say anything else about that night or about me?"

"Not that you didn't hear for yourself." Carrie smiled faintly, then sobered to add, "Trust me, I wish I could give you more. It's clear she wants you so bad that it's affecting her day and night."

"She's still not sleeping well?"

"Not even close. Last night she woke up screaming so loud, I thought someone was killing her. She was kicking and shoving like there was something on top of her. I tried to wake her up and she yelled at me to leave before he hurt me, too. I have no idea who or what that— Ooh, wait, she's looking. What do you say to another kiss?"

Duane's gut knotted as Carrie's words sank in. She might not know who or what her sister had been dreaming about but he could guess well. Candace had been dreaming about him, about him losing control and hurting her.

Son of a bitch, why couldn't he get it through her head that he was safe, that he would never harm her again?

"Yes? No? Decide something fast before she looks away."

Decide something, like that maybe their coming here wasn't such a good idea. That maybe his being with Candace wasn't even a good idea, not when attaining his dream came at the cost of her suffering. The thought was too heavy and crippling to think of now, so he forced flippancy into his tone and smiled at Carrie. "Are you sure that brother complex is really an issue and you aren't just out for another kiss?"

She looked first shocked and then mortified. "Ew, yes. It is so an issue. If it weren't for the fact I haven't had a date in ages, let alone kissed someone, I'm sure I wouldn't even have thought of the last one as nice."

Duane's interest rose at that first part and he latched onto it as a way to temporarily forget his own problems. "Why is that?"

"What?"

"That you haven't had a date in so long? You're an Anderson, which pretty well means good looking, charismatic and loaded. On top of that, you're in a business college whose student body is made up of more than seventy percent men." Something he'd hated when he'd been attending but, for a woman, it had to be a plus or at least a factor in her date book. "How the hell can you not have guys asking you out?"

Carrie pulled her attention away from his to concentrate on peeling the label off her beer bottle. "There have been a few."

In the five years she'd been going to the university, he'd be willing to bet there had been a lot more than a few. She might routinely wear a ponytail and prefer baggy clothes to tight ones but, as he'd noted already, she was still an Anderson. Still had the tanned, blonde good looks they all shared. She wasn't as sensually appealing as Candace but she was cute as hell. "I'm betting a lot more than a few."

She huffed out a breath and shrugged. "Fine, there have been quite a few but I just haven't felt the sparks."

"Isn't that the point of the date, to give the sparks a chance to happen?"

Carrie glanced up from the beer bottle and frowned. "I just... I'm picky. I have a certain type of man in mind and I won't settle for less."

Something about her tone, or maybe the way the emotion in her eyes didn't match her frown, had Duane asking, "He have a name?"

"Who?"

"The man you have in mind."

Her eyes went wide for an instant, then narrowed to accusing slits. "I didn't say I had 'a' man, I said I have a 'type' of man."

No, she had "a" man. He didn't need to telepathy or even finely attuned senses to know that either. The emotion he'd witnessed before now came clear. It was one he himself experienced every time he was around Candy. Carrie was in love or, at least, deeply in lust. Perhaps that explained why she was doing so much to help him out with Candace. "Right."

"What is *that* supposed to mean?"

The snide tone and deadly glare were too much not to laugh over; they looked like Candy to a tee. "You know, you're a lot more like your sister than I ever realized. Well aware of what you want, but afraid to make it known."

"Shut up and kiss me already."

He laughed again. "See what I mean. Bossy as hell. Gotta love that in a woman."

"This woman is not free to love," Carrie bit out.

"Right, because you already gave your heart to another."

She hissed out a breath, then leaned toward him and brought her hand to the side of his face. "If you want my help, start playing your part. I have plenty of other things I could be doing right now than being on a date with your sorry butt."

"Other men, too, by the sounds of things."

She blew out another jagged breath and, chuckling, Duane brought his mouth to hers. He brushed over her lips with just enough pressure to make it look more intimate than what it was. Carrie angled the hand at his face, shielding their mouths while she twisted her head to the side to make it look as though she was taking the kiss deeper. Duane started to pull back when Candace's thoughts slammed into his mind.

The big, fucking idiots. That is not real. They are just messing with me, so help me they are.

Yeah, they were and a part of him was still feeling guilty about it. A bigger part was thinking she was getting just what she deserved for not only dressing the way she had for her date but for all but launching herself into Andy's arms from across the table. The fact she'd done both had him moving closer to Carrie yet and pretending to kiss her with a savage hunger he could never feel for any woman but Candace.

* * * * *

He shouldn't have come back to this house. Duane hadn't been able to stop himself. He'd dropped off Carrie shortly after midnight to find that Candace was still out with Andy. He'd gone home then, but hadn't made it inside. He'd sat on the front porch in the moonlit darkness, letting the crisp air of early April infiltrate his senses while he wondered where Candy was and what she was doing. The possibilities that coursed through his mind had been endless and yet consistent, in that each one of them involved her naked, sweaty and moaning in the arms of another man.

That wouldn't happen. He wanted to trust her judgment enough to believe she herself would stop it from happening. Only he couldn't. Not when he knew how desperate she was to move past her feelings for him. So he'd done the one thing he'd promised himself just last night that he wouldn't do again. He'd returned to Candace's house in his wolf form and stood sentinel in the shadows outside her bedroom window. Not that his waiting here would help her should she need him somewhere else, but at least this way he would know if she made it home safely, or at all.

Twenty-some minutes had passed when Andy's truck pulled up the drive. The air cruised from Duane's lungs in thanksgiving, then quickly rushed back in when Andy and Candace stepped from the vehicle. Their voices carried to his perceptive ears as clearly as if they stood beside him and his tension built with each word.

Candace had made the right choice tonight in saying her goodnight to Andy at her front door—where the two currently stood talking—but, by the sounds of things, she didn't plan to follow that course for long. She was telling Andy what a wonderful time she had, how she hoped they could go out again tomorrow. How she'd think of him every moment until then.

She was full of shit. She hadn't had a good time, she didn't want to go out again, and she sure as hell wasn't going to spend her time thinking of him. Candace didn't want Andy. Only, the sound of her throaty sighs as Andy pulled her close and kissed first her mouth and then her neck sounded a whole damned lot like want.

Andy's hands slid down, cupping her buttocks through her long jacket and too-damned-tiny-skirt, and Duane's frustration turned to hostility. Loathing tunneled up as a feral growl from deep within his throat.

No one but him touched *his* woman that way! And Candace was his. They all knew it. If Andy didn't yet, then he was about to find out.

Heart hammering in his ears, Duane bounded from the shadows and straight for the couple on the front porch. He was halfway to them when Andy relinquished his hold on Candace's ass, said a last goodnight and turned for his truck. Duane stopped short, blood singeing between his ears and through his limbs. Fuck, he couldn't move in any closer and rip out the man's tongue the way he burned to do. Unless he wanted Candy to both despise him and be frightened of him the rest of her life, he couldn't do a damned thing but retreat to the shadows.

Bridling his temper, he slinked back to the side of the house and camouflaged himself amidst the row of shrubs that lined it. Andy got into his truck and, after Candy went inside the house, backed up the drive and pulled away.

Duane had no choice but to follow. If he made his claim on Candace to Andy when she was in listening distance, she would deny it with either repulsion or laughter, possibly both. For the sake of the man's safety and what might happen to him should he continue to date Candace, Duane had to get him alone and make it clear that she was already taken. Make it even clearer that, if Andy chose to ignore that fact and pursue her anyway, the outcome was liable to be painful, if not deadly. It wouldn't come to that though; somehow he would figure out a way around anyone getting hurt.

Winding the scent of exhaust, Duane started after Andy's truck. He caught up with the glow of taillights after several minutes and continued to follow the vehicle to the narrow, winding road that ran the length of the Dorr National Forest and through the sprawling Eagleton Mountain Range. The truck veered off the main road to head up one of the steeper, wooded paths and Duane stopped short.

Where the hell was he going and why? No one came into this stretch of the mountains in the middle of the night, no one outside of predatory animals and those humans who were close enough to predatory animals to not fear the creatures that lived here. Then again, Andy wasn't from around here. He probably didn't know any better.

Wasn't that laughable? He'd followed the man to warn him away from his woman and what would happen if he didn't stop seeing her. Instead, it looked as though he would be warning him from far worse dangers than himself.

The red glow of taillights disappeared from sight and Duane snarled. He couldn't waste his time sitting around trying to figure out Andy's reason for coming here. He had to catch up with him before he did something stupid, like get out of his truck for a moonlit stroll through the mountains.

Duane took off at a sprint, quickening his pace as he hurdled over fallen trees and through overgrown thickets and dense patches of swampy marshland. The foliage grew thicker the higher he climbed, then split away suddenly to reveal a rolling glen, engulfed in moonlight. He'd been to this place before, the few times he'd given in to the pack howls of other wolves — both were and natural — and joined in their monthly rituals. He'd believed this is where he would find Andy. Only Andy wasn't around. Judging by the silence of the glen — only the occasional howl and the gentle stirring of the wind punctuated it — no one or nothing was.

Even as he thought it, the wind picked up, turned to a rushing whip that had his fur standing on end and his nostrils flaring with awareness. His senses went on full alert while his blood pumped through his veins in a violent crescendo. He'd been wrong before. Someone or something was here.

Branches snapped behind him. Duane spun in a circle, opening his mouth to reveal his fangs as he eyed the woods through night sensitive eyes. He couldn't make out anything but forest. He could scent something though. Something that smelled dead.

From somewhere to his left, a feline hiss rent the night air. Releasing a warning howl, he turned toward the sound and connected with the glowing yellow eyes of a panther. There were no panthers in this area, they couldn't live in this environment. Only, there *was* a panther. One that let out an ear-shattering caterwaul as it leapt at him.

Chapter Six

Candace woke from a nightmare to have her already pounding heart leap into her throat. Duane was in her bedroom, his eyes glowing an eerie yellowish-green from where he was haunched down in the corner in his wolf form. Her own eyes adjusted to the darkness and her mad heartbeat slowed as realization settled in. Duane wasn't in her room. It was just that damned stuffed wolf. That wolf she'd moved out of her room this morning. Clearly, Carrie had moved it right back in.

That just went to show how accurate Candace had been tonight at dinner.

No matter how much Duane and Carrie had touched and kissed, it hadn't meant a thing to either of them. It had all been for the sake of making Candy jealous.

It hadn't worked. She hadn't been jealous in the least. Truth be told, she'd forgotten all about them and their numerous displays of affection and focused solely on her date. Going into the evening, she might not have been attracted to Andy. But by the time the night was through, she'd been more than ready to give in to the invitation in his eyes. She'd been burning to bring him back to her bedroom and show him that, while her name might sound sweet, her bedside manner was anything but. She would have done just that too, if it weren't for the fact Carrie had already been home and asleep. She didn't want to wake her sister with her screams of ecstasy.

And if that wasn't the biggest load of shit to ever cross her mind, nothing was.

Growling in the back of her throat, Candace laid back and stared at the darkened ceiling. It was *so* not fair. She'd wanted to want Andy. She'd tried everything short of crawling under the table, unzipping his jeans and taking his cock into her mouth to get herself hot for him. Nothing had worked.

She'd learned a lot about him tonight, enough to move past her old impressions of him as a carefree bad boy and respect him as a trustworthy friend. But that's it, just a friend. Even that long, deep goodnight kiss he'd planted on her hadn't gotten her a little wet. It was hopeless. Only it couldn't be. She had to want Andy. Once she returned to work she wouldn't have time to track down another man who could speak to her compassion enough to make her forget Duane. And she wouldn't put off forgetting him another day.

Candy.

Candace shot up in bed and nearly screamed at the thought that darted through her mind. A thought that wasn't her own but sounded a whole lot like one of Duane's. She inhaled automatically and his odd scent filled her senses and had heat curling to life in her belly and her libido firing on high.

Wonderful. She'd spent over five hours with Andy and, as much as she'd tried, she couldn't even work up a little wetness for him. All she had to do with Duane was think he might be in her room and her pussy was dripping wet and her nipples hard as rocks. Yeah, she'd been right the first time. It just wasn't fair. Or sane, for that matter.

She reclined back in the bed and tugged the covers up around her, closing her eyes. "I know you aren't real and I wouldn't hear you, even if you were."

A low wheezing sound somewhere between a yelp and a sigh drifted to her ears and brought her pulse thrumming to chaotic life. He wasn't really here, she reminded herself. It was just like Friday night. She'd thought she smelled him then, too, but she hadn't. Not really.

Candy, sweetie. I'm real. Turn on the light.

"No, you aren't," she snapped, aware how irrational it was to be yelling at a stuffed animal and still unable to stop herself. "I'm just...dreaming."

She laughed at the irony in the words. The visions her mind had conjured up the last few nights were not dreams. They were nightmares that haunted her damned near every second. And it was all Duane's fault. If he could have just left her alone after that first time she probably would've been able to move past it, past him. But he wouldn't leave her alone. He just kept pushing his way into her life, her thoughts. Her bed.

Her blood pumped harder with the idea of him being in bed with her right now. Of feeling his cold, wet nose on her naked thigh the way she thought she had last night. That dream had morphed in to a nightmare but at first it hadn't been one. At first, as his long, rough canine tongue suckled at her pussy and rasped over her clit, it had been like the most wicked kind of heaven.

And that was wrong on too many levels to count.

Candace lifted her head to glare at the corner of her room. The curtains fluttered inward from the windows she left cracked open every night and, just to the right of those curtains, were eerily glowing eyes that looked far too intense to be made of glass. "Why the hell can't you just leave me alone?"

Need you.

"What's the matter, Carrie didn't live up to your expectations?" Nice. Now was she not only talking to a stuffed animal in her sleep but she was making it pretty damned clear she'd been jealous of Duane dating her sister.

Don't need…Carrie. Need you. Turn on…the light.

"Sorry, but I don't have a Clapper." And there was no way in hell she was getting out of this bed and walking over to that light switch with that damned stuffed wolf ogling her naked ass. Then again, this was a dream. Perhaps if she clapped her hands, the lights would come on, even without the handy-dandy mechanism that made The Clapper work.

Candace drew up into a sitting position and brought her hands together in two short claps. Darkness loomed on, broken only by the sound of the wolf's next thought.

What...you doing?

Acting like an idiot. "Nothing. Why aren't you talking to me anyway? Every other time I've dreamt about you, you've talked to me."

Can't talk...when wolf. This...only way... Light...

He couldn't talk when he was a wolf and apparently he couldn't think very well either, because his thoughts were coming across disjointed and hard to follow. Why she was even trying to comprehend them was beyond her. It was a dream. A stupid dream she needed to wake up from before her last few sanity cells decided to go the way of all the rest she'd lost this year, thanks to the big pain in her ass known as Duane Livery.

Huffing out a breath over his name and the stimulating effect just thinking it had on her body, she flung herself back in bed and growled, "I don't want to turn on the light. I want to wake up. I'm going to pinch myself now and end this hellish dream, so goodbye."

Not...dreaming. Light. Please.

Forcing the thought from her mind, Candace reached to her left forearm with her right hand and gave the skin a hard pinch. Pain shot up her arm and she squeaked out a gasp that turned to a snarl when the darkness waged on along with the suddenly intense sound of labored breathing that wasn't hers.

Son of a bitch, this wasn't real. It wasn't. But it sounded real. The subtle movement of the wolf's big body against the billowing curtains seemed real. The pleading glint in his eyes seemed so real it was frightening. "Damn it, I don't want you here. Go away!"

Can't. Hurt. Light.

Hurt? Candace's fear of the situation at hand evaporated as a new kind of panic burst forth, bringing emotions barreling up her throat and into the backs of her eyes. She worked as an emergency room nurse, she should be immune to feeling alarm over injury. But she wasn't immune to it, not when it was Duane who was the one in danger.

And he was in danger. She couldn't deny it any longer. Couldn't shut out his wheezing breaths and the way his eyes had dipped to half moons, as if he couldn't keep them open any longer. She couldn't dismiss his pleading quests to turn on the light. She could only face reality. Duane was in her bedroom in his wolf form and he was in pain.

Candace couldn't deny it and yet she also couldn't make herself get up and turn on the light. Not until she had some idea what to expect when she did finally see him. "What do you mean, you're hurt? Why are you hurt? How? What's wrong with you?"

Help…me. Light. Please…

Shit. He wasn't going to tell her. He was just going to keep begging her until he couldn't beg any longer. That he was begging at all said something and it was that she couldn't lie in this bed a second longer.

Wrapping the top cover around her and tucking its end between her breasts, Candace moved from the bed and over to the light switch. She flipped it on, then held her breath as she slowly turned around. Her heart constricted at the sight before her while the air cruised from her lips on an agonizing gasp.

She'd seen Duane in his almost-wolf form that night he'd lost control but she'd never seen him completely as a canine. He looked exactly as he had in her dreams and nightmares. Exactly, but for his wounds. Flesh and fur hung lifelessly from numerous gashes. Dried patches of crimson stained his chestnut coat, singeing the air with the metallic tang of blood. A wide, jagged laceration ran over his left eye and the tip of his nose seemed to be hanging on by little more than a thin strip of cartilage.

Candace's stomach turned over and whispers of fear chased along her spine. Pushing both sensations away, she rushed to Duane's side and dropped down to take his face into her hands and examine his injuries more closely. His tongue slipped from his mouth to hang limply at one corner and his eyes faded to slits that seemed to scream suffering. Her belly tightened anew, her heart balling into a fist of anguish for his pain, while a blinding truth slammed into her mind and soul.

She'd thought that Andy was her solution to forgetting him, to moving past her feelings for him, but she would never be able to do either of those things. She cared about him too much. Cared about him beyond everything, including anything that might have happened between them in the past. Even more than what he was.

She couldn't think about feelings now or the mistakes she'd made these last months in not giving him the chance to prove himself when he said he could maintain control no matter how intense things might become. All that mattered was helping him and that meant distancing herself from the situation, from the man and the wolf. The only way to distance herself from Duane was with anger.

Shutting out the caustic turning of her belly and insistent press at her heart, Candace lifted her hands from his face and stood. She stepped back and, fisting her hands at her hips, glared at him. "What the hell happened to you?"

His eyes flickered open. *Panther.*

There were panthers in Clarion Heights? That was extremely creepy. Not to mention impossible. Unless they weren't normal panthers. Unless they were werepanthers. Oh, God, when had her mind gotten so warped that she could even consider something like that as being real? Probably about the same time she'd given her heart away to a werewolf whose favorite late night snack was her breasts.

She shivered at the thought then, remembering what she had to do here if she was to be any help to Duane, forced sarcasm into her tone. "Right. A panther. Because there are just *so* many panthers in Clarion Heights."

His eyes lulled shut again and he sprawled onto his belly. *Don't know. Help. Please.*

"Stop saying 'please'! Or thinking it." She couldn't even pretend to be angry when he was pleading with her that way.

She also couldn't pretend she knew what to do, because she didn't. "You should never have come to me, you idiot. You need serious help. A doctor."

Need you. Can't...shift. Weak.

"Then a vet. The point is I can't help you, Duane. I don't know anything about treating werewolves. Hell, I don't know anything about treating regular wolves."

A low howl escaped him and he slumped onto his side. Torn flesh and muscles glistened with the tint of red and Candace closed her eyes against a threatening wave of tears. She sucked back her emotions and opened her eyes. She tried to glare, to stay where she was and act pissed. She couldn't do either.

The emotions returned in a wash and this time she was powerless from caving to them. Sniffing at the tears that slid over her cheeks, she dropped to the floor and leaned over Duane's body, touched a finger to his broken flesh, wondering, if he looked this bad on the outside, what did it say of the shape of his insides? He whimpered in response to her gentle probing and her own fearful sigh slipped free.

"God," she whispered, "you're injured in so many places. If you die, I swear I will—"

His head lifted a bit, angled toward her until she could see his pale, watery eyes. His lips curled back in what she guessed to be a smile. *Can't...kill...me....then...*

For his benefit, Candace forced her own smile while inside her guts twisted into searing knots. He was right. If he died, she couldn't kill him. And that was exactly why he couldn't do it. Life might be easier without him around but it would be a hell of a lot less worth living too.

She rocked back on her heels and narrowed her gaze. "You won't die! You hear me, Duane, you will *not* die! That's an order and I don't want to hear anything else about it, so just...shut up."

His head returned to the ground and his tongue lolled back to the side of his mouth. Eyes closed, his thoughts came through slowly, drunkenly. *Y-ou...f-ix...m-e....*

The uneven sound of his breathing slowed and his thoughts tapered off to nothing. His body lay inert, save for the barest of movement with his heartbeats. If ever she believed he possessed magic, she knew now she'd been wrong. If he were magical, he would fix himself. He wasn't, he was just human. In a wolfish sort of way.

Candace fisted her hands to keep from reaching out and pummeling him. Not because she wanted him to suffer any more pain, but because she knew he was no longer with her — at least consciously — and she was clueless what to do to help him.

"Wake up, Duane," she ground out. "Goddammit, you cannot pass out on me! I don't know what to do." She added in a gentler tone, one thick with emotion, "Please, wake up for me. If you wake up, I will do whatever you want. I'll give in, Duane. I'll admit you were right about us all along. Just open your eyes and look at me."

His body remained silent, his thoughts the same, and she closed her eyes and blew out a ragged breath. Shit. *Shit, shit, shit!*

She had to get herself together. Had to take stock of his injuries as best as she could and do everything in her power to try and fix them. She had to because he wasn't going to die. He couldn't. Because if he did, she would never be able to forgive herself for not admitting to the way she felt about him.

* * * * *

"Candace."

At her whispered name, Candy turned back from where she stared out the window at the dawning of a new day. Dim light bled into her bedroom from between the curtains and onto the bed where she'd managed to maneuver Duane when he'd been semi-coherent several hours ago. His eyes were open and he watched her with alertness that spoke to fact he was more than semi-coherent now. He was awake and...alive. Her heart squeezed with near painful relief.

Thank God, he was going to be okay.

Try as she might, she hadn't been able to distance herself from him last night. She'd battled with panic and sorrow the entire time she'd spent tending to his injuries, suturing those wounds that needed it and applying gauze and tape to the remainder. She'd experienced those emotions right up until a few short hours ago when she gave him one of many washcloth baths in the hopes of keeping his fever down.

She had almost completed the task of wetting his fur with cold water when his body moved under her hands. She'd held her breath, prayed he was regaining consciousness. Only he hadn't regained consciousness. Instead, he'd shifted. The sound of bones grinding together as they changed shape and size had had her belly roiling in an instant. The sight of his naked, sweaty human form beneath her palms when the shifting process was over had the roiling in her belly turning to a pang of hunger that settled much farther down than her stomach.

Due to Candace's fear of covering him and bringing his temperature up in the process, Duane was still naked now and her gaze automatically moved over his body. She tried to view him as a patient, tried to take in his many wounds and the way they already seemed to have significantly improved. Tried not to notice how long and lean and perfect he looked laying in her bed, his dark head resting on her pillows. She failed on all accounts the moment he shifted his leg to reveal a quickly lengthening erection.

Her own body pulsed to life with the sight of his strong, sturdy cock jutting up from a thick patch of chestnut brown hair. Juices flowed deep within her pussy and dampened the crotch of her cotton shorts. She hadn't had time to worry over underwear or a bra last night; she'd barely even had time to throw on a T-shirt and shorts. Since she wasn't about to look down and check, she could only assume her wetness was visible against the pale gray cotton.

Wrenching her attention from his groin, Candace crossed to the side of the bed. Duane's nostrils flared at her approach and she sensed her own response on instinct, inhaling his intoxicating scent and making her clit tingle with awareness.

God, she wanted to touch him. To prove to herself he really was here in her bed and looking so much healthier than he had even four or five hours ago. She couldn't touch him. Not now, when he was still her patient. And, more importantly, not until they had a chance to talk about things. Since she planned to follow up that talk with action of the most pleasurable kind, it wasn't happening until he was completely better.

"You're awake," she finally said, stunned by the sound of her own voice. The house had been dark and silent for so long. She hadn't even heard Carrie leave for her sadistic morning run.

Duane's gaze left hers and he looked down at his body. He glanced back at her and his brow furrowed as he croaked out, "When…"

Candace reached for her glass of water on the nightstand and brought it to his dry lips. He lifted his head but didn't even try to maneuver the drink himself and that told her even more than his low, scratchy voice that, while he might be feeling some better, he was still in a good deal of pain. "Drink slowly and only a little bit, or you'll get sick," she said in her nurse's voice.

His question returned to her as he drank and she fought off a shiver over the renewed memory of his shifting. "A few hours ago, when I was giving you a cool-down bath. Between the fact I never expected it to happen and I never imagined when it did happen it would sound so incredibly disgusting, it's safe to say you scared the fuck out of me."

He took a last sip of water, then laid his head back on the pillow and closed his eyes. "I'm…sorry."

"Don't talk." By the sound of his rasped words, it hurt him to do so. Even if it didn't, it still hurt her, squeezed pressure at her heart and had her chest swelling with ache for him. "You're doing better, unbelievably so, but you still aren't in the clear. You need more sleep."

Duane's eyes popped open and he shook his head. "No—"

"Damn it, yes," Candace snapped, instinctively responding to him the way she always did when he acted difficult, with temper. "I am the professional here, remember? You want to be a pain in the ass tomorrow or whenever it is you're able to get your butt out of my bed and go home, fine. Today, we do things my way. And that means you go back to sleep."

He stared at her, his eyes searching her face for several long seconds, and then they closed again and he rolled onto his stomach, emitting a yelp in the process. She opened her mouth to tell him to roll back over, that it wasn't smart to be lying on his stomach when his wounds were still so fresh. Nothing made it out short of a whimper.

Candace took a step back to keep herself from giving in to the temptation his ass presented. Tight. Taut. Perfect. She wanted to grab a cheek in each hand and squeeze. She wanted to turn him back over, straddle his groin and grab hold of his buttocks as she drove herself onto his magnificent cock. She wanted to forget about waiting on the talk and say the words right now so she didn't have to feel so damned guilty about standing here, ogling him. She didn't do anything she wanted but crossed her arms over breasts made heavy by arousal and turned her back on him.

"You were right."

Muffled by the pillow beneath him, Duane's words were barely audible and brought her swiveling back around to ask, "What?"

He placed a palm flat on the mattress near his shoulder and, groaning with the effort, rolled back over to eye her somberly. It was an expression she'd seen on his face only one other time. Last year, when he'd realized the way his savage behavior had hurt her.

Whatever he was about to say had to be life altering, or at least close to it. That knowledge took any residual heat she was feeling from that spectacular view of an even more spectacular ass and destroyed it. "Whatever it is you seem to think I was so right about, just tell me already."

"We don't belong together."

Candace's belly lurched, her pulse skittering while her mind turned with disbelief. He was wrong, damn it! She had *not* been right. It didn't happen often—okay only twice in her whole entire life—but it had this time. They belonged together. And he knew it, too. "You're sick, Duane. Probably even hallucinating from the pain medicine I gave you. You don't mean what you're saying."

"Yes, I do. You are my mate, the only woman I will ever want, but that doesn't matter any more. I would rather be alone forever than let this—" he lifted the hand he'd placed at his ribs to gesture to his wounded body, "—be your life. It isn't a life and I won't let you go through it again. I shouldn't have last night. I just..." He broke off on a wheeze that quickly turned to a rasping cough and shook his entire frame. When the coughing ceased, he finished on a whisper, "I didn't know where else to go."

Because there had been no other place. She'd been scared, unsure how to treat him, and yet she'd known, almost from the moment he'd shown up in her room, she wouldn't have wanted him to go to anyone else for help.

Once more the urge to touch him coursed through Candace. She dropped her arms to her sides and, fisting her hands, eased that impulse away. Soon. Very soon. Now he needed the woman she hadn't been able to be last night, the strong, stubborn one who relied on severity to get her out of many a tight situation.

She narrowed her gaze and said firmly, "You did the right thing in coming here, Duane. Now be quiet and go to sleep. You're tiring yourself out and wasting your breath over nonsense."

"I scared you," he murmured.

The shit out of her and then some. "Outside of when you shifted, which, I already told you the effect *that* had on me, you didn't scare me."

His mouth twitched, started to turn into a frown that edged into his goatee, then instead sparked into a weak smile. "I could sense your fear last night, Candy, sweetie. I can still sense it now."

And she could sense the number that sexy smile of his was doing to her shorts.

God, she could *so* not think about the insistent throbbing of her pussy right now. "If you think so, then your sensors are seriously in need of a checkup. I was worried last night, if anything. Worried my sister would come in and find you in my room. Worried about how I would ever get your blood out of my carpet. Worried about getting even a wink of sleep." *Worried once he closed his eyes he would never open them again.*

Candace pushed away the thought, refusing to let it affect her emotions and start up the tears she'd cried too many of last night. "That's all it was, just worry."

Duane's smile faded and he eyed her down hard. He didn't have to tell her she'd been anxious enough right then to have her thoughts coming through to him loud and clear, the bite in his lowly spoken words was clear. "Don't lie. I hate it when you lie. It makes me angry. It makes me want to get out of this bed and take you over my knee."

That wasn't supposed to be an invitation she thrilled in and had her cunt flooding with excitement but somehow it managed to still affect her that way. "You're not getting out of that bed," she growled, determined to get him back to sleep even if it took all morning. "I didn't save your sorry ass just so you could go and die anyway."

He snarled at her and the sharp points of burgeoning fangs showed just past his lips. "Then tell the truth."

In the past, the sight of those fangs had brought Candace fear, now they seemed nothing more than a part of him. A part of the man she cared deeply for and, if she was ever going to have the opportunity to prove it to him, the man she had to get healthy again. "That's what it's going to take to get you to listen to reason, the truth?"

He looked thoughtful, as if he were contemplating if she seriously meant to tell him, and then nodded. "Yes."

"Fine. I was scared. I was scared shitless, as a matter of fact, and it wasn't about my sister, the carpet or any damned thing else but you."

Duane pulled in an audible breath. "Because I was a wolf and you thought I would hurt you the same way I did before."

"No, you idiot, because I thought you were going to lose consciousness and never wake up again. I thought... I thought I would never get to say I was sorry." Candace's voice broke on that last and she rolled her eyes and cursed her stupidity. She did not want to talk to him about feelings now and, if she started in with the blubbering again, there wouldn't be a single damned way around it.

Curiosity filled his eyes and he asked quietly, "For what?"

"Nothing. For nothing. I'm just rambling. I do that when I'm tired. I only got an hour of sleep last night thanks to someone. Now go to sleep, so I can do the same."

To her astonishment, Duane closed his eyes as if in agreement. Ten minutes passed and his breathing evened out. Relieved to finally have him asleep, so she could do the same, she crept toward the bed. She'd almost reached it when his eyes snapped open and he looked at her. "Where?"

"Where what?" she asked, halting in her tracks.

"Will you sleep?"

Where she'd been en route to when he'd made it clear he was still awake. The same place she'd lain last night, right on the bed beside him. True, he hadn't been conscious then, or human and gloriously naked, but once he was asleep that wouldn't matter. She hoped. "That's for me to know and you never to find out. Now get your ass to sleep before I decide to kick it out of this house."

* * * * *

Duane opened his eyes and took in his surroundings. Soft beige walls, white lace curtains that revealed the late afternoon sun, a deep green comforter wrapped around him and a woman who smelled of slumber and orange blossoms curled in his arms.

He was in Candace's bed and Candace was in it with him.

Her hand was at his back and it moved now in a gentle caress. The rush of her warm breath feathered along his chest. She was awake. Awake and under the belief he wasn't, Duane realized in the next instant, as she moved away from him and pulled back the covers. His eyes were closed and yet he could feel the heat of her gaze as it roved over his body. She was checking on his injuries, the rational parts of him knew, and yet those parts didn't seem to care any more than the irrational ones.

His blood hummed to life. His cells heated as well, when her fingers returned to his body, sliding along his torso with a teasing lightness that spoke to every male part of him. His cock grew, thickened, throbbed. Candace's startled gasp ensured she hadn't missed the almost instantaneous transformation from nearly flaccid to stiff as stone.

Duane knew it was time to open his eyes, to face her and what would happen now that he was healthy again. And he was healthy, healed—just one of the benefits of being a werewolf. Not that accelerated healing would've helped if that panther had killed him—not even werewolves could come back from the dead—but it hadn't and he wasn't going to think over the outcome if it had.

He opened his eyes to find Candace leaning over him, her long blonde, sleep-tousled hair nearly brushing his groin as she stared in the general direction of his lap. Her fingers moved to his inner thigh, probed, while her tongue slipped out to dab at her lips. His shaft pulsed in response to the wet pink tip gliding over her full lips and his erection bobbed toward her face. With another gasp, her gaze snapped to his. The two connected and she jerked her hand away, leaned back. The look in her eyes went from inquisitive to furious in a heartbeat.

He chuckled at her angry look, relieved beyond measure to see real temper on her features again and not just anger that she tried at for his sake. He needed to hear her laugh as well. To see a smile on that mouth that had been turned down in concern for over sixteen hours, happiness shimmering in eyes that had been murky with tears. He had been unconscious on many levels last night and early this morning, but he'd still been aware of her unyielding presence, of her pain, her fear. He wouldn't think of those things now. Now they needed levity.

Duane took hold of her arm, so she wouldn't try to run, and grinned. "See anything you like down there?"

Candace's cheeks deepened with pink and she tugged on her arm, relenting when it became clear it was pointless. "That is *so* not funny, you idiot! I was checking on your wounds, making sure they weren't infected or anything."

"And were they?" he asked, not letting up on his hold, not trusting her to stay.

Her upset was replaced with awe as she nodded. "You're healed. There are a few lingering marks, but nothing worth worrying over. Nothing that won't be gone tomorrow morning if your progress so far is anything to go by."

Her expression and tone were both too serious, with no trace of the humor or even the passion he craved. Needing those things as badly as he'd needed the water she'd made him drink this morning, perhaps even more so, Duane gave her arm a squeeze and jerked his head toward his feet. Her gaze followed his, right to the swollen length of cock standing thick and tall and throbbing in wait of her touch.

He looked back at her and allowed his grin to become wicked, wolfish, for the hunger that had clamored to life the moment he'd spotted her eyeing his groin to reflect in his voice. "Thanks to you, I'm even better than healed."

Candace's nostrils flared and she again tugged at her arm. Thoughts tumbled around frantically in her head, spiraling into his. *Give in. Run. Give in, then run.*

Finally, she said, "Don't think just because I kept you alive it means that I care about you or that I want you or anything like that. I don't."

No? Then why had she acted so alarmed when he'd voiced his thoughts about them not belonging together? About her being better off without him? He hadn't wanted to admit that for the world but he also didn't want to think about her having to tend to his wounds whenever he chanced by a pissed off panther or bear or whatever it might happen to be the next time. And what if next time there were no wounds that could be healed, what if he didn't make it through? Even worse, what if *she* didn't make it through? If they were to be together as mates, as the family he'd dreamt of being with her for so long, it meant her becoming a werewolf, too.

The "what ifs" had been more than enough reason to do her bidding and agree to stop pursuing her. But that had been before Duane had heard her deny his words, before he read her thoughts of how much she too still believed they belonged together. Well before she—God forbid—admitted she'd been wrong. Maybe she hadn't said the words aloud but she'd thought them, meant them. She wanted to give him—them— another chance. A real one this time.

Duane's heart swelled with that knowledge and he smiled up at her. "I think you do care, Candy, sweetie. I think the idea of my being dead scared the hell out you, even more than the idea of my being a werewolf."

He tugged at the arm he still held, this time with enough strength to take her off guard and have her collapsing onto his chest. The weight of her breasts rubbed at his flesh, her nipples peaking into rigid points that had the softest of sighs tripping from her lips. She wiggled her groin against his cock, pulling at his resolve, awakening both the urges of wolf and the too-long unfulfilled hunger of the man from their semi-dormant state. He couldn't stop himself from pulling her the rest of the way up his chest and feasting on the sight of her plump pink mouth.

Candace's hands moved to either side of his head on the mattress, her pupils deepening to gold, dilating. Her tongue came out, moved over her lips in an impatient little flick. Her full sweet lips glistened from the action. His blood pumped harder, his tongue moved in his mouth, ready to plunge into hers, to give, to receive. To succumb.

"You want me, Candy. Just like you want this kiss."

No longer willing to hold back and wait for the moment when she'd finally admit her desires aloud, Duane buried a hand in her hair and tipped his head to bring his mouth to hers. She met him halfway, her tongue the first to imbibe, to slip into his mouth and stroke, to rub against his with raw need and urgency. One of her hands moved from the mattress to feather through his hair, tangle in the short, thick strands, caress his scalp. Her tongue moved faster, diving in and out in a carnal move she soon mimicked with her hips, pistoning against his engorged cock, grinding the hard ridge of her pelvic bone and the far softer, wetter slit of her cunt with demanding pressure.

His blood boiled, his cells ached. He felt as though they would explode with the need to change, to shift, to take what was rightfully his, what they'd both wanted for years now. Only he wouldn't do that, not this first time. Not when it was clear she was still fighting some residual concerns. Soon though. Very soon.

You want me, Candy. Just as I want you. You care about me. Just as I do you. We're family, you and me. Soul mates. It's the reason I can't leave you alone, sweetie. The reason I gave you that wolf, so I knew the woman I love more than anyone or anything else in this world felt soothed, watched over, protected, when I couldn't be here to see to it myself.

Candace pulled back with his thoughts, tugged her hands from his scalp and sat back. Straddling his groin, she touched her fingers to her lips, looked at him through eyes dark with desire and yet something more, an emotion he couldn't name.

"I-I shouldn't," she admitted in a breathy voice.

"Because you're afraid of me?"

"No. Because…just because."

Duane didn't know what that "because" was and, judging by her thoughts, neither did she. What he did know was she wasn't lying this time when she said she didn't fear him. She also had no intention of moving off of him and tossing him out of her room the way she'd threatened to do several times in the last sixteen hours. She wanted him and she sure as hell cared. "Sorry, sweetie, but 'because' isn't gonna cut it with me."

"I know—" the emotion he hadn't been able to place left her eyes and she dropped back onto his chest while a seductive smile curved her lips and happiness lit her gaze, "—that's why I'm not going to listen to it."

Chapter Seven

Candace reveled in the feel of Duane's long, lean body beneath hers. She hadn't wanted to have second thoughts. Last night and this morning she didn't even think she could have them. This afternoon, as evening fast approached and it became clear Duane would be fine, the enormity of it all—of giving in to her worst fear even if she claimed it wasn't—had caught up with her and had her retreating to her more severe persona.

Between the way his stimulating scent grew stronger when he was aroused, the passion that had filled his kiss and his true reason for giving her that wolf—because he cared for her and wanted to see her protected—that persona hadn't stood a chance.

Any panic she might have felt was gone in a blink and then it had all come down to the order of events. She'd wanted to talk with him first, get out the things she'd been feeling, thinking. She hadn't made it that far.

Or maybe she'd made it farther, Candace realized on a whimper as Duane's mouth returned to hers, his hands slipping beneath the waistband of her shorts. His tongue plundered, took, demanded, while his large, rough palms cupped the heated flesh of her buttocks. Rubbing her tongue against his own, she melted against the exquisite feel of his hands kneading her skin, his masterful mouth overtaking her senses, the hard press of his swollen cock against her inner thigh.

He pulled away from her mouth and looked up at her, his eyes an eerie shade of yellow. His voice laden with an almost painful sounding rasp, he asked. "Are you sure?"

If she had been feeling any lingering anxiety, it vanished with the question, the sincerity of his expression. He had her right where he'd wanted her for months—make that years—where they both had wanted to be, and he was giving her the opportunity to retreat. It showed two things on his part. He was in control and he cared for her more than what she'd ever even hoped to realize.

Candace's heart beat faster and her pulse took off with the understanding that his thought from a moment ago had been authentic, that he truly did love her. That he'd chosen her to be his family— something she'd always known he'd never had but, until now, hadn't realized how badly he ached for. "I am *so* sure." The thrill she felt came through in her words, lit them with happiness. "I'm more sure of this, of us, of the way I feel for you, than anything else in my life. I'm even more sure if we don't get started soon, I'm going to come just thinking about it."

Duane chuckled and his mouth curved into the delicious grin that made her wet and hot every time it appeared on his handsome face. Bringing that sexy grin to her lips, he kissed her softly, sweetly, in a way he'd never kissed her before. No man had. There was such emotion, such tenderness and, beyond that, quiet control.

It was the control that spoke to her the loudest. He was keeping his desire in check at a cost to himself. There was no reason for that, because she trusted him to let loose and still not hurt her. If there was ever a time he was going to turn wild on her, then it should have been in the small hours of the morning, when he'd been in his wolf form and extreme pain.

Candace brought her hand to his face, stroked his cheek. She rubbed her thumb over the crisp hair of his goatee, imagining how it had felt on her feminine lips that night in the storage closet of the church. Her pussy exploded with juices at the memory of the way he had tongued her. It had lasted only a few seconds before she'd felt his claws and ended things, yet it had been so amazing… "Give in to me, Duane." She allowed a fraction of demand to enter her voice. "Succumb. It will be okay."

His eyes filled with an indefinable emotion and then he pulled her tightly to him and laughed long and hard. Sobering, he loosened his hold to pin her with a serious look. "I've been saying that same damned thing to you for months, that if you just gave in to me, it would be okay—better than okay. You didn't believe it, so why should I?"

Here it was, the moment of truth. One she'd only just realized a short while ago. One that took the desire she'd been feeling and temporarily sedated it. "I did," she admitted quietly.

"What?"

"I did believe it. At least, part of me did. The truth is..." Candace faltered at that and tried again, forcing her voice to ring steady, clear, "The truth is you didn't hurt me so much that last time. You did some but you scared me more than anything. Enough to make me fear what might happen if there was a next time. If the pain would get worse or if maybe...maybe there would be no pain. Maybe if I just gave you a second chance it would be just the way you promised it would. That you would stay in control." She inhaled deeply, then said on a heated rush, "I thought I wanted that, you staying in control, but I don't. I want you to give in to me and show me the way you really feel, not hold back for fear the truth will scare me away. I'm a hell of a lot stronger than that. We both know it."

"What are you saying?"

"I want you to let loose, Duane. Succumb to the wolf."

His features lit with elation. But then he shook his head. "Not this first time. Next time, yes. Absolutely. But this time is for you, to make you understand that, while the wolf might be a part of me, it isn't what rules me. It isn't what makes me want you. It isn't what made me fall in love with you years ago. That's all about you, Candy. About the remarkable woman you are."

To hear him say he loved her again, that he had for years and well before he'd changed, swelled Candace's heart with joy and yet she couldn't ignore the tautness of his limbs and his body beneath hers. "You're too tense like this. I can feel it, taste it. You can't even enjoy yourself."

Humor flashed in Duane's eyes. He shifted beneath her, rubbing his thick shaft against her thigh and pooling a fresh course of desire in her sex in the process. "Do you feel that, sweetie? Does that really feel like I'm not enjoying myself to you? I am. Very much so. And soon I will be even more. Now shut up and kiss me already."

Part of Candace still wanted to deny him, wanted to demand he give in to his baser urges the way she could sense he craved to do, but the rest of her responded to the delicious friction of his cock sliding along her heated flesh. Her pussy pulsed with the thought of him plunging into her, slamming his shaft deep into her wet channel. She needed that, had needed it for so long.

Placing her palms on the defined muscles of his chest, she scooted down his body, until his erection brushed against her mound and had fire flaming to life deep in her womb. She slid her hands lower, curled her fingers over the sides of his chest and leaned back to grind against his long, thick cock. Her clit flamed with each intense rub and her cunt throbbed for so much more.

"Is that all you want, Candy?" Duane taunted, his voice a low growl and his eyes afire with appetite. "Just to rub against me with your clothes on? Or do you want more? Do you want me to tear off those shorts and ram my cock deep inside you?"

Between the explicit suggestion and her ceaseless grinding, she was breathless, achy, on the verge of exploding. "Yes," she panted. "That's what I want. I want you wild. Feral. I want you to show me my limits and take me past them. Please, Duane. Give me what I want."

Duane had already said he wouldn't let loose the werewolf this first time and he planned to stick to that promise. He hadn't said a word about letting the darker urges of the man come forth and give her everything she pleaded for.

Pulling her flush to him, he rolled them over so that he straddled her from above. He moved down her body, until he reached the heart of her, the heat. The scent of her arousal was thick, musky and he inhaled it and let it affect him just enough to grant her the most pleasure possible and yet still allow him to remain in his human form. Mostly, anyway. His cock throbbed, burned as it grew thicker, longer, skirting the edges of the one he claimed as a wolf. His tongue lengthened as well, grew wider, stronger, while the very tips of his fangs emerged.

Power rippled through him with even those minor changes and he took that power and turned it on Candace. He pushed her knees up and her thighs wide, buried his face against the darker gray area of her shorts. The cotton was damp against his nose, damp and sexy as hell. He rubbed his nose against her pussy through the shorts until she whimpered and brought her hands to his head and then he dug the short edges of his fangs into the material and wrenched his head to the side.

The cotton tore free as if it was hooked together by no more than a single stitch and then her pussy was before him, dark blonde curls damp and parted and her lips splayed wide, gleaming with her essence, heavy and pink from her excitement. He sniffed her and her hips arched up, all but pushing her cunt into his face.

"Please…" Candace breathed. "Don't keep me waiting."

He couldn't even if he wanted to. His tongue was on fire to thrust into her, lap at her cream, feel her tremors of ecstasy as she exploded into his mouth. Gripping her thighs, he pushed into her, drove his tongue all the way to her core and, fitting his mouth to her feminine lips, suckled.

"Holy shit!" Her hips pumped against his mouth, pistoning her pussy against his tongue, making him take her harder and deeper yet. "That is so…so deep. I can feel you… Oh, God, it's like you're in my throat. I can feel you in my throat!"

A laugh bubbled up at both the awe and artlessness of her words. He pushed it back. There would be plenty of opportunities for laughter through the years, right now her pleasure was tantamount.

Stop thinking and let go, Candy. Just feel. Don't question.

"I don't know if I ca...aan." Her words died on a moan as he pulled back and drilled his tongue into her again.

Duane glanced up at her face through the vee of her legs. Her cheeks were crimson and her eyes pinched shut, her tongue rimming her lips. If she needed speed and silent demand to make her stop thinking, then speed and silent demand he would provide. Gladly.

He retracted his tongue and let loose her hips to part her sex with his fingers. He pulled back the hood covering her clit and rubbed his goatee along it in a slow, sensual caress and then fitted his mouth over the nub and suckled. She arched up again, her fingers diving back into his hair, her short nails scraping his scalp. He rasped the edge of a fang along the sensitized bundle of nerves and her pussy trembled as she screamed out, "What the fuck are you doing?"

Once more laughter bubbled up. One more he fought it back.

You like it.

"Yes, but what is it?"

What it was wasn't important, that she admitted to liking it was, because if she liked the feel of his fangs on her clit, then she would love it when it came time to make her his mate, his werewolf. His family. His cells tingled with the thought, his cock pulsated with the need to do so now.

Soon. Very soon, he assured himself.

For now there were other matters to see to. Matters he planned to enjoy to the utmost. Sliding his tongue past his teeth, Duane moved his fang back over her clit and this time when she arched, when she screamed, he drove his tongue deep inside the warm, wet walls of her cunt. He fucked her with his tongue while his fangs rubbed again and again over the distended nubbin of her pleasure.

Candace thrashed beneath him, the bite of her nails letting up on his scalp as the tremors of her pussy grew. He applied more pressure, slamming his thick tongue into her the same way he would soon be doing with his cock and, with a shudder that shook her entire frame and a scream that had to be heard by the entire neighborhood, she came around him. Her muscles contracted, pulled at his tongue, struggling to take it deeper, to bury it inside her permanently. He drew back from that commanding grip and lapped at her cream for several lazy seconds, then he pounced up and over her, his hands on either side of her head, and drove his cock hard into her still-spasming cunt.

Her eyes went wide, turned brilliant gold as they connected with his, and a breathy gasp escaped her swollen lips to be cut off when he filled her mouth with his tongue. She sucked at his tongue, licked at her cum that still lined it and lifted her hips to meet him, thrust for needy thrust. Feeding from her mouth, he pumped into her until the tremors returned, telling him just how close she was to falling over that edge again, and as the first cries of her orgasm mumbled against his lips, he gave into his own climax.

This first time Duane had allowed it to happen fast, because he knew that was what she'd wanted, and also because his body ached to get to the next time. To that time when he would first make her his mate in body and then in form. To that time he'd dreamed of for years. To that time that was now upon them.

Candace's breathing began to return to normal and she pushed at his chest, as if she thought they were done, that he should roll off and away from her. They weren't done. Not even close. He reared back and thrust into her again to prove it.

Her eyes went wide. "No way. You're still... But I felt you—"

"And I felt you." He grinned. "I will again. Soon. We both will." Only this time it would be the way she'd wanted before. The way he craved.

He kissed her softly, slowly and then moved down to expose her breasts. He pushed her T-shirt up and the pale, heavy globes sprang forth. The scars from the first time they'd been together, when he'd been drugged by her taste, her scent, her blood, and had bitten her too hard and in far too many places, caused him a moment of hesitation. Then he remembered those scars would soon be nothing more than a memory and that it was Candace herself who had asked for this, for him to cut loose and let the wolf emerge. To make her his mate in every way.

Duane tweaked a hard nipple, enjoying her answering squeak, and then bent his head to lavish her breasts with hot, wet kisses. She stiffened beneath him when his teeth scraped over a nipple, then relaxed again when he moved on without so much as a teasing nip. Returning to plying her breast with damp kisses, he rubbed his thumb over her other nipple until he could feel its sensitivity and then moved that hand to the place where they were connected. Her pussy still dripped with wetness and he coated his fingers in her cream and slid one into the seam of her ass.

On a gasp, Candace wrenched forward. Her eyes flared wide. "What the hell are you doing?"

Duane slipped a second finger inside her buttocks, readying her, testing her for when he would fill her with his cock. He fondled the interior walls of her ass and she reared against his fingers, her wetness growing, this time from her own anticipation. "What you wanted," he said thickly. "What you asked me to do."

She shook her head even as she reared back again, her dampness continuing to grow. "I never asked for this."

Maybe not in precise terms, but she still wanted it and he wouldn't stop until he gave her all that she desired.

He pulled his fingers and shaft free and, gripping her around the waist, turned her over and placed her onto her belly. The air rushed from her mouth on a squeak. Aware that squeak would soon be turning to a sigh of pure rapture, he rimmed the seam of her buttocks with his cock, then slipped the lubricated head inside.

Candace tensed beneath him, pushed up with her hands against the mattress and shook her head. "I don't want this, Duane. I don't."

Yes, she did. He knew it. She knew it as well. She'd even said so. Said she wanted the wolf to come out, to take her, to finally make her his and this is how that happened. "Yes, you do, Candy. Just relax, sweetie. Relax and let it happen."

Splaying a hand at her belly, Duane eased inside her buttocks. Her sphincter muscles tightened around his shaft and he paused, reached a hand down and captured her clit between his thumb and forefinger, pulled at the aroused bundle.

She bucked against him on a moan that quickly turned to a broken shout. "Stop it! Goddammit, stop...please... I don't want this."

"You said you did," Duane snarled, hating the sound of her fear, the way it twisted his gut, and hating even more that she could claim to be strong, to trust him not to hurt her, only to prove she wasn't strong and she didn't trust him at all. It made him want to push into her all the way, to take her hard and deep, to sink his fangs into her neck and not care if she screamed in pain the entire time.

That last thought was too much. It wasn't him that wanted those things, to punish her for not believing in him; it was the beast within. Before that beast threatened to overtake him and hurt Candy in the process, he moved off her, to the side of the bed, and stood. She rolled onto her side and faced away from him.

The twisting in Duane's gut turned to a bitter knot. She feared him so much she couldn't even look at him now. But no, she didn't fear him. She couldn't, not having experienced what he just had, having tasted the passion and longing in her kiss. And most of all because he didn't sense it. She was giving off something, possibly even something close to fear, but not the real emotion.

Whatever it was that she felt, he didn't want to make it worse and yet he couldn't stop himself from biting out, "Damn it, Candace, you told me you wanted the wolf to emerge. You fucking asked me to succumb!"

"I didn't mean like that."

The words were spoken low, shakily, so much unlike his Candace. His Candace was all attitude, stubbornness, spoke her mind loudly and frankly. She would never cower in a moment like this.

What would it take to get his Candace to come out? More questions, more pressing her for action? "*That* is how it has to happen, Candy. *That* is how you become mine."

Her shoulders shook and a sniff reached him. "Then I don't want to be yours. I don't even care about you."

He almost laughed. Others had tried to do this to him too, treat him so tenderly, so lovingly, to go so far as to actually admit they cared about him, only to change their minds. Those others he might have believed when they said they didn't care any longer, but he would never believe Candy. Not when she'd spent the night seeing to his welfare and foregoing sleep in the meanwhile. Sure as hell not when she'd cried over him, let alone given in to him for sex of any kind. "You do care, Candy. That is one thing you can't lie to me about."

"Fine. I care but not enough to let you do that to me."

"Do that? *That* is nothing. I told you that you would enjoy it if you relaxed, if you trusted me enough to give me a chance to show you. If you won't even relax for that, then what will you do when I change you?"

The shaking of her shoulders came to a halt. She rolled onto her back and looked at him through murky eyes. "What do you mean, change me?"

"When I make you my mate forever. My wolf."

"Your wolf…"

Candace sat and shook her head. No. No way could he mean that. She hadn't even been prepared to have him take her from behind, she could never accept becoming a werewolf. The former had taken her aback, left her disturbed, distressed. The latter had rage born of fear shooting to life deep within her soul.

She narrowed her eyes, flared her nostrils. "There is no way in hell I'm becoming a werewolf. It's bad enough that you are, that I can feel something for you knowing that you are. I can't become one myself. I won't!"

Duane's eyes glowed, fangs showed just past his curled upper lip. "You will do it. You will become my mate and you will enjoy it. You will because you know we belong together, that we're family. You must submit to me."

Never. Not at the price he demanded of her. She cared for him, had wanted to be with him for years, but it was just too much. "The only thing I *must* do is kick your ass out of this house."

"I'm not going any goddam—"

"Candace?"

They both turned toward the partially opened bedroom windows, to the shout that drifted past the billowing curtains, followed by loud knocking. It was Andy's voice and, if his agitated tone were to be believed, then he'd been out there for a while. A glance at the alarm clock told her why. They had a date tonight. A date that should have begun ten minutes ago.

"Shit." Candace moved off the bed and jerked her robe from its hanger near the door. Andy's shout came again and she growled in the back of her throat.

Why hadn't Carrie answered the door? Come to think of it, why hadn't her sister checked on her even once today? Candace never left her door closed during the day and she certainly never spent it sleeping unless she was deathly ill. Then there was the matter of the shouting, not to mention the elated screams and squeaking bed. Carrie had to have heard it all. Unless she wasn't home. Had she even been home last night when Andy had dropped off Candace? Carrie's bedroom door had been closed but she'd never actually heard her sister inside the room.

"Maybe she decided at least one of you deserves to be happy and ran off to be with her lover."

And maybe he should just stay the hell out of her head, Candace thought with a cutting glance at Duane. "Right, Carrie with a lover. I don't think so."

"You sure as hell thought so last night when it was me she was with."

"I don't want to think about last night." Or this morning, or any time in the last twenty-four hours. God, how was it possible for things to go from perfect to perfectly miserable in such a short amount of time?

She had to get rid of Andy, then somehow convince Duane to leave as well. She needed distance. Time to think, to sort out all the thoughts and feelings jumbled together in her head. She reached for the doorknob, twisted.

"What's the matter, Prince Andy turn out to be a toad?"

Candace closed her eyes and blew out a hard breath at the resentfulness clear in Duane's words. She felt guilty over it, like she owed him an explanation. Like she should tell him the truth, that Andy hadn't done anything for her one way or the other. Only she couldn't tell him the truth, because he would think she wanted him around. And she didn't. At least, not right now.

Andy's pounding came once more and Candy knew what she had to do. Use the man's presence as her ticket out of this house and away from Duane. "Andy was wonderful. Too much so to keep him waiting another second."

Before Duane could respond, she stepped out the door and closed it tightly behind her. Praying he wouldn't follow, she went to the living room and opened the door far enough so that Andy could see her face and little more. Candace had been prepared to voice an apology, to explain she wasn't quite ready and would meet him at the restaurant in twenty minutes. The sight of him stilled the words in her throat.

His face was cut in several places and a dark purplish-black bruise ringed his left eye. She should have felt sympathy for him and whatever had happened since he'd last seen her. Instead, Candace thought of Duane, of the way he'd looked when he'd come to her last night. How afraid she'd been of losing him. She'd thought he would die. That she'd never get to admit that she cared. That she'd never get to tell him she wasn't half as afraid of him as what she let on, that most of her anxiety was due to her own overactive imagination and too-damned-lifelike dreams.

Was it that same anxiety that ate at her now? She certainly wasn't afraid of Duane and the things he wanted of her because she'd experienced them in the past. She had no idea what it would be like to have him take her from behind any more than she did to be a werewolf. Maybe she would even like it, them. Maybe even if she didn't like them, it would be worth enduring to be with him, to be his lover, his family.

"She's busy."

Candace's thoughts evaporated at the sound of Duane's sharp tone coming from just behind her. His arm wrapped possessively around her middle, pulling her back into the house and against his hard and very naked chest, while he opened the door the rest of the way with his other hand. Andy looked from her to Duane and back again and his gaze turned shrewd and knowing.

So much for using him as an excuse to get out of here. She pried Duane's arm from her waist and swiveled to glare at him. "I don't need your help."

His lips curved in a predatory smile. "In that case maybe I should just go back to bed and wait for you." Before she could get out so much as a gasp in response, Duane nodded at Andy's face. "Rough morning?"

"Late night walk gone wrong."

Duane's smile slipped away and his gaze narrowed on the other man. "Shouldn't go up in the mountains at night. Dangerous place."

Candy frowned at the odd remark. "What makes you think he was up in the mountains last night?"

"Those marks on his face are from an animal, a canine one, so unless he got into it with a damned big dog, I'm guessing he came across a wolf. The only place I've ever seen wolves in this area is up in the mountains."

Her stomach rumbled with the words, with the accusation that seemed to fill them. The guilty look that flashed through Andy's eyes made the rumbling all the worse.

The look passed and Andy said, "Part right, anyway; it was a canine, a damned big one. I stopped to pet an Akita only to figure out she wasn't feeling any too friendly."

Duane chuckled, the sound low and mocking. "Bullshit, you did."

Andy's gaze narrowed. Temper flared in his eyes and turned their blue-green shade stormy. There was something happening between the two men, something Candy couldn't name and yet she could feel it, stifling the air around them.

Not about to let it happen, whatever "it" was, she snarled at Duane, "Leave."

"I was just about to," Andy said.

Candace looked back at Andy. "I was talking about him, not you."

"Doesn't matter. You two obviously have things to work out. I'm not sticking around to hear them."

Andy turned and headed for his truck. Candy closed the door and swiveled around. She fisted her hands at her hips and glared but it was Duane who spoke first. "You don't want him, Candy."

"You don't know what the hell I want." And frankly neither did she, outside of time away from him. She strode toward her bedroom, intent on slamming the door in his face and locking herself safely inside.

"Yes, I do. I know you don't want Andy, because he's just like me, but worse."

The sobriety of Duane's proclamation stopped her mad stride. She spun back to find his eyes held the same serious note his voice had. "What is *that* supposed to mean? He's 'like you'?"

"He's a panther and, if the idea of mating with and becoming a wolf scares you, you don't even want to think about what it would mean to be with him."

He's…a…panther…

Candace huffed out a breath and closed her eyes, not wanting to believe it. The flash of fangs in candlelight sprang to mind, followed by the guilty look in Andy's eyes both last night at dinner and this evening at her door. Shit. The man was a panther. And, like the idiot she was, she'd all but thrown herself into his lap in the hopes of forgetting another just like him or close enough to it for her piece of mind.

The accusation in Duane's words when he called Andy a liar returned to her and she realized what he'd meant. "You think he's the one who attacked you?"

Duane nodded. "I don't think, I know. I followed him last night after he left your place. He went up into the mountains and his truck disappeared. Next thing I knew, a panther was on me. Those marks on Andy's face aren't from any dog, they're from me."

If she hadn't spent the last ten months coming to terms with the fact there were werewolves and her feelings were wrapped up in one in particular, Duane's comment about the marks on Andy's face being from him might have bothered her. She had spent the last ten months coming to terms with it and the only thing she heard was that he'd followed her date after the man had left her house. And she knew why. Because in Duane's mind she was his to control. He thought she should lay down her sense of self for him, give in to his every demand. Turn into a werewolf and howl at the fucking moon until her throat hurt too badly to speak. Only she wouldn't be speaking because werewolves couldn't talk. At least, not outside of her dreams and nightmares.

She might not know what the lifestyle of a werewolf was like but she also wouldn't be finding out. Not when it came at the expense of being controlled by a man, of being made to do every damned thing he wanted whether she was comfortable with it or not. Not even if choosing not to become one meant walking away from a man she cared about more than she would ever care for another.

"You're right. I don't want him. I don't want either of you. I just want my normal life back. If you truly love me the way you say you do, then you'll give me that. You'll leave right now and never again say a word about what you are or what the two of us are meant to be."

Chapter Eight

"Can you stay four over?"

Candace turned from her locker where she was grabbing her street clothes to change into when the head nurse's question reached her. It was a pointless one, since Nikki asked it at least once a week and every time Candace said, "Sure thing."

Why shouldn't she? It wasn't as though she had anything else to do.

She couldn't even pass time by bickering with Carrie. Her sister was back in school and apparently taking her studies very seriously, in that she was spending all her evenings and even some of her nights at the campus library.

There was always the alternative of going home and attempting to catch up on all the sleep she'd missed these last weeks. Only Candace knew damned well that would never happen. Just like she would never ask any of her family members if they'd seen or heard from Duane in the past month.

That wasn't to say they didn't try to tell her without her having to ask. At some point in time, everyone in her family had attempted to confront her about him and what had happened between them. As much as she'd been tempted, she hadn't been able to open up, not even about those parts of their relationship that didn't border on the surreal. It was her inability to do so that led to the thing she did instead of sleeping at night. She stared at the ceiling and thought of Duane, wondered how he was doing, if he was spending his time overseeing the neighboring city's Sportie's shop now that late spring was upon them, or if he was at another location altogether. And, the worst thought of all, if he'd been serious when he'd said she was his only one, that he would never take another woman for his mate, for his family, or if he'd already moved on to someone new and far more receptive to his needs.

Refusing to think of another woman in his bed, howling her rapture as he took her over the edge, Candace rehung the shirt she'd taken out and closed the locker door. She forced a smile for Nikki. "Sure thing. I'll just grab a soda and be over."

"Great. Thanks."

After stopping at the cafeteria to down a diet soda, Candace made her way to Trauma. Mount Mercy was a large hospital and the registration area was situated in the middle of the waiting area and the dozen plus examination rooms. She stopped at the check-in desk to see if help was needed anywhere in particular. Before she could even get the question out, the piercing wail of an ambulance filtered in from the automatic doors that led outside.

Instinctively, Candy ran to meet the ambulance crew. A doctor and nurse carting a gurney followed closely on her heels. The EMTs transferred the injured man from the rig to the cot and, after rattling off his information, vitals and injuries, handed him off to the hospital's care.

"Still can't believe he hit a wolf in that area," the driver of the rig said to his partner moments later, as the two men started for the registration desk to fill out the necessary forms. "Never heard of one being that far down from the mountains."

Candace had been moving on rote, doing her best to help the injured man relax and, along with the other nurse, assisting the doctor in whatever way she could. She froze now, her heart pummeling into her throat, and looked from the patient's pale face to the EMT who'd just spoken. He was several yards away with his back to her. More than likely she'd heard him wrong. But what if she hadn't? "Did you say a wolf?"

He turned to her and nodded. "Yeah, over at Fifth and Hill."

Fifth and Hill. A few blocks from her house. A wolf.

The words slammed into her one by one, each sending her pulse to beating a little louder between her ears, her heart into thumping harder against her ribs.

"How is he?" she asked, struggling to keep her welling panic at bay.

"Like I said, lower half of the leg's shattered from where he tried to brace himself when he crashed but, other than that, minor cuts and bruises. He got lucky."

Candace's fingers curled with the half-wit response. She wanted to reach out and shake the idiot. She settled on gritting her teeth and moving closer to snap at him, "Not the man, the wolf! How is the wolf?"

He frowned, then, "Dead. Guy was going almost forty. Happened on impact."

Dead. As in dead? Like D-E-A-D, dead?

Her mind spun, lightheadedness swamped her. She shook her head, forcing it off. She couldn't faint. She had to know more. She had to know that it wasn't Duane. It couldn't be him. It was impossible. Because…just because.

"Candy, they need you in room three."

She heard the request, recognized the voice and yet couldn't get herself to turn and acknowledge it. She couldn't break eye contact with the EMT. If she did, he would leave and he couldn't leave. Not until she had all the facts. Not until he told her the truth, that Duane wasn't dead. "What color was the wolf?"

Once more the man frowned but then answered, "Brown."

Oh, God… Not brown, any color but brown. It was too uncommon. Wolves were gray or white or…something. Not brown. Not many. One was. Shit.

Sucking in a calming breath, she moved closer to the man, stopped just short of grabbing his shirt front and shaking. "Brown, like chestnut brown?"

"Never been big on colors but sure, I guess you could say so."

"No." No, she could not. And neither should he, because the wolf hadn't been brown. It hadn't. But it had. The man said it had!

This wasn't happening. Damn it, it could *not* be happening!

"He a friend of yours or something?"

Candace laughed hysterically as the stupidity of that question rolled over, reached deep down inside. No, Duane was *not* a friend. He was her everything. He was the man she cared about more than anyone or anything else in this world. No, not cared about. He was the man she loved. Her family. And he was dead.

No…

Emotions charged up her throat, tears stormed into her eyes. She pushed them back, pushed calmness into her voice. Just managed to quell the renewed urge to grab the man by the shirt collar and shake. "Are you sure he's dead? Maybe he was just badly hurt. Maybe he just needs—"

"Candy, they need you in room three. Stat."

The word "stat" was the only reason that Candace turned to the speaker of that last request, which sounded much more like a command. Nikki stared at her, her expression somewhere between speculation and annoyance.

Candy nodded numbly. "Right. Room three." But, no, not right. She couldn't stay here and pretend like nothing was wrong. Like Duane didn't need her help. He needed her help, because no matter what the EMT had said, he wasn't dead. He was just hurt badly and, with a little care from her, he would be fine in the morning. "No. I-I can't. I have to go. I… I forgot. I have a dentist appointment."

"Cancel," Nikki said firmly. "I need you here. In that roo—"

"I'm sorry," Candy snapped back, "but someone else needs me more."

Nikki spoke further words but Candace had no idea what they were, she was already running out the door and through the parking lot for her car. She didn't even have her damned purse she realized as she flung open the car door and jumped inside. That was okay though, she didn't need her purse. She kept a spare ignition key in the back of the glove box. All three of her brothers had told her it was a stupid thing to do. It didn't seem stupid now; it seemed like the smartest thing she had ever done in her life.

Except for telling Duane she cared. Only she hadn't followed that caring through with trust. Goddammit, why hadn't she been stronger for him? For both of them.

She started the car and backed out of the lot, pulled onto the street with an angry screech of tires. She'd gone a few miles when she realized she didn't even know where she was going. They wouldn't have left a dead wolf on the side of the street. They would have taken it somewhere. But where? The city morgue? No, not for a wolf. More likely Duane's body had been taken back to animal control by whatever cops had responded to the accident.

Duane's body. The thought ricocheted through her mind, down her throat and tore at her heart. *He's not really dead. He's not really dead.* So long as she kept telling herself that he wouldn't be. He couldn't be.

Three miles from the police station, Candace realized she was in front of Nate and Kelsey's house. She didn't want to take the time to stop and yet instinct told her she had to. It was almost six o'clock. Her brother always watched the news. What if the accident was on there? What if he recognized the wolf and figured things out for himself?

That couldn't happen. She had to be the one to tell Nate his best friend was dead. That he was never coming back. That he'd died feeling unloved and alone because she was a heartless bitch who'd been too afraid to believe in him and try something a little different with her life.

Dead. Dead. Dead.

The words chanted through her mind as she flew into Nate's driveway, threw the shifter into park and shot out of the vehicle and up the front porch steps. She pushed the door open at the same time that someone opened it from the inside and collided hard with her brother.

Nate caught her shoulders and stilled her. In that jarring moment, reality hit Candy like a slap in the face. She'd been so afraid of Nate seeing Duane's dead body on TV but the truth was Nate didn't even know that Duane was a werewolf. Duane was dying, maybe already dead, and here she was, standing in her brother's doorway, wasting impossibly precious time.

She shook her shoulders, fought at his grip, trying to get him to loosen up, but his hold remained firm, his look one of intolerable dread.

"Candy, what the hell's the matter with you?"

Shit. She had to tell him now. She had no choice.

She opened her mouth to speak but no words came out. No sound. She tried again, managed a whispered, "It's…it's Duane. He's… Oh, God, Nate, he's…he's dead."

The dread on his face waged on and she guessed he was taking it in slowly, digesting it and coming to term with the reality his best friend was no more.

Nate let her shoulders go then tossed back his head and laughed. Hard.

He stopped laughing and smiled at her. "I think you seriously need to consider taking a longer vacation next time, sis. Duane isn't dead. He's in the kitchen with Kelsey and Mom and Dad."

Candace's throat closed up. Her heart seemed to stop as well. She closed her eyes and focused on getting air into her lungs, to making her heart beat normally again. When she felt as though she wouldn't pass out, she opened her eyes and looked at Nate. Replayed the words in her mind, then barked out, "*What?*"

He nodded. "We're having dinner. What most normal people do this time of night instead of working themselves into an early grave or, in your case, a panic attack."

She narrowed her eyes at the accusation. A panic attack? He thought she was having a fucking panic attack? His best friend was dead and he thought— But no, Duane wasn't dead. Nate had just said so. He'd said Duane was in the kitchen.

The reality behind those words crashed through her in a temporarily blinding haze. She froze for a moment, unable to move so much as an inch, and then she pushed past Nate and bolted into the kitchen.

"Candace!" he shouted after her.

"Candy, honey, what's the matter?" her mother asked, concern etched into her tone.

Candace shut out both voices and focused on the man looking at her from the far end of the table. His hazel eyes filled with very real and very alive emotion.

Duane's nostrils flared and she knew he was sensing her fear, reading into her thoughts. He knew what was going on in her mind and still she couldn't stop herself from murmuring it aloud, "You're alive. Not dead. Alive."

He smiled slowly, sexily, sensuously. "Looks that way to me."

Why, the idiot! She ought to smack him for looking so good, so alive. Alive. What he was. Not dead. But alive. "Someone hit a wolf a few blocks from here and it died," she said on a rush. "I thought... I thought you were dead."

"Why in the hell, with all the traffic around here, would you think he was the one who hit the wolf?" Nate asked from where he'd entered the kitchen behind her.

"I didn't think he hit the wolf. I thought that he—"

"I'm fine, Candy," Duane cut her off. "I'm not hurt, not even scratched."

The sudden intensity of his look caught up with her and she realized what she'd been about to admit. She truly was having a panic attack if she would come so close to sharing Duane's secret with everyone here. "I'm sorry," she said, focusing on him, hoping her look conveyed the truth of that. She backed toward the door. "I should go."

"Stay for dinner, Candy," Kelsey said from her seat next to Duane. "There's plenty to go around." Her face lit with a dimpled smile as she added, "Not to mention I'm dying to tell someone else what an incredible time we had in the Caribbean."

"No. I-I can't. I have to get back to work." If she even still had a job after the way she'd run off.

Duane pushed back his chair and stood, rounded the table. "Let me walk you out." *Please.*

As much as she had to talk to him, to explain what a fool she'd been, she knew she didn't want it to happen here, in her brother's house, where everyone would hear. Only, Duane's silent plea and the concern that had overtaken his face, now that he was facing away from the others, were too much to ignore. "Okay."

Candace said a quick goodbye to her parents. Then, after promising to stop by soon and hear all about Nate and Kelsey's honeymoon, she walked with Duane into the living area that led to the foyer. Now that the bulk of her panic was over, she felt incredibly stupid for acting the way she had. In the past, she might have written it off with sarcasm. Today, she couldn't do that. Not with Duane.

She stopped walking and turned to him, licked her too dry lips and met his eyes. "I'm sorry about that. I just thought—"

"That someone finally killed me the way you're always threatening to do?"

His grin sparked and she ached to close the short distance between them and melt against him. She couldn't do that. She couldn't seek comfort in his arms until she had out all those things she needed to say. And then, only if he took her back.

Her belly pinched tight. He had to take her back. They belonged together. They both knew it. He had for a long time, she finally did as well and with a level of understanding that before she could only have imagined. She thought succumbing to him meant giving up her sense of self, giving in to his every demand. It didn't. And he'd tried to tell her as much on several occasions. For some reason his words had never sunk in before today. They did now and she understood succumbing to him meant him succumbing to her in return, to giving and taking in equal shares, to broadening her sense of self and attaining an even stronger awareness. Of being a family.

"I panicked," she admitted. "I thought you were gone. I thought I'd lost you."

His grin slipped away and he narrowed his gaze. "I thought's what you wanted?"

"So did I but I was wrong," she said solemnly, then added on a lighter note, "I know that's hard to believe, me being wrong twice in the same month, but I was." She sobered again and gave into her urge to step forward, to reach a hand to his face, rub her thumb over his cheek and down along his goatee.

"What I want isn't for you to go away," she said softly. "What I want is for you to stay. To be with me, so I can be with you. What I want is everything, Duane. I said that before but that time I didn't know enough to mean it. This time, I do. This time, I'm sure. I want to be a wolf, Duane. I want you to make me your—"

"I don't think you should be driving."

The distressed sound of Nate's voice cut Candace off. Refusing to remove her hand from Duane's face, even if the intimate touch would cause her brother to jump to conclusions—ones that were one hundred percent accurate—she turned toward Nate.

He stood just outside the kitchen door, an odd look on his face somewhere between shock and mystification. "You aren't making any sense, Candy. People don't just become wolves. Maybe in the movies, but not in real life. Tell her, Duane."

She was caught up in emotion, still feeling fragments of residual panic, and yet Candace heard the hesitation in her brother's words. He wasn't just asking for her sake, he was asking for his own. Did he somehow know? Could Kelsey's brother have told him about Duane? Did Kelsey even know about Andy? Did Nate?

I doubt either of them know about him. But Nate, at least, knows something isn't right with me. One day I'll tell him why. We will together. Just not today.

Duane followed that thought up with a nod of accord. "He's right, Candy. You can't go back to work in your condition. Maybe not even tomorrow." He looked to Nate. "Don't worry about her, man. I'll take her home and see that she gets to bed."

Nate glanced from Candace to Duane, his mouth edging somewhere between a smile and a frown, as if he couldn't decide how he felt about the two of them being together. Finally, he nodded. "Fine. Just…be nice to her."

"I won't do anything she doesn't want me to do," Duane promised.

Nate opened his mouth to say something in response but then shut it and waved toward the door. "Just go and take care of her already."

* * * * *

Duane had done exactly as he'd promised Nate, took Candace to his home and saw that she got to bed. Being the overachiever he was—at least when it came to a certain woman and certain situations that involved that particular woman—he even took it one step further and climbed into bed along with her. Sleep, well, it was a good thing he hadn't promised Nate to see his sister got any of that, as there didn't appear to be any on the foreseeable horizon.

Candy was gloriously naked and on her knees on the king-sized bed, her breath coming in jagged pants, her breasts heavy with arousal and filling his hands. His cells were on fire with the need to finally make her his, in body if not yet in form. Yet he stopped himself from pumping into her buttocks the way he burned to do and asked one last time, "Are you sure you want this?"

"Yes," she breathed, rearing back against his rock-hard shaft, trying to get him between her butt cheeks by her own means. "I want it. I want you, Duane. I love you."

The words were remarkable, ones he could hear every day of his life and never tire of. He planned on doing just that, just as he planned on speaking his own in return every day, night and numerous times in between.

After rubbing his cock along the seam of her ass one last time, he pushed the pre-cum-lubricated head inside until he reached her sphincter muscle. She tensed for an instant, the muscle tensing in turn, and then both loosened again as she demanded, "Now! I want you inside of me now."

Candace reared back against him again and this time he met her thrust with one of his own in the opposite direction. He pumped his cock deep inside the slick valley of her ass and she squealed out with the rapid entry while her fingers dove into the sheets, clawing against the navy silk and turning her knuckles white.

"Too much? Tell me if it is, sweetie. Tell me to stop." It very well might kill him to stop now but, if she asked, he would do it. There would always be another day, another time for them to become mates in more ways than just in hearts.

"You will not stop!" she bit out. "You will move!"

He chuckled at her demand. If those weren't the sweetest words he'd ever heard, then he didn't know what were. Actually, Duane realized as he gave in to her request and his own burning need, pulling his cock almost all the way out of her buttocks and then thrusting into her again to the sound of her ecstatic screams, he did. He voiced them now, "I love you, Candy. Always. Forever. You're my family. Everything I've always wanted. Dreamed of. Mine."

Her body trembled beneath his, her muscles tugging at his cock, urging him to release inside her, to spurt his seed and finally make her his. He leaned down over her, until her back was flush with his chest, and pulled at her nipples, teasing, toying, twisting until fevered cries rang from her lips. He took her neck in his teeth then. Let his fangs emerge ever so slightly and bit down.

Candy's tremors turned to shakes and her moves to jarring slams, her buttocks grinding hard against his groin and her pussy dripping with her juices against his balls. The scent of her sweet arousal filled his nostrils, had his cock growing thicker, longer, wider within her ass, his fangs emerging to sink farther in her neck. For a moment, he feared it was too much and then she shouted a euphoric, "Ye-esss!"

She reared back one last time and her sphincter contracted around him, tugged at his cock until he was powerless to giving in. He didn't even try to prolong it. He had no reason to. He could feel the orgasm sliding through her, hear its effects in her thoughts and feel them as the cum drained from her body and soaked his balls and the bed beneath them. As his own shot into her buttocks, filled her up in a warm, wet stream, she turned her neck against his mouth and growled, "Mine."

"Yours, huh?" Duane asked teasingly moments later as he pulled her into his arms and kissed the bite marks on her neck.

Candace smiled back, her eyes dark gold and filled with love. Her voice was anything but, biting out, "Yes, you're mine. To control. To have whenever I want. To demand you give me endless pleasure."

He chuckled, aware just how much truth there was to the venomous tone — not very damned much. Moving to her lips, he kissed her soundly. "Don't forget about taking you hunting at night for road kill and field mice, every werewolf's entrée of choice."

She laughed, then sobered. "I seriously think you need an education if you think that's what us werewolves like to eat."

All humor drained away with her seriousness. "'*Us* werewolves'?"

She licked her lips and nodded. "I'm ready."

Ready. As in, ready to change. Ready to become his in more than just heart and body. In form. "You're sure?"

"You said it wouldn't hurt, right?"

Duane recalled the way she'd responded to his tonguing her that afternoon after he'd met up with Andy in his wolf form. She'd more than enjoyed the scrape of his fangs against her clit, just as she'd enjoyed them on her neck now. "Did you like becoming my mate?"

Her eyes widened slightly, her pupils dilating just enough to tell him she'd liked it and then some. "If you really have to ask that, then you truly are an idiot."

"I don't, but I love it when you get bitchy with me." To the sound of her gasp, he moved down her body and settled his hands on her thighs, pushed her legs up. "Open up, sweetie. Your inner wolf's down here, just waiting to come out and play."

Parting her thighs, she raised an eyebrow. "Down there?"

"Oh, yeah." He planted a kiss on the ticklish pear-shaped birthmark that lined her upper thigh. To the squeal of her laughter, he moved lower still and sniffed at her arousing scent. He brushed his goatee over the sodden curls that covered her mound, then parted those curls and sank his tongue deep inside her warm, waiting wetness. Slowly, he allowed the wolf in him to take over, to emerge. To become whole.

The grating sound of bones shifting and changing filled the air for several seconds and then faded away to nothing but the excited sound of Candace's panting breaths.

Duane looked up at her through his wolf's eyes and brushed his cold, wet nose over her clit, followed it with the gentle rasp of a fang. Her pussy pulsed in response, let loose a flood of juices. Her eyes darkened and her fingers dove into his long fur. He moved his fangs to either side of her clit and sank them into the delicate flesh that surrounded it as he plunged his tongue deep inside her core. Her hips bucked up off the bed and her fingers clenched in his hair.

"Oh, God, Duane," she breathed as he increased the pressure of his sucks, his thrusts. "I want to become a wolf at least once a day. On second thought," she bit out a on a harsh pant as his tongue lengthened and widened to its fullest, "make that twice."

Epilogue

Candace pulled into the parking deck of Vaughn Technologies, fighting off anxiety. Joe was going to be ecstatic, just as the rest of the family would be about her news. Still, Candy hadn't expected this day to ever come, let alone so soon, and the idea of telling her oldest brother she was engaged had her belly coiling with tension. Deep down, she knew the truth. She wasn't anxious about sharing the news she and Duane were getting married, but that the outcome of that marriage would be children they both wanted badly and soon, yet also ones she had no idea of what to expect. Would they be human? Wolves? Mixed breeds like their parents?

According to Duane and what he'd learned in speaking with others of their kind, they would be the latter, but more than likely come out in their wolf form. And that was the real cause of her nerves. Before that day came, they would have to tell her family the truth about them, not to mention find an obstetrician who wasn't afraid of delivering werepups, potentially a whole litter of them.

First things first, though. Sharing her happy news with Joe.

Mentally calming herself, Candace made her way from the closed-in ground-level deck to the third floor of the technological building that housed Joe's office along with numerous others. It was after five already but she knew her brother well. He was working an extra hour or two a day now to compensate for next month, when his son was due and he'd want to take off several days in a row, if not more.

Reaching his closed office door, she heard the echo of his deep voice from inside. Just like she'd guessed, working late.

Candy took one long, nerve-fortifying breath, then turned the doorknob, pushed in and…came to a mind-jarring halt.

The deep voice she'd heard seconds ago was louder now, far more understandable, and didn't belong to her brother for a second. It also wasn't her brother who stood on the opposite end of Joe's spacious office. That man was clad in nothing more than black suit pants, his dark hair shot with gray at the temples, and in his hand was a whip. A whip he brought down soundly on the bared and reddened backside of a blonde.

Candace's speeding thoughts came to a grating halt at that last observation. Forcing herself to look past the actions of the man, she concentrated on the woman. On the blonde. The one who was bent over and manacled to the arms of Joe's desk chair and shouting out her pleas for mercy. Pleas that sounded more like ecstatic requests for the man never to stop. Pleas that rang out in a voice Candy recognized to a heart-stopping certainty, just as she recognized the woman's fair blonde hair. It wasn't in a ponytail now, the way she always wore it, but that didn't change the facts.

Good God, Carrie?

But, no, it couldn't be. Her sister never wore her hair down. Didn't even seem the least bit interested in men. She sure as hell wasn't subservient—that trait wasn't built into the Anderson gene pool. Then there was the little matter of Carrie being at the university library this evening, cramming for a coming exam. That's what she'd told Candy this morning. Had told her almost the same damned thing the morning before that and the one before… Oh my… No. No way. She couldn't have been lying that whole time. This couldn't be her sexually reserved little sister—

The blonde's head fell back suddenly, her facial features coming into clear view, and Candace all but swallowed her tongue. She blinked back her stupefaction, her shock, the sensation she was going to pass out, to gasp, "Holy shit! Carrie?"

"Oh. My. God." The words tumbled from Carrie's lips on a squeak. Candy repeated them silently, only with far more strength. Their overprotective older brothers were going to freak.

Well, Candace did still owe Nate for making her stand up with Duane in his and Kelsey's wedding. Not that she was actually upset about that anymore. Or that she planned to get retribution by telling him their baby sister was not only seeing a much older man, if the gently graying hair was any sign, but one that was into whips and handcuffs. Judging by the elated look on Carrie's face just before she'd spotted Candy and horror overtook her expression, Carrie was in to it every bit as much herself.

Oh, dear Lord. And she'd thought her secret was big.

Enjoy this excerpt from
Naughty Mistress Nita
© Copyright Jodi Lynn Copeland, 2003

Chapter One

Jordan was dead.

At least she would be when Anita Roemer got her hands on her. Her so-called best friend had contacted her in major panic mode this morning, with a request no one in their right mind would have agreed to.

'Meet my appointment for me and tell him I can't make it,' Jordan had said. 'I've tried calling, but there's no answer. He's prepaid and I can't just leave him hanging.'

Meet her appointment, Anita thought now with a snort, easier said than done considering Jordan worked as a professional dominatrix. Not to mention this particular appointment was nowhere near to Jordan's office, but in a tiny cabin nestled so deeply in the Picanti Mountains no one would've guessed it even existed.

And as far as being in her right mind, clearly Anita wasn't, since at this very moment she stood knocking on the hardwood door of that particular secluded cabin. Worse than lost marbles, and the reason she was going to ring Jordan's neck was the appointment in question didn't even appear to be around.

She'd committed a major transgression—at least for her anyway—and driven the forty-mile trip ten miles over the limit to make it here on schedule. And for what, to spend her time knocking on the door of an empty cabin while the gods of thunder streamed non-stop insults around her?

She should leave right now. She had far better things to do with her Friday evening than stand here knocking away. Cleaning needed to be done...or arranging her bookcase...or, well, she could always pay that visit to her parents she'd been putting off for too long now. Only what if Jordan got in trouble because of it? Worse, what if her friend thought she'd never made the trip in the first place, and tossed out another remark like the one she'd flung at her earlier today. The one that pushed Anita over the edge and made her agree to come to this ramshackle shed in the middle of nowhere.

Jordan's words burned through her mind even now. *"If you aren't up to telling him I can't make it, you can always be my stand in."* And then she'd laughed loud and long.

Was it really so hard to imagine Anita letting loose enough to make a man her slave? Yes, she was uptight at times. Maybe even a bit on the prim and proper side. Certainly as uniform and statistical as the balance sheets she handled through her job at the accounting firm. All of those things were a direct result of her stern upbringing. None of those things meant she couldn't control a man, bend him to her every whim.

Her sexual exploits might be limited to two very tidy, organized sessions of standard missionary-style sex, but that wasn't because she was following in her mother's goody-two-shoes footsteps. Or that her minister father's numerous sermons about premarital sex being sinful had convinced her to abstain. It was merely because she had yet to find someone she cared to go a second round with, let alone experiment with outside the norm.

At twenty-five she was still plenty young. If and when a man came along, who revved her engine in all the right ways, then she'd cut loose and try all those things she'd dared to fantasize about. Until then, she was fine and dandy with her conservative ways.

A loud rumbling shook Anita from her musings. Through the dense canvas of elm, pine and sycamore trees, she peered warily at the dark, roiling sky. Hitching her purse strap higher on her shoulder she breathed in the unmistakable scent of the forthcoming storm mingled with the forest greenery. For Jordan's sake, she'd wait a few more minutes. Either that or until the rain gods decided to join forces with the thunder gods.

Less than a minute had passed when, with an ominous hiss, the sky opened up. Cold, hard rain pelted down, instantly soaking her through to the skin. Expelling a rare curse, Anita twisted the cabin's doorknob. It turned in her hand, the door pushing inward. She dashed into the building's warmth, closed the door behind her, and turned to face the room. Her breath caught as she took in the cabin—make that, pigsty—before her.

"Good gracious, the man's a slob."

How could anyone live like this? Clothes lay strewn across the faded couch and recliner that centered the small building's sitting room. Several books were tossed about on the scarred coffee table and the T.V. was on!

Who on earth would go away and leave the T.V. on? Unless he was home.

Anita shook the excess rainwater from her hair and sweater and then opened her purse to the business card section. She pulled out the card Jordan had handed her earlier that morning. Zane Matthews was emblazoned on the card's front in brilliant gold. She stifled a laugh at his title—architect. Maybe that explained how he managed to stack his clothes so high without fearing they'd topple.

"Mr. Matthews?" she called out, weaving her way through the chaos and into the only other room aside from the bathroom—a good-sized bedroom in nearly the same appalling state as the main room.

Crinkling her nose, she called his name again. Still no answer.

Dang. She couldn't stand around all day waiting for him. Just a few more minutes, she promised herself again. Until then she'd do a little straightening. Whoever the guy was he'd surely appreciate some tidying. And maybe her selfless efforts would help smooth things over when he realized she'd entered his home without permission.

Forty-five minutes and one moderately clean cabin later, Anita had had enough. Her back was sore, her feet hurt and darn she was tired. The big, pine-framed bed called to her from the corner of the bedroom, and it was all she could do to stop from whimpering. She could test it out, make sure she'd gotten the corners tight enough when she'd made it. After all, she'd hate to think she was doing something halfway.

"Just a quick test," she murmured as she lay down on the soft, forest-themed comforter and inhaled the mixed aroma of man and pine.

She'd get up in a second...or maybe two, she thought fleetingly as her eyes drifted closed. Or three. Really, what was her hurry anyway, all she had waiting for her at home was more work. Four minutes and then she was really, really going to get up.

* * * * *

"Son of a bitch," Zane Matthews vented as he yanked off his sopping wet flannel shirt and tossed it onto the hardwood bedroom floor.

It wasn't enough the fish weren't biting, or that he'd gotten stuck in the worst thunderstorm to hit the Picanti Mountain range this spring, subsequently drenching every inch of him during his trek back from the lake to his temporary home. But now he had to find a goddamned woman in his bed! A woman whose services he'd flatly refused each and every time his buddies suggested he spend a little time at her hands.

Enjoy this excerpt from
Son of Solaris
Taurus
© Copyright Jodi Lynn Copeland, 2004

The smile that Tristan had ready for the moment when Cara stepped out of the bathroom fell flat the second she materialized before him. She'd gone into the bathroom looking like a prostitute and come out looking like the angel he knew and loved. Her green eyes were wide and luminous and her skin alive with natural, glowing color. "*Mio dio*, you're beautiful."

Her pace faltered for an instant. Wrapping her arms around her body, she continued across the room. She pinned him with a frosty look. "Well, that's a step up from a hooker anyway."

He bit back an apology. He didn't have anything to apologize over. She had looked like a hooker. From the neck down she still did. Now, at least, she looked like a hooker in the privacy of his hotel suite. Remembering his plan for when she walked out of the bathroom, he smiled and gestured to the wheeled cart positioned next to a small round table in the dining area. "Looks like they brought more than just a steak."

Cara glanced at the uncovered cart, which held a vat of simmering chocolate surrounded by fat, red strawberries. Her eyes went from narrowed to adoring. "Oh, God, is that Godiva?"

The breathy quality of her voice ensured he'd hit his mark. If there was one thing that could turn Cara's head, or in this case stop her feet from walking out his door, it was Godiva chocolate. The strawberries were a bonus, one he hoped reminded her of their first night together.

He allowed his smile to grow into a knowing grin. "Is there any other kind?"

She looked back at him and a myriad of emotions crossed through her gaze. Finally, she shook her head. "You are an evil man, Tristan Manseletti."

Maybe. Or maybe just a man who knew the right strings to pull. "It's here now. It would be a shame to let it go to waste."

She glanced at the cart and back at him. "I'm supposed to be leaving, remember?"

Judging by her tone, she'd spoken those words in an attempt to remind herself she was supposed to be leaving as much as she had to remind him. She hadn't needed to, because she wasn't going anywhere. They both knew it. It was a simple matter of acceptance on her part.

Tristan crossed to the cart and dipped a lush strawberry into the dark chocolate. He brought it to his lips slowly, licking the sweet substance away from the berry, savoring the rich flavor aloud. Cara watched him with trembling lips and a knitted brow. In her eyes was want. A desire that Tristan could feel burning deep within her. One that went far beyond chocolate and fruit.

He selected a second juicy strawberry from the plate and dipped it into the chocolate. Holding it above his opened palm, he crossed to her and offered the berry. "What's a few more minutes between old friends? Go ahead, enjoy."

She looked from the berry so near to her mouth and back at him. Her eyes watered and her words came out terse. "I can't!"

Frustration charged through him with her declaration and Tristan fought the urge to toss the berry across the room. He drew several calming breaths and asked a question he was already too aware of the answer to. "Because I'm paying for it, right?"

Her eyes watered further. She sniffed back tears and shook her head while her full lower lip quivered. "No. Because I already had my chocolate this morning."

Both the destituteness of her expression and the absurdity of her response had laughter bubbling up in his throat. He checked the humor, and asked calmly, "You're on a once a day diet?"

She nodded, sniffing back more tears. "I have to be to stay in shape."

The amusement he'd known with her first sniff vanished, rage returning in an instant and boiling through his blood as loathing. He looked away in an effort to check his temper, but when he looked back it was still there. "So you can undress?"

Cara's tears seemed to dry in an instant. Defiance entered her eyes and she set her chin in a stubborn gesture he'd come to know well through the years. "So I can dance."

No. So she could undress. So she could flash her breasts and most the rest of her body to drunks and lowlifes who would go home and fuck themselves to sleep while thinking of her raunchy show.

Damn it, how could she do that to herself? She was too damned smart and talented to degrade herself that way. She'd claim she did it for Joey, but if seeing to her little brother's welfare truly meant so much to her then she would have stayed working for Tristan even after they'd broken up. There had to be some other reason.

Did she find it stimulating? Would he? "Show me."

Her eyes went wide and she took a step back. "*What?*"

"Show me how you dance. If it is just dancing, then you won't mind."

She shook her head wildly. Her long red hair swished over her shoulders, giving him an idea how it would look when she was undressing. The ends of the thick, fiery strands caressed her breasts and drew his attention to her nipples. They were erect beneath her thin black shirt, the shape of them too definable for her to be wearing a bra. Definable and truth telling. Clearly she did find stripping stimulating. And as his cock throbbed restlessly beneath his slacks and briefs he realized he too was suddenly looking at her undressing in a whole new light.

Cara crossed her arms firmly, blocking his view of her breasts. "Absolutely not. You've seen me dance before, you know how I do it."

"Only once, years ago. I wasn't watching your body that night, but your mind."

Her lips pinched tight. "Stay the hell away from my mind."

Tristan sighed at the anxiety he felt storming through her. She would agree to stay with him tonight, he could already sense her relenting, but would one night of pleasure make a damned bit of difference in the long run? Her expression said it all, as had her words. She was scared of him. It wasn't a surprise, he'd always known she was scared of his powers at times, but the strength of her fear concerned him. How could he ever compete with it?

About the author:

Jodi Lynn Copeland resides on 30 acres of recreational woodland and farmland, minutes from Michigan's state capital. She has been writing since her junior year in college when she began a romantic suspense novel. Since then she has written numerous books, which range from single title mystery to erotic romance, and has won various writing awards. When not writing, she enjoys time in the outdoors—hunting, fishing, playing ball, or just spending time with her family and pets. Weekdays are spent on her day job as a technical writer, graphic designer, and web programmer for a national engineering firm, and evenings and weekends bringing tales of passion, romance, and adventure to life.

Jodi is a member of Romance Writers of America (RWA), Greater Detroit Romance Writers of America (GDRWA), Mid-Michigan Romance Writers of America (MMRWA), Cata-Romance, and a dedicated critique group.

Jodi welcomes mail from readers. You can write to her c/o Ellora's Cave Publishing at 1056 Home Avenue, Akron OH 44310-3502.

Why an electronic book?

We live in the Information Age—an exciting time in the history of human civilization in which technology rules supreme and continues to progress in leaps and bounds every minute of every hour of every day. For a multitude of reasons, more and more avid literary fans are opting to purchase e-books instead of paperbacks. The question to those not yet initiated to the world of electronic reading is simply: *why?*

1. *Price.* An electronic title at Ellora's Cave Publishing and Cerridwen Press runs anywhere from 40-75% less than the cover price of the exact same title in paperback format. Why? Cold mathematics. It is less expensive to publish an e-book than it is to publish a paperback, so the savings are passed along to the consumer.

2. *Space.* Running out of room to house your paperback books? That is one worry you will never have with electronic novels. For a low one-time cost, you can purchase a handheld computer designed specifically for e-reading purposes. Many e-readers are larger than the average handheld, giving you plenty of screen room. Better yet, hundreds of titles can be stored within your new library—a single microchip. (Please note that Ellora's Cave and Cerridwen Press does not endorse any specific brands. You can check our website at www.ellorascave.com or

www.cerridwenpress.com for customer recommendations we make available to new consumers.)

3. *Mobility.* Because your new library now consists of only a microchip, your entire cache of books can be taken with you wherever you go.

4. *Personal preferences are accounted for.* Are the words you are currently reading too small? Too large? Too...**ANNOYING**? Paperback books cannot be modified according to personal preferences, but e-books can.

5. *Instant gratification.* Is it the middle of the night and all the bookstores are closed? Are you tired of waiting days—sometimes weeks—for online and offline bookstores to ship the novels you bought? Ellora's Cave Publishing sells instantaneous downloads 24 hours a day, 7 days a week, 365 days a year. Our e-book delivery system is 100% automated, meaning your order is filled as soon as you pay for it.

Those are a few of the top reasons why electronic novels are displacing paperbacks for many an avid reader. As always, Ellora's Cave and Cerridwen Press welcomes your questions and comments. We invite you to email us at service@ellorascave.com, service@cerridwenpress.com or write to us directly at: 1056 Home Ave. Akron OH 44310-3502.

erridwen, the Celtic Goddess of wisdom, was the muse who brought inspiration to storytellers and those in the creative arts Cerridwen Press encompasses the best and most innovative stories in all genres of today's fiction. Visit our site and discover the newest titles by talented authors who still get inspired - much like the ancient storytellers did, once upon a time.

Cerridwen Press

www.cerridwenpress.com